The Fifth Target

The Fifth Target

Gloria Duncan

Northshore Noir Press

Northshore Noir Press

Toronto, Canada

www.northshorenoir.com

ISBN: 978-1-998648-43-6

eBook ISBN: 978-1-998648-44-3

Contents

Chapter 1

Rachel Fenimore came back to herself like a swimmer breaking the surface—sudden, gasping, and with no memory of the depths. Rain stippled her face in cold pinpricks. A streetlamp twenty feet away flickered, its stuttering yellow-white transforming the wet pavement into a mirror of broken light. She lay on her side, one arm pinned beneath her body, the other sprawled across rough concrete. The world smelled of garbage and rain and something copper-bright and familiar that made her stomach twist before her mind could name it.

Blood.

She pushed herself to sitting, her sweatshirt clinging to her chest and stomach. Not with rain. With blood. Dark crimson patches spread across the gray fabric, still wet enough to gleam under the faltering streetlamp.

"No," she whispered, the word dissolving into the steady drum of rain.

Her fingers trembled across the wet fabric, searching for a wound, a source. Nothing. No pain anywhere, no break in her skin. Not her blood.

A soft gurgle drew her attention.

Three feet away, a man lay curled on his side, his back to her, shoulders hunched as if warding off a blow that had already landed. His clothes—layers of jackets and shirts despite the summer night—were dark with rain and more. One hand clutched at his midsection.

"Sir?" Rachel's voice sounded strange to her own ears, borrowed from someone else. "Sir, can you hear me?"

The man made another wet, bubbling sound. Rachel moved toward him on hands and knees, her palms slapping against the wet concrete, the knees of her jeans soaking through instantly. When she reached him, she placed a hand on his shoulder. Warmth radiated through all those layers. Still alive.

"I'm a nurse," she said, the words automatic as breathing. "I'm going to help you."

She rolled him onto his back with gentleness. His face was gaunt, skin stretched tight over sharp cheekbones, a graying beard matted to his chin. The whites of his eyes showed as he stared past her shoulder at something far away. A horrible sucking sound accompanied each shallow breath.

Rachel's training took over, pushing aside confusion. She placed her fingers against his throat, feeling for a pulse. It fluttered beneath her touch, fast and thready.

She looked down at his midsection, where his hands were clutched. Blood seeped between his fingers, mixing with the rain. She moved his hands away and caught her breath. The wound gaped open beneath his sternum, a deep puncture that had torn upward through vital organs. With each struggling breath, pink froth bubbled from the opening.

His lung was collapsed. And from the amount of blood, something else was hit too. His liver maybe. Or his spleen.

"What's your name?" she asked, though she knew he couldn't answer. His lips moved silently, eyes rolling. "I'm Rachel. I'm going to get help."

There would be no help. There was nothing to be done for a wound like this, not here in an alley with nothing but weeds as witnesses. Not with her bare hands. He needed surgery, blood, drainage tubes. He needed a hospital ten minutes ago.

"Hang on," she said, the words pointless. She fumbled in her pocket for her phone, her fingers leaving smears of blood on the screen as she pulled it out.

The man had a name. All men did. But she didn't know it. In the hospital, he would be a John Doe until someone identified him. Here, in this rain-slicked alley with death already settling into his features, he was just a stranger. No, not even that. He was a patient. The last patient she would ever fail.

She knew his face now, though. Gray-white beneath the weather-beaten tan. Eyes a pale blue that was turning milky even as she watched. Late fifties, maybe older—hard living aged a person faster than calendar years.

"Nine-one-one, what's your emergency?" The voice on the other end of the line was clear, professional.

"I need an ambulance," Rachel said, her voice cracking. "There's been a stabbing." She looked up at the street sign visible at the mouth of the alley. "Corner of 8th and Porter, in the alley behind the Chinese restaurant." She swallowed hard. "Hurry. He's critical."

"Is the victim conscious?"

Rachel looked down at the man. His eyes were still open, but no one was home anymore. She pressed her fingers to his throat again. Nothing.

"No," she said. "No pulse. I'm starting CPR."

She set the phone down without ending the call, positioned her hands over the man's sternum, and began compressions. It was futile. With that wound, she was only pushing more blood out of his body. But she couldn't stop. Not yet. Not while someone on the other end of the line was listening.

One-two-three-four. She counted silently as she pushed down on his chest. The rain mingled with sweat on her forehead, dripped into her eyes. Blood seeped between her fingers.

What am I doing here? The thought struck her between compressions. I was at home. In bed. I took my medication. I did everything right.

The sleepwalking had begun when she was eight—her parents finding her in the kitchen, or curled up on the couch. Minor incidents that grew worse as she aged. In college, her roommate had woken to find Rachel trying to leave their dorm room at three in the morning, fully dressed. After that, locks with keys she kept far from her bed. Medication. A sleep specialist who told her it was stress-related.

For five years, she'd been careful. Controlled. Few incidents, nothing dramatic.

Until this.

She had gone to bed at ten in her apartment, six blocks from this alley. She had taken her medication with a glass of water. She had checked the locks twice. And then—

Nothing. Just darkness between closing her eyes and waking up here.

But the blood. God, the blood on her clothes. On her hands. This man, with a wound that could have been made by a knife. A knife she might have held.

The sound of a distant siren wailed over the rain. Rachel's hands stilled on the man's chest.

She looked down at her bloody clothes, at her bloody hands. At this man, a stranger, dead beneath her fingers, his blood literally on her hands. She took a deep breath.

The flicker of the streetlamp intensified, throwing wild shadows across the alley walls. For the first time, Rachel noticed a metal dumpster hulking behind her, its green paint peeling. A stack of broken pallets leaned against the restaurant's back door. A small dark movement that was either a large rat or a small cat. No witnesses. No cameras that she could see.

Just her and a dead man in the rain.

And a siren getting closer.

The rain fell harder now, plastering her hair to her scalp, running in rivulets down her neck and beneath her blood-soaked sweatshirt. She sat back on her heels beside the man's body—not a patient anymore, just a body—and stared at her hands, sticky with someone else's life. The siren wailed closer, then cut off abruptly. First responders, arriving at the scene. Police would be with them. They would ask questions she couldn't answer.

What happened here?

How did you find him?

Why are you covered in blood?

Rachel pressed her palms against her thighs, leaving dark handprints on her jeans. Her sleepwalking episodes had never taken her this far from home before. Never for this long. Never with such consequences.

She had walked six blocks in her sleep. Had she ever done something so bad?

Once, at nineteen, she'd woken up in her dormitory's common room with a kitchen knife in her hand. Her roommate had found her standing there, staring at nothing, gripping the handle so tight her knuckles were white. Rachel had no memory of taking it from the drawer. No memory of what she'd planned to do with it.

The sleepwalking always worsened with stress. Finals week. Bad breakups. The first month at a new job. Her therapist said it was her subconscious mind trying to resolve problems her conscious mind couldn't.

But what problem was her mind trying to solve with this man's blood?

"I couldn't have," she whispered to herself, but the words sounded hollow against the drumming rain. "I'm a nurse. I save people."

The siren had stopped, but no red and blue lights painted the alley walls yet. They must have stopped on the main street. Any minute now, flashlight beams would sweep the alley, find her sitting there with a dead man and his blood all over her.

Rachel's breath quickened. Her heart knew what was coming. Arrest. Questions. Headlines.

NURSE ARRESTED IN HOMELESS MAN'S MURDER.

She could claim innocence, tell them about her sleepwalking. But what jury would believe her? What hospital would ever hire her again? Her entire career, the only thing she'd ever wanted to do, would be over. Eight years of education and training reduced to an asterisk: *Lost license after being charged with murder.

"I didn't do this," she said to the dead man, as if he could absolve her. His open eyes reflected the flickering streetlight. Accusing her.

Rachel stood on legs gone wooden with dread. Water ran down her face—rain or tears, she couldn't tell anymore. She looked down at the man one last time.

He wore three layers of clothes despite the summer night: a faded denim jacket over a flannel shirt over what might have been a thermal undershirt. All soaked through with rain and blood.

What was his name? Had she asked? It was unimportant. More important was his condition, his wound, his pulse. Professional to the end. But now she wanted to know. Needed to know.

Because he wasn't just a body. He was a person, and people deserved names, especially when they died alone in the rain.

"I'm sorry," she whispered, though she didn't know what she was apologizing for. For not being able to save him? For leaving him? For something worse she couldn't remember?

A thin beam of light swept across the mouth of the alley, thirty feet away. A flashlight. Voices murmured, indistinct beneath the rain.

"The call said the alley behind the Golden Dragon—"

"This one here—"

The blue and red strobe of police lights colored the alley walls, diffused by the rain into watercolor smears that crept closer with each pulse. Rachel's medical training and her duty as a citizen told her to stay. To explain what she knew, which was almost nothing. To help identify the man, give what details she could about his wounds.

She heard a car door slam. The sound punched through her, primal and final.

Rachel turned and ran deeper into the alley, away from the light. Her sneakers slapped against wet pavement, splashing through puddles. The alley doglegged left, then right, emerging onto a narrow one-way street lined with parked cars. She kept running, the stitch in her side growing with each step, the blood on her clothes growing tacky as it thickened.

Where was she going? Home was to the east, but she couldn't go there. Her clothes, her appearance—someone would notice, would call the police. A woman covered in blood running through the streets after midnight? She wouldn't make it two blocks.

Think. Think. Rachel forced herself to slow, to stop beneath the awning of a closed bakery. She stood in the shadows, watching the empty street, trying to steady her breathing.

She needed to get inside somewhere. Needed to get clean. Needed to think.

The YMCA was three blocks south. They had showers. They had lockers where members could leave clothes. They were open 24 hours.

And she had a membership card in the pocket of her jeans.

No damned way could she show up like this.

She pushed away from the wall and started walking, shoulders hunched against the rain. Each step felt like moving through mud, her body resisting the direction her mind had chosen. A car passed, headlights sweeping over her. She ducked her head, turned to examine a dark storefront as if interested in whatever was displayed there. The car continued on.

Two blocks later, she heard sirens again, closer this time. More units responding. She pictured the police spreading out from the alley, looking for witnesses, checking nearby streets.

Looking for her.

She broke into a run again, no longer caring if she looked suspicious. The rain had slowed to a drizzle, no longer washing the blood from her clothes. She ran with her head down, arms pumping, breath coming in ragged gasps.

At the next corner, blue and red lights flashed a quarter-mile down the cross street. Rachel froze, then bolted in the opposite direction. She ran past shuttered storefronts and darkened apartment buildings, past a late-night convenience store where the clerk watched her pass with wide eyes, past a taxi letting out passengers who turned to stare.

She ran until the buildings around her became unfamiliar, until she no longer recognized the street names, until her legs threatened to buckle beneath her. Still, she ran.

Away from the body in the alley.

Away from the name she would never know.

Away from a truth she wasn't sure she could face.

Chapter 2

Rachel stood before the weathered door of her apartment, keys clutched in her bloodstained hand. The rain had stopped, but water still dripped from the ancient gutters above, each drop hitting the back of her neck like an accusation. Two flights up, behind a door with three locks she'd installed herself, lay safety—or what passed for it. But first she had to get past her own reflection in the scratched glass entrance. Past her neighbor, who should be asleep. Past Harper, who might still be awake.

She wiped her hand on her already ruined jeans, unlocked the door and pushed through. The vestibule lobby smelled of someone's forgotten takeout, the scent of garlic and grease hanging in the air. She quickly locked the door behind her. Rachel hurried up the stairs then slowed. Safer. Fewer chances of being noticed.

The stairs stretched before her, concrete and steel, each flight identical to the last. Her legs burned with the effort after all the running, but pain was better than discovery. Black spots danced at the edges of her vision. On the second floor landing, just two apartment doors. She paused outside her door, listening for sounds within. The television murmured behind the wood and plaster—the late-night news, probably. Harper had trouble sleeping. Always had, even when they were together.

Rachel slid her key into the first lock, then the second, then the third, each click louder than thunder to her ears. She eased the door open, stepping into the narrow entryway that fed into their cramped living room. The lights were off. Only the blue glow of the television illuminated the space. Maybe Harper had fallen asleep on the couch. Maybe Rachel could slip past, make it to the bathroom, dispose of these clothes.

She took one silent step, then another.

The overhead light snapped on, flooding the room with harsh brightness. Rachel froze, a startled animal caught in headlights.

Harper Langston stood by the light switch, one hand still raised, the other wrapped around a mug of steaming tea. Her dark hair was pulled back in a loose ponytail, tendrils escaping around her face. She wore the faded Mercy General Hospital T-shirt she'd stolen from Rachel when they were still sharing a bed instead of just an apartment. Her eyes, the deep brown that Rachel had once written bad poetry about, widened as they took in the sight before her.

"What the hell happened to you?" The mug clattered onto the coffee table as Harper crossed the space between them. "Rachel, Jesus—is that blood?"

"It's not—" Rachel began, then stopped. Of course it was blood. Denying the obvious would only make Harper more suspicious. "It's not mine," she finished.

Harper's expression shifted from shock to professional assessment. Five years of living with an ER nurse had trained her to see blood as a problem to solve rather than something to fear. "Whose is it then? What happened?"

Rachel's mind raced, constructing a story from fragments of truth. "Emergency at work. Multiple car accident on Riverside Drive. They called me in." The lie tasted bitter on her tongue. "Trauma case. Bad one."

"You weren't scheduled tonight." Harper's voice was flat. "I checked your calendar when I got home. You were off."

"They were short-staffed." Rachel tried to move past her, toward the bathroom, toward escape. "You know how it is. Someone calls out, they start going down the list."

Harper blocked her path with a step to the left. "Bullshit. What happened?" Her eyes narrowed.

The apartment shrank around Rachel, walls pressing closer. The ceiling lowered. The air thickened. Their apartment had never been large—a living room that doubled as a kitchen, two bedrooms hardly bigger than closets, a bathroom with cracked tiles and perpetually low water pressure—but now it felt like a prison cell. Nowhere to run. Nowhere to hide.

"Special circumstances." Rachel's voice sounded distant to her own ears. "All hands on deck."

"Try again." Harper stepped closer, her eyes cataloging details. The spatter pattern on Rachel's sweatshirt. The way the blood had dried in the creases of her palms. The tear in the knee of her jeans that hadn't been there this morning. "You're lying."

"I'm not." But the protest sounded weak even to her. "I just—I need a shower. It's been a long night."

"Rachel." Harper reached out, her fingers hovering just above Rachel's trembling hands. "You were sleepwalking again, weren't you?"

The words hit like a physical blow. Rachel took a step back, bumping into the edge of their secondhand dining table. A salt shaker toppled over, spilling tiny white crystals across the scarred wood.

"No." The denial came out too quick, too sharp. "I took my meds. I checked the locks." But even as she said it, she knew how it looked. The blood. The confusion. The missing time.

"Then where were you?" Harper pressed. "Because you weren't at the hospital working multiple injuries, in your street clothes."

Rachel felt a chill spread through her chest. "I just…" Rachel struggled to find words that would make sense, that would explain without condemning her. "I couldn't save him."

The moment the words left her mouth, she knew they were a mistake. Harper's face went still, all the animation draining from her features. She took a step back, putting distance between them.

"Who, Rachel? Who couldn't you save?"

"A patient." The lie came fast now, desperate. "At the hospital. That's all I meant."

But Harper wasn't listening anymore. She'd moved to the side table where her phone lay charging. Her hand hovered over it.

"What are you doing?" Rachel asked, though she knew the answer.

"I'm calling Dr. Shepherd." Harper's voice was gentle now, the way she spoke to patients in distress. "Your sleep specialist. This is serious, Rachel. If you're sleepwalking again—"

"I'm not." Rachel moved forward, faster than she meant to. Harper flinched, and the sight of it—her ex-girlfriend, her best friend, flinching away from her—broke something inside Rachel's chest. "I would never hurt anyone," she said, the words coming out raw and desperate. "You know that, right? You know me."

For a long moment, Harper said nothing. The silence stretched between them, filled with everything they'd once been to each other and everything they weren't now.

"I thought I did," Harper said at last.

Rachel pushed past her toward the bathroom. "I need to shower," she said, unable to look back at the hurt and fear in Harper's eyes. "We'll talk after."

But as she closed the bathroom door behind her, Rachel wondered what she could possibly say to make this right. How could she explain what she didn't understand herself?

Behind her, she heard Harper pick up her phone and begin to dial.

Rachel locked the bathroom door and leaned against it, her breath coming in shallow gasps. The bathroom was small—toilet, sink, and shower crammed into a space big enough for one person to turn around in. The overhead light buzzed and flickered, casting her reflection in the medicine cabinet mirror in alternating shadow and harsh illumination. A stranger stared back at her—hair wild, face pale beneath streaks of drying blood, eyes too wide and desperate. She hardly recognized herself.

Harper's voice drifted through the thin door, the words indistinct but the tone unmistakable—concern mixed with fear. Calling Dr. Shepherd at this hour. What would she tell him? That Rachel had come home covered in blood? That she suspected Rachel had hurt someone?

Had she?

The question froze her in place, her hand still on the doorknob. The blood on her clothes, her hands, under her fingernails—it belonged to someone. To that man in the alley. But how had it gotten there? How had she gotten there?

"No time," Rachel whispered to herself. "No time to think about that now."

She turned to the shower—an ancient fixture with rust stains blooming like dark flowers where the porcelain had chipped away. The shower curtain, a dollar-store special with faded tropical fish, hung limp from plastic rings that squeaked when she pulled it aside. She reached in and twisted the hot water knob as far as it would go. The pipes groaned behind the wall, a sound like something in pain, before water spurted from the showerhead in an uneven stream.

Rachel glanced again at her reflection. Behind her, steam began to rise from the shower, fogging the edges of the mirror. Soon it would claim the whole glass, erasing her image. She welcomed the thought.

She stepped into the shower fully clothed—sneakers, jeans, sweatshirt, everything. The water hit her like a judgment, scalding hot against her skin, but she didn't adjust the temperature. She deserved the pain, the heat. It might be the only thing that could cleanse her.

The water turned pink around her feet almost immediately, swirling blood from her clothes, her hair, her skin. She watched it flow toward the drain in hypnotic patterns. The man's blood. His life, washing away down metal pipes to join the city's waste.

What was his name?

The question returned, sharper now. She had asked him when he was still alive, but incapable of answering. Or she had not heard. Too focused on the wound, the blood, the failing pulse beneath her fingers. Too professional to remember the human behind the patient.

She pressed her palms against the shower wall, watching rivulets of diluted blood trace paths between her splayed fingers. How much of this blood had been on her hands before she tried to save him? How much had come after, during the futile CPR?

The water ran clearer now. Rachel peeled off her soaked sweatshirt, the fabric heavy and clinging. Her t-shirt beneath was stained too, darker patches visible despite its black color. She removed it as well, then bent to unlace her waterlogged sneakers. Her jeans were last, the wet denim fighting her efforts until she had to sit on the shower floor, the hot water pelting her back, to work them down her legs.

She left the pile of clothes in the corner of the shower and stood under the spray, naked and shivering despite the heat. The water couldn't seem to reach her core, where a cold knot had formed the moment she'd seen that man's eyes go vacant. She grabbed Harper's fancy shampoo—the expensive kind that smelled like some tropical fruit Rachel couldn't name—and worked it into her hair, scrubbing her scalp until it hurt. Then body wash, then conditioner. Mechanical actions. Normal actions. Things a normal person would do who hadn't woken up in an alley with a dying man.

When the water began to cool, Rachel shut it off. The silence pressed against her ears. She could no longer hear Harper on the phone. What did that mean? Had she gone to bed? Called the police instead of Dr. Shepherd?

Rachel stepped out of the shower onto the threadbare bathmat, leaving wet footprints on the cracked tiles. The mirror was fogged, her reflection a pale ghost. She wiped a section clear with her palm and stared at herself again. Clean skin. No blood. But her eyes still held the same wild, hunted look.

She grabbed a towel and dried herself, movements sharp and efficient. Then she turned to the pile of wet clothes in the shower. She couldn't leave them there.

Rachel reached into the shower and picked up her sweatshirt first. She twisted it over the drain, watching as pink-tinged water squeezed from the fabric and disappeared down the dark hole. Then her t-shirt. Her jeans. Each item twisted until no more water came out, then placed in the plastic laundry basket that stood in the corner next to the toilet.

They would need to be washed properly. Soon. Tomorrow, when Harper was at work. For now, hiding them in plain sight would have to do.

Rachel wrapped the towel around herself and sat on the closed toilet lid, her mind racing back to the alley. To the man. To the wound in his chest that she couldn't have made. Couldn't have. She was a nurse. She saved people. That's what she'd trained for, what she'd sworn to do.

But the sleepwalking. The blackouts. The lost time.

She pressed the heels of her palms against her eyes until colors burst behind her eyelids. There was a gap in her memory. She had gone to bed in this apartment, in her own room with its three window locks and door alarm. She had taken her medication—she was certain of it. The little orange pill with its bitter taste. She had set her phone to charge. Had closed her eyes.

And then—nothing. Until the rain on her face in that alley. Until the dying man beside her.

Six blocks. She had walked six blocks in her sleep, through rain-slicked streets. What else had she done? What had happened in those blank hours?

The last time she'd sleepwalked, even with the current medication, she'd woken up in her apartment building's laundry room at three in the morning, barefoot, with no memory of how she'd gotten there. Her therapist had called it a stress response. Said her mind was trying to solve problems while she slept.

What problem had her mind been trying to solve with a knife and a homeless man?

Rachel's breath caught in her throat. She hadn't thought about a knife until now. Hadn't seen one in the alley. But the wound in the man's chest—the upward angle, the depth—it had been made by a knife. She was a nurse. She knew knife wounds.

She looked down at her clean hands, turning them over slowly, examining her palms, her fingers. No cuts. No defensive wounds. If there had been a struggle, if she had—

No. She couldn't have. Wouldn't have.

But the blood had been on her clothes before she tried to help him. She was sure of it now.

Rachel stood up, her legs unsteady beneath her. She had to think clearly. Had to piece together what had happened. But first, she needed to face Harper. Needed to convince her that everything was fine. That Rachel was fine.

Even if she was beginning to suspect that nothing would ever be fine again.

Chapter 3

Detective Carolyn Hall stepped out of the unmarked sedan into a morning that couldn't decide if it wanted to rain again. The sky hung low and gray over New Hanan, the color of a bruise that wouldn't heal. Six-thirty in the morning, and already the day felt used up. She adjusted her blazer, squared her shoulders against the damp chill, and nodded to her partner, Robert White, who heaved himself from the passenger seat with a grunt that spoke of too many late nights and early mornings strung together like cheap beads on a thread about to break.

"Third one this month," White said, his voice thick with sleep. He hadn't touched the coffee they'd picked up on the way, the cup still wedged in the center console, steam fogging the lid. "Something in the water lately."

Hall didn't answer. Her shoes crunched over broken glass as she ducked under the yellow crime scene tape stretched across the mouth of the alley. She checked in with the scene officer and stopped. The scene was lit with portable floodlights that cast harsh shadows, turning every puddle into a mirror and every piece of trash into something worth a second look. Uniforms milled at the perimeter, their faces blank with the particular boredom that came from standing guard over death.

The alley smelled of rain and the coppery tang that rose beneath the scent of wet concrete. Blood had a way of announcing itself, even when you couldn't see it yet. Hall had smelled it at a hundred scenes before this one. She would smell it at a hundred more, if she lived that long.

"Detectives." Officer Meacham nodded as they approached. His notepad was damp at the edges, the ink bleeding into blue halos around each word. "Body was called in at 2:15 this morning. Female caller, didn't give a name. Said there was a stabbing victim in the alley behind the restaurant."

"She stay on scene?" Hall asked, though she already knew the answer. People who stayed were the exception, not the rule.

"Negative. Paramedics arrived at 2:23, found the victim VSA. He coded before transport. We're working with 911 Services to get contact information on the caller."

White sniffed, rubbing a hand over his stubbled cheek. "Any cameras back here?"

"One at the loading dock entrance, but it's been busted for months. Building's been empty since Millerton Textiles went bankrupt last year." Meacham gestured toward the shadowed bulk of the mill, its windows dark eyes watching their movements. "Nearest working camera's at the convenience store on the corner, but it points toward the street, not down here."

Hall stepped further into the alley, her eyes adjusting to the play of light and shadow. Water pooled in the uneven pavement, reflecting the floodlights in broken patterns. At the center of the scene, a dark shape lay beneath a white sheet that glowed in the artificial light, its edges fluttering in the morning breeze.

"What do we know about him?" she asked.

Meacham consulted his notes. "Ira Lewis. Had a food card from the Saint Christopher Shelter in his pocket. They confirmed he's been staying there on and off for about eight months. Before that, no idea."

"Age?"

"Shelter intake form says fifty-eight, but he looks older." Meacham shrugged. "Hard living."

Hall had seen it before. Life on the streets aged a person faster than calendar years. She'd interviewed men she thought were in their sixties who turned out to be forty. Women who looked ninety but weren't yet seventy. Time wasn't fair that way. It charged some people interest.

"Anyone talk to the shelter yet?" she asked.

"Morning shift just came on at six. We called, but they said most of the overnight staff had gone home. They're calling them back in now."

Hall nodded, trying to picture it. Ira Lewis, sixtyish, alone in an alley at two in the morning. What brought him there? Who was the woman who called it in? The pieces didn't fit together yet, but they would. They always did, eventually.

"Let's take a look," she said to White, who followed her to the covered body.

One of the crime scene techs looked up from where he was collecting evidence near the body. His badge identified him as Yeung. "We're still processing, Detectives. Try not to disturb anything, yeah?"

Hall nodded, careful where she stepped. The rain had turned the ground into a slurry of dirt and debris. Any footprints left by the killer—or the caller—were long gone, washed away or trampled by first responders.

She crouched beside the body, lifting one corner of the sheet. Just enough to see the face. Ira Lewis stared back at her with cloudy blue eyes that had once, perhaps, been sharp enough to see the world clearly. His skin was waxy in death, gray-white beneath a weather-beaten tan. A graying beard covered his lower face, neatly trimmed despite his circumstances. Not the wild, untended growth she sometimes saw on the chronically homeless.

"Someone cared about you," she murmured, noting the trim. Maybe he'd done it himself. Maybe someone at the shelter. But someone had cared enough to make sure Ira Lewis didn't look like what the world expected a homeless man to look like.

She let the sheet fall back.

"Single stab wound to the abdomen," White read from the preliminary report one of the uniforms had handed him. "No defensive wounds noted. ME estimates TOD at approximately 2:20 A.M., give or take."

"He was alive when the woman called," Hall said, straightening up. "But not for paramedics."

"That's what she said, anyway. You thinking robbery gone wrong?"

Hall surveyed the scene. The rain had washed away so much. Blood, evidence, footprints—all diluted and dispersed by water that didn't care about human concerns like justice.

"Maybe. Homeless doesn't mean he had nothing worth taking."

"Or maybe he knew something someone didn't want known," White suggested. "Saw something he shouldn't have."

Hall nodded, but the theory didn't sit right. Murders like that—silencing witnesses—were usually more efficient. A blow to the head. A slit throat. Not a single stab to the abdomen that left the victim alive long enough for someone to call for help.

"The caller," she said. "That's our first priority. Find out who she is, why she was here, what she saw."

"And why she ran," White added.

"And why she ran," Hall agreed, her eyes still on the shape beneath the sheet. There were reasons people fled crime scenes. Fear of the police. Outstanding warrants. Involvement in the crime itself. None of them reflected well on their mystery caller.

"We've got work to do," she said, turning away from Ira Lewis's covered form. Behind her, the restaurant's windows watched, dark with old secrets. In front of her, the city of New Hanan was waking up, unaware that one of its forgotten children had bled out in the rain while it slept.

Hall watched White disappear around the corner of the dumpster, beginning his ritual perimeter sweep. In the years they'd worked together, White had found three murder weapons, two witnesses who thought they'd hidden themselves well enough, and once, improbably, a suicide note that had blown thirty feet from the victim's pocket. Hall turned toward the center of the scene where Dr. Trinity Reid crouched beside Ira Lewis's body, her gloved hands precise as she documented the wound that had ended his life.

Dr. Reid had pulled back the sheet entirely now, exposing Lewis to the gray morning light. She worked with a quiet efficiency that Hall had always appreciated. No wasted movements, no unnecessary words. Just the business of death, conducted with the respect it deserved.

"Morning, Detective." Reid didn't look up from her examination. Her voice carried the rasp of someone who'd been up all night, or maybe just someone who'd been up too many nights across too many years. "Busy night. Three overdoses, a hit-and-run, and now Mr. Lewis here."

"What can you tell me?" Hall asked, crouching beside the doctor. Up close, the smell of blood was stronger, mingling with the sharp antiseptic scent of the gloves Reid wore.

"Single stab wound to the abdomen, angled upward through the liver and into the right lung." Reid indicated the wound, a dark puncture just below the sternum. "The blade went in at least six inches deep. Not a hesitation wound. Whoever did this committed to it."

"Defensive wounds?"

Reid shook her head, lifting Lewis's hands for Hall to see. Paper bags. "Bagged, but I doubt we'll find anything. The nails were fairly clean. No cuts or bruises on the knuckles or forearms that might indicate he'd tried to fight off his attacker."

"Suggests he knew his attacker, or he was taken by surprise," Hall said.

"Or he was too impaired to fight back." Reid said. "Won't know until the labs come back, but his eyes and skin shows signs of long-term alcohol abuse. Could have been drunk."

"May I?" Hall asked, gesturing to the body.

Reid nodded, sitting back on her heels to give Hall room.

Hall looked more closely at Lewis now. He wore layers despite the summer night—the outermost a faded denim jacket stiff with dried blood. Beneath that, a flannel shirt, and under that what looked like a thermal undershirt. All of them soaked through. His jeans were worn but not filthy, suggesting he'd had access to laundry facilities recently. They'd been sliced open.

"The body position—"

"Moved, of course. Paramedics rolled him. Cut his pants, shirt," Reid said, pointing to the ECG pads.

Hall had seen enough death to know its variations. Some fought. Some were saved. Some lost.

"Time of death?" she asked, though she already knew the answer.

"I declared at 3:28 A.M. But paramedics said he was VSA shortly after they got here, around 2:20 A.M., give or take." Reid glanced at her watch.

"He was alive when the caller phoned it in."

Reid nodded. "Apparently, but not for long. With a wound like this, he was bleeding internally from the moment the knife went in. Even if paramedics had gotten here five minutes after it happened, his chances would have been slim. The blade nicked the hepatic artery. He bled out quickly."

"But not instantaneously," Hall said, thinking of the woman on the phone. The one who'd called for help and then disappeared. "He had time to talk, if someone had been there."

"Possibly. Shock sets in fast with injuries like this. But yes, he might have been coherent for a minute or two after it happened."

Hall stood, her knees protesting the movement. She was forty-three, not old by any standard, but old enough to feel the concrete through her slacks, old enough that crouching beside bodies wasn't as easy as it had been when she made detective at thirty.

She walked toward the CSU technician, Yeung, who was scraping something from the ground near where Lewis had fallen.

"Find anything useful?" she asked, already knowing the answer from the tight set of his shoulders.

Yeung looked up, his face drawn with the particular frustration of a scientist whose laboratory had been contaminated. "The rain washed away most of it. Blood's diluted, spread across half the alley. Whatever other evidence was here—footprints, fibers, the weapon—it's probably gone."

"No weapon?"

"Not yet, but…" He gestured at the cluttered alley. Beside the dumpster, a pile of construction debris from some long-abandoned renovation project created a dozen hiding places for a knife. "Even if we find it, the rain's probably destroyed any prints or DNA."

Hall nodded, unsurprised but still disappointed. Cases like this—homeless victims, outdoor crime scenes, bad weather—they were the ones that so often went unsolved. Not for lack of trying, but for lack of evidence. For lack of witnesses willing to come forward. For lack of people who cared enough to keep asking questions when the trail went cold.

"Keep looking," she said. "Sometimes we get lucky."

"Sometimes," Yeung agreed, but his tone suggested this wouldn't be one of those times.

Hall thanked him and turned away, scanning the alley for her partner. She spotted White leaning against the brick wall at the far end, his face tilted up toward the morning sky, eyes closed. Not sleeping—White never slept on duty—but processing. It was his way. When a case presented too many questions and not enough answers, he found a quiet corner and let his mind work without the distraction of other people's theories.

She walked toward him, her shoes splashing through puddles that reflected the gray sky above. The rain had stopped, but the morning remained damp, the air heavy with moisture that clung to her skin and clothes. Around her, the investigation continued—photographers documenting the scene, technicians collecting what little evidence remained, uniformed officers canvassing nearby buildings in search of witnesses who probably didn't exist.

All this activity for a man who had lived invisibly. Ira Lewis, whose death now commanded the attention his life never had.

White opened his eyes as she approached, straightening from his slouch against the wall. His expression told her he'd found nothing useful in his perimeter search. No murder weapon. No convenient clue dropped by a careless killer.

"So," he said as she reached him. "What's your take?"

Chapter 4

Hall watched White's face for a moment, noting the lines around his eyes that deepened when he was processing a difficult case. The morning's thin gray light did him no favors, emphasizing the pallor beneath his five o'clock shadow. White rubbed his jaw, a gesture as familiar to Hall as her own handwriting after seven years of partnership.

"Found a witness," White said, keeping his voice low. "Night shift worker from the warehouse next door. Guy named Nikolai Ware. Security supervisor."

"And?"

"And he was outside having a cigarette around two this morning." White glanced toward the mouth of the alley where uniformed officers still maintained the perimeter. A trash truck rumbled past on the street beyond, its hydraulics hissing like some great metal beast. The smell of exhaust drifted into the alley, momentarily overpowering the copper scent of blood. "Says he heard a dog bark somewhere, but didn't see or hear any else until about 2:15. Then he spotted a woman running from this direction."

Hall considered this. "The 911 caller?"

"That's what I'm thinking. Timeline matches up."

A police photographer crouched near the spot where Ira Lewis had died, his camera clicking as he documented bloodstains that the rain hadn't washed away. The sound reminded Hall of crickets in tall grass, a summer memory from childhood that seemed out of place in this damp concrete corridor.

"Tell me about Ware," Hall said.

White shifted his weight, his leather shoes squeaking against the wet pavement. "Forty-seven, divorced twice, works security at Kingman Storage. Been there eight years. Before that, ten years in the Army, honorable discharge. No record except a DUI from 2012."

"And he's sure about what he saw?"

"Says the woman came running out like the devil himself was on her heels. Dark clothes, couldn't make out her face. She headed east on Porter." White gestured in that direction with his chin. "By the time he thought to follow, she was gone. Then the police showed up, lights and sirens, so he figured whatever happened, they were handling it."

"But he didn't come forward."

"Not until uniform canvass found him this morning." White shrugged. "Said he didn't think it mattered. People come through alleys in this part of town all the time. It wasn't until he heard someone died that he connected it."

Hall turned to look back at the body. The sheet had been removed, and Dr. Reid was directing the transport team as they prepared to move Ira Lewis to the morgue van. Lewis looked small in death, his body collapsed in on itself like a building after the support beams were removed. That single knife wound had drained him of more than blood. It had taken whatever dignity he'd once had.

"What's your working theory?" she asked.

White exhaled slowly. A drizzle had begun again, so fine it was more mist than rain, beading on their coats and hair. "Unknown female suspect. Someone Lewis knew from the shelter or the street. They get into an argument. She stabs him, panics, calls 911, then runs."

"Why call at all?"

"Guilt. Shock. People do strange things when adrenaline's pumping." White pushed himself away from the wall. "Maybe she didn't mean to stab him. Maybe it was self-defense."

"No defensive wounds on Lewis," Hall reminded him. "Hard to argue self-defense when he never raised a hand against her."

"Could've been a threat. Or maybe she thought he was going to attack." White's eyes tracked the movement of an evidence tech who was bagging something near the dumpster—probably nothing more than another cigarette butt or scrap of trash, but they had to check everything. "Doesn't have to make sense. Street crimes rarely do."

A pigeon landed on the fire escape overhead, its wings creating a soft flutter that echoed in the narrow space. It watched them with a single bright eye, head cocked as if trying to understand their presence in its domain. Hall wondered what the bird had seen last night, whether it had witnessed Ira Lewis's final moments from that same perch.

"So our 911 caller," Hall said, bringing her focus back to the case. "You think she's our killer?"

White tugged at his collar where raindrops had slid beneath it. "Possible. Maybe probable. But I've seen stranger things. Could be a witness who didn't want to get involved. Could be someone who found him after the fact. Could be the person who sold him his last bottle."

"But you don't believe that."

"No." White's voice was flat. "I think she stuck the knife in him. I think she panicked and called 911, maybe hoping to undo what she'd done. Then she ran because she knew it couldn't be undone."

Hall nodded, considering. "Street crimes are messy."

"And contradictory," White agreed. "People who live on the edge don't follow the same patterns as those who don't. Their motives get tangled with survival instincts. Their decision-making gets warped by necessity."

The pigeon took flight suddenly, startled by something only it could sense. Its wings beat against the damp air as it disappeared over the rooftop. Hall watched it go, thinking about freedom and the illusion of it. How even that bird was constrained by the city, by the weather, by the constant search for food and safety.

"We need to find her," Hall said. "Before the trail gets any colder."

"We will." White's certainty was forced, a professional habit rather than a genuine belief. They both knew that cases like this—homeless victim, minimal evidence, uncooperative witnesses—had the lowest clearance rates of any homicides. "The 911 call gives us a starting point at least. Better than nothing."

Hall looked toward the street, where life continued uninterrupted. A delivery truck had parked across from the alley, its driver unloading boxes onto a hand truck. A woman walked her dog along the opposite sidewalk, her phone pressed to her ear, laughing at something the person on the other end had said. None of them glanced toward the crime scene tape. None of them paused to wonder about the life that had ended just yards away from their morning routines.

"Better than nothing," she echoed, but her voice held no conviction.

The radio on a nearby officer's belt crackled, voices cutting through the morning air with the clarity of church bells. Hall turned at the sound of footsteps approaching—firm, measured steps that belonged to someone with purpose rather than the tentative shuffle of the crime scene techs. Officer Gentry, a uniformed veteran whose face carried the permanent squint of someone who'd spent too many years watching other people's tragedies unfold, ducked under the crime scene tape and made his way toward them, a small notebook clutched in one hand.

"Detectives." Gentry nodded at them both, his voice carrying the gravel of a twenty-year smoking habit he'd quit five years too late. "Got a hit on that 911 call."

Hall straightened, her attention sharpening. In the distance, a car horn blared, the sound bouncing between the buildings like a pinball searching for an exit. The noise felt intrusive, a reminder that the world continued its business while they stood in this bubble of stopped time.

"The call came from a cell phone registered to a Rachel Fenimore." Gentry glanced down at his notebook, though Hall suspected he didn't need to. Gentry had one of those minds that cataloged information with computer-like efficiency. "Lives at 148-B Waller Street."

"Dispatch try calling her back?" White asked, pulling out his own notebook.

"Multiple attempts, no answer." Gentry shrugged. "Phone's either off or she's ignoring it. Uniform's been dispatched to the address, but no response there either."

"Prior record?"

"Clean as a whistle. Not even a parking ticket." Gentry closed his notebook, tucking it back into his breast pocket. "That's all I've got for now. I'll let you know if anything else comes in."

Hall thanked him, and Gentry retreated, pausing to exchange words with another officer near the perimeter. The morning had warmed, burning off some of the earlier mist, but dampness still hung in the air like an unfinished thought. From somewhere nearby came the sweet, cloying scent of rotting fruit, probably from a dumpster behind one of the restaurants on the block.

"Rachel Fenimore?" White's voice had changed, a note of recognition softening his usual professional tone. "I had a nurse by that name at Mercy General."

He touched his hip lightly, an unconscious gesture that Hall had seen a hundred times since that night two years ago. White's face tightened, eyes narrowing against a memory that still had physical weight. Hall remembered the blood—so much of it, pooling on the cracked linoleum of the abandoned warehouse where they'd tracked a suspect who'd turned out to be far more dangerous than their intel had suggested.

Two shots fired in the dark. One missing White entirely. The other finding a home just below his belt, tearing through muscle but missing his femoral artery. The doctors later said he'd been minutes from bleeding out. Hall had used her belt as a tourniquet, had pressed her hands against the wound with all her strength, had whispered fierce encouragements that sounded like prayers even to her own ears. She'd ridden in the ambulance with him, her hands still red with his blood, and had sat in the surgical waiting room for eleven hours, unable to wash her hands because that might somehow jinx his survival.

"The one with the dark hair?" Hall asked, searching her memory. Those days after White's surgery had blurred together, a haze of hospital antiseptic, bad coffee, and the constant beeping of machines. "Quiet, efficient? Seemed to know when you needed pain meds before you asked?"

White nodded. "That's her. Wonder if it's the same person."

Hall thought back to the woman she remembered—or thought she remembered—from those hospital days. Medium height, slim, with the kind of face that was designed to fade into the background. The type you could pass in a hallway five times and still not recognize on the sixth encounter. But there had been something about her eyes that Hall had noticed. Something watchful. Intelligent. The eyes of someone who saw more than she let on.

"Could be a coincidence," Hall said, though neither of them believed in coincidences. Not in their line of work. "Not an uncommon name."

"No," White agreed, "but not that common either." He shifted his weight, wincing. The old wound still troubled him on damp days, a permanent barometer built into his flesh. "Let's head to Mercy General. Someone there will know her schedule, her whereabouts. Then we can find out if it's the same Rachel Fenimore."

A gust of wind swept down the alley, carrying with it the scent of someone's breakfast—eggs and bacon from one of the apartments above—momentarily overwhelming the crime scene smells of blood and wet concrete. Hall's stomach growled, reminding her she hadn't eaten since yesterday's lunch, a sandwich consumed at her desk between witness statements on another case.

"Let's go," she said, turning toward where they'd parked. Behind them, the crime scene techs were finishing their work, packing equipment into black cases, labeling evidence bags. Dr. Reid supervised as attendants lifted Ira Lewis's body onto a gurney, his form now hidden in a black bag, the stains of his death contained and cataloged. Soon there would be nothing left in this alley to indicate that a man had bled out here in the rain except a faint darkening of the concrete that would wash away with the next heavy downpour.

As they walked toward their car, Hall thought again about the woman running from the alley. What had Rachel Fenimore seen—or done—that sent her fleeing into the night? And why call 911 if she was responsible? Questions without answers, at least for now. But they had a name, and a place to start looking. In Hall's experience, that was often enough to unravel even the most tangled of threads.

Chapter 5

Mercy General Hospital rose before them, a twelve-story slab of concrete and glass that reflected the morning's weak sunlight like a dull mirror. Hall pulled into the visitors' lot, the car tires crunching over scattered pebbles that had escaped from a nearby landscaping bed. White complained about the thirty-dollar parking fee, despite the fact that Hall was paying.

"I'll get reimbursed, you know," Hall said as she tucked the ticket into her wallet.

"Highway robbery," White scoffed.

The air smelled of rain-washed pavement and distant exhaust as they stepped in, the hospital's automated doors parting with a whispered hiss that reminded Hall of secrets being told.

The emergency department buzzed with controlled chaos. A child with a bleeding forehead clung to his mother in the waiting area. An elderly man dozed in a wheelchair, his breathing a raspy counterpoint to the muted television mounted in the corner. Three nurses behind the central desk, their faces set in the neutrality of people who had seen too much pain to react to it anymore.

"Second time this week I've been here," White said, his voice low. "Brought my nephew in Tuesday night. Kid broke his wrist skateboarding." He absently touched his hip, a gesture Hall had seen a thousand times since his injury. "Place never changes. Same smell."

Hall knew what he meant. Beneath the surface notes of hand sanitizer and floor cleaner lay something more fundamental—the unmistakable scent of human frailty. Fear and pain and relief and grief, all mingled together in a cocktail that permeated the very walls.

White scanned the room, his eyes narrowing as they moved from face to face. Then his body stiffened. "That's her," he said, nodding toward the far end of the nurses' station. "Rachel."

Hall followed his gaze to a woman in blue scrubs, her dark hair pulled back in a simple ponytail. Rachel Fenimore bent over a computer terminal, her fingers wrestling with a mouse. She was younger than Hall remembered, mid-thirties perhaps, prettier. But there was something in the set of her shoulders, a tension that didn't match the easy movements of the other staff.

"You're sure?" Hall asked, though she already knew the answer.

White nodded. "Positive. She was on the rehab floor when I was recovering. Always punctual with the pain meds. Quiet type. Kept to herself, but good at her job."

Hall studied Rachel, taking in details with the eye of someone who had spent time translating physical cues into insights about the people who displayed them. Rachel's scrubs were pristine, recently laundered. Her movements were precise, economical. But her left hand strayed repeatedly to her neck, fingertips pressing against the spot where her pulse would be strongest, a self-soothing gesture Hall had seen in countless interview rooms over the years.

As they watched, another nurse—a heavyset woman with a riot of red curls escaping her cap—passed behind Rachel and paused, leaning in to murmur something in her ear. The woman's eyes flicked toward Hall and White, and she gave Rachel a subtle elbow to the ribs before moving on. Rachel's shoulders tensed further, but she didn't look up. Didn't turn to see who had entered. Just kept her eyes fixed on the screen before her, her fingers now motionless on the keyboard.

"She knows we're here," Hall said.

"Seems that way." White's face had taken on the flat, professional mask he wore when approaching a suspect. All traces of the man who had once been this woman's patient were gone, replaced by the detective who saw her now as a potential link to a dead man in an alley.

Hall took a step forward, then paused as a doctor rushed past, the hem of his white coat fluttering. A new patient was being wheeled in—an unconscious woman on a gurney, her face covered by an oxygen mask, a paramedic straddling her body performing chest compressions. For a moment, the emergency room's attention shifted toward this fresh crisis. All except Rachel, who remained frozen at her terminal, a statue amid motion.

"She's afraid," Hall observed. "Look at her hands."

Rachel's fingers now gripped the edge of the counter, knuckles white with pressure. Her breathing had changed too—quick, shallow inhalations that made her chest rise and fall in a rhythm too rapid to be casual.

"Guilt or fear?" White wondered.

"Sometimes they look the same from a distance."

A nurse called Rachel's name, and she startled, head jerking up like a puppet whose string had been yanked. She turned toward the voice, and for the first time, Hall saw her face clearly—pale skin with faint shadows beneath her eyes, lips pressed into a thin line of concentration or worry. As Rachel moved to respond to her colleague, her gaze swept across the room and for a fraction of a second, she locked eyes with White.

Recognition bloomed in her expression, followed immediately by something that might have been alarm or might have been resignation. Her step faltered before she continued toward the patient room where she'd been summoned.

"She remembers you," Hall said.

White nodded, his expression unreadable. "Question is, does she remember what happened this morning?"

They watched as Rachel disappeared into the examination room. Through the partially open door, Hall could see her checking an IV line, her movements automatic, her mind visibly elsewhere.

"What else do you recall about her?" Hall asked, keeping her voice casual though her mind was cataloging every detail, building a profile of the woman they needed to question.

White considered for a moment, rubbing his jaw. "Quiet. Some of the other nurses were chattier—weekend plans, dating problems, the usual stuff. Not her. Kept to herself." He paused. "There was something, though. One night, late shift, she was doing her rounds. I was having trouble sleeping—pain was bad. She sat with me for a bit. Mentioned she had sleep problems too."

Hall filed this information away. Sleep. Who didn't have sleep problems?

"Ready?" she asked, nodding toward the examination room where Rachel was finishing up with her patient.

White straightened his tie, a gesture that had less to do with appearance and more to do with preparing for a confrontation. "Let's find out what she knows about Ira Lewis."

As they crossed the emergency room floor, Hall noticed the red-haired nurse watching them, her expression a mix of curiosity and concern. She leaned toward another staff member, whispered something that made them both glance toward Rachel's room. Word was spreading. The white wall of medical solidarity forming, perhaps. Hall had seen it before—the instinctive closing of ranks around one of their own when outsiders approached with questions.

They paused outside the examination room, waiting for Rachel to emerge. Hall positioned herself where she could observe the nurse's face when she saw them—that critical window when surprise might reveal truth before defenses could be raised. White stood slightly behind her, his presence a solid weight at her back, familiar and reassuring in its constancy.

The door opened, and Rachel Fenimore stepped out, her eyes cast down at the chart in her hands. One step, two, and then she looked up.

Rachel froze mid-step, her eyes widening before her professional mask slipped back into place. Something flickered across her features—recognition, certainly, but something else too. Something that made Hall's instincts prickle like the air before a lightning strike. Rachel clutched her clipboard tighter against her chest, a shield of plastic and paper between herself and the two detectives who now blocked her path in the narrow hospital corridor.

"Ms. Fenimore?" Hall stepped forward, her badge already in her hand. "Detective Carolyn Hall. This is Detective Robert White. We'd like to ask you a few questions."

White offered a small smile. "We've met before, actually. You might not remember."

Rachel's gaze shifted to White, her throat working as she swallowed. "Detective White, yes. I—" She paused, one hand rising to touch her employee badge, fingers tracing its edges like a worry stone. "You were shot, if I recall. Two years ago?"

"Two years, three months," White confirmed, his voice neutral despite the memory it carried. "You were part of the surgical team."

Rachel shook her head, a quick, nervous gesture. "No, that's not right." Her voice was softer than Hall had expected, with a slight rasp at its edges. "I'm an ER nurse, not surgical. I was working in Rehabilitation then." A faint flush colored her cheeks. "I helped during your recovery. Changed dressings, administered medication. That sort of thing."

Her fingers moved from her badge to her watch, adjusting its position on her wrist though it hadn't been out of place. The watch was expensive, Hall noted. A Merten with a leather band, incongruous against the practical scrubs. A gift, perhaps, or a personal indulgence that spoke of a life outside these antiseptic walls.

"You have a good memory," White said, his tone conversational though his eyes remained sharp.

"I remember the serious cases." Rachel's gaze dropped to the floor, then to the wall behind them, then back to White's face. Never settling, never still. "You were lucky. The bullet missed your femoral artery by millimeters. Are you doing okay?"

A passing orderly pushed a cart of supplies, the wheels squeaking against the polished floor. The smell of microwaved food wafted from the staff break room down the hall—something with fish, the scent intrusive and out of place in the clinical environ-ment. Rachel's nose wrinkled, the most natural reaction Hall had seen from her so far.

"Ms. Fenimore," Hall said, drawing the nurse's attention back, "we're investigating an incident that occurred early this morning. A stabbing near the Chinese food restaurant on Porter Street. In a back alley." She watched Rachel's face, looking for any tell that might betray foreknowledge. "A man died."

Rachel's composure slipped, just for a moment—a tightening around her eyes, a quick inhalation. But she recovered quickly, her features schooling themselves back into professional concern.

"That's terrible," she said. Her hand moved to her neck, fingers pressing against her carotid pulse. "But I'm not sure what that has to do with me."

White shifted his weight, the movement drawing Rachel's gaze. "Emergency services received a 911 call about the victim. The call came from your cell phone."

The clipboard trembled almost imperceptibly in Rachel's hands. "There must be some mistake."

"The call was placed at 2:15 this morning," White continued, his voice level. "Caller reported a stabbing victim in an alley behind the textile mill. When paramedics arrived, they found a man with a slicing wound to the abdomen. He died shortly after."

Rachel's tongue darted out to wet her lips. "I was asleep at 2:15 this morning. At home. In bed."

"Can anyone verify that?" Hall asked.

"No."

"The call definitely came from your phone, Ms. Fenimore," White pressed. "Your number is registered in our system."

Rachel's fingers found the hem of her scrub top, twisting the blue fabric. "My phone was with me all night. It was charging beside my bed." She hesitated, then added, "I take medication to help me sleep. I wouldn't have heard it if someone called."

"We're not talking about someone calling you," Hall clarified. "We're talking about someone using your phone to call 911."

Rachel looked down at her shoes—white nursing clogs, practical and unmarked. When she raised her head again, her expression had changed. The nervousness remained, but now there was something else beneath it. Something calculating.

"I don't know what to tell you," she said. "I don't know anything about the stabbing. I don't know how my number could have been used."

White's patience was visibly thinning. "Technical errors don't usually include accurate details about crime scenes. The caller knew where the victim was, what his injuries were."

Rachel's gaze dropped to White's hip—the spot where the bullet had torn through him two years before. A gesture so brief Hall might have missed it if she hadn't been watching so intently.

"I think," Hall said, her voice gentle but firm, "that it would be better if we continued this conversation somewhere more private."

Rachel's head snapped up, her eyes meeting Hall's for the first time. Something passed between them then—a current of understanding, perhaps, or recognition. For a heartbeat, Rachel's mask slipped. The frightened nurse vanished, replaced by someone altogether different—someone with depths Hall hadn't anticipated.

"There's a break room," Rachel said quietly. "We can talk there."

The break room was tucked at the end of a narrow hallway, far enough from the ER's constant motion that the beeps and voices faded to a distant hum. Hall followed Rachel's stiff back, noting how the nurse's shoulders had risen closer to her ears with each step away from the bustle of the emergency department. The smell of someone's leftover lunch—something with garlic and tomato sauce—lingered in the air, growing stronger as Rachel pushed open the break room door.

The room was small and institutional—a square box with beige walls and speckled linoleum flooring that had seen better days. A round table with three chairs occupied the center, its laminate surface scarred with coffee rings and pen marks. The overhead LED panels cast a shadowless light that made Rachel's skin look paler than it had in the corridor.

Hall took the chair facing the door, a habit born from years of interviewing witnesses and suspects. White settled beside her, his bulk making the metal chair creak in protest. Rachel hesitated before taking the seat across from them, her fingers trailing along the table's edge as if testing its solidity.

"I owe you an explanation," Rachel said, the words coming out like something practiced. Her eyes fixed on a spot just past Hall's left shoulder. "I did call. I found him and I called 911."

White leaned forward, forearms resting on the table. "Why don't you start at the beginning? Tell us about last night."

Rachel's tongue darted out to wet her lips. A ceiling vent kicked on with a soft rattle, sending a cool current of air through the room.

"I worked late last night," Rachel began, her hands twisting together in her lap. "We had a multi-car accident come in around ten, three critical patients. By the time we stabilized everyone and got them moved to ICU or surgery, it was past midnight." She paused, swallowing. "I clocked out around 1:30. I always walk home when the weather's decent. It helps me decompress."

Hall noticed the slight hesitation, filed it away. "That's a late shift. You must have been tired."

"It happens in emergency medicine." Rachel's shoulders relaxed fractionally. "You learn to function on whatever sleep you can get. I'm sure you detectives know exactly what that's like."

A nurse with cropped gray hair pushed through the door, nodding at the three of them before heading straight to the refrigerator. As she opened it, Hall caught the yeasty scent of cold air and leftovers. The woman pulled out a yogurt, paused, then headed for the door without speaking. Hall cataloged the reaction, noting how the woman's pace quickened as she left.

"My apartment is a few blocks from here," Rachel continued. "I was cutting through that alley on Porter—it shaves about ten minutes off my walk. That's when I found him."

Rachel's eyes lost focus. "He was already on the ground when I found him. There was so much blood. I could tell immediately it was a stab wound. Deep. The knife went into the lung. I could tell from the bubbling blood."

"What did you do then?" Hall asked, watching as Rachel's fingers found the edge of her name badge.

"What any nurse would do. I assessed him, tried to apply pressure to the wound. But it was... it was a severe wound." Rachel's eyes lost focus. "I called 911. I had my phone in my pocket. I told them where we were, what I could. I started CPR, but it was futile."

"And then?" Hall prompted when Rachel fell silent.

"I heard the sirens getting closer. I knew they would take him, try to save him." Rachel looked down at her hands. "But I also knew they wouldn't succeed. His injuries were too severe."

"So you left," White said, the words flat.

Rachel nodded. "I didn't want to be in the way. There was nothing more I could contribute."

Hall leaned back in her chair. "Most people would stay. Give a statement to police."

"I'm not most people." Something hard lived behind Rachel's eyes. "I have issues with authority figures. Bad experiences. I panicked when I heard the sirens."

"Did you know him?" White asked. "Ira Lewis?"

Rachel shook her head. "No. Never saw him before. That was his name? Ira?"

"Yes," Hall said, watching for any flicker of recognition. There was none. "He stayed at the Saint Christopher Shelter occasionally."

"I didn't know that." Rachel's shoulders slumped. "I didn't know anything about him. Just that he was dying, and I couldn't stop it."

White closed his notebook with a soft snap. "Thank you for being honest with us, Ms. Fenimore."

There was a weight to his words that Hall recognized—the pressure of suspicion not quite voiced. Rachel heard it too. Her fingers went back to her badge.

"I'm a nurse," she said, as if the title itself was an alibi. "I try to save people. Not harm them."

"I never said you harmed him," White said, head cocked.

Hall stood, signaling the end of their conversation. "We understand, Ms. Fenimore. We may have more questions as the investigation continues."

Rachel nodded, relief washing over her features at the prospect of returning to her work. But as they prepared to leave, Hall couldn't shake the feeling that Rachel Fenimore had just told them a story with crucial pieces missing.

The emergency room had changed in the twenty minutes they'd spent in the break room. A fresh wave of patients had arrived—an elderly woman coughing, an angry drunk with two police escorts, and a teenager with a wrist bent at an unnatural angle. Hall breathed in the complicated scent of the ER and watched as Rachel Fenimore stepped back into this world with visible relief.

"Thank you for your time," Hall said.

Rachel nodded, already half-turned toward the central desk. "I'll let you know if I remember anything else."

White said nothing, his silence its own form of skepticism. They watched Rachel move away from them, her steps quickening. A small boy sat on the edge of a chair, his face wet with tears. Rachel approached them, kneeling to the boy's level, her face softening into genuine warmth.

"She seems really nice," Hall said.

White snorted. "That's not how I remember her."

Hall turned to him, curious. "No?"

White started walking toward the exit, and Hall fell into step beside him. "When I was in rehab, she was a drill sergeant. Always on my ass about exercises, pushing me to do one more set, walk one more lap around the floor."

Hall smiled. "She was your rehab nurse, White. Getting on your lazy ass was literally her job."

"She made me do leg lifts while I was trying to watch the playoffs," White grumbled.

"Sounds like she was good at her job. You were back on active duty three weeks ahead of schedule."

"Fuck off," White said, the words light, familiar.

Hall's smile widened. "That's Detective Fuck Off to you."

Hall paused as they passed the central nursing station. One of the nurses—her name badge read MARTINEZ—looked up as they approached.

"Can I help you?" Martinez asked, her tone suggesting she hoped the answer was no.

Hall produced her badge, holding it at waist level. "Detective Hall, New Hanan PD. Just wondered if I could ask you something quick."

Martinez regarded Hall with weary skepticism. "Make it fast. We're short-staffed to-day."

"What was the ER like early this morning?" Hall kept her tone casual. "Around one, two in the morning? Chaotic?"

Martinez frowned. "No, it was quiet. Just the usual overnight stuff—a couple of drunks, broken ankle from a guy who fell off his porch, college kid with alcohol poisoning. Nothing special."

Hall nodded. "I guess Rachel's patience comes in handy with the drunks, huh?"

The nurse's fingers stilled on the keyboard. She glanced toward where Rachel was still with the boy.

"Rachel?" Martinez's brow furrowed. "Rachel wasn't working last night."

The words landed between them, simple and devastating. Hall kept her face neutral, but beneath the professional mask, her mind accelerated.

"Oh? My mistake," Hall said, her voice revealing nothing.

Martinez shook her head. "No, I'm sure she wasn't here. I was on shift myself. Rachel called out yesterday morning—said she was fighting a migraine. She wasn't due back until this morning at seven."

"Still, sounds like an easy night," Hall said, stepping back from the counter.

White joined her, his expression questioning. Hall shook her head—not here—and continued toward the exit. They walked in silence through the automatic doors and into the parking lot, where morning sun had broken through the clouds, turning puddles from last night's rain into mirrors.

Only when they were twenty feet from the building did Hall speak. "Rachel wasn't working last night."

White stopped walking, his body going still. "There were no reports of multi-vehicle accidents last night. Just checked Traffic Service's feed. She lied."

"Straight to our faces." Hall squinted against the sudden brightness.

White's face hardened. "Why? Why lie about something so easy to check?"

"That," Hall said, "is the question worth asking."

They reached the car in silence, the gravity of Rachel's lie settling between them. Hall leaned against the driver's side door, key fob in hand but making no move to unlock it. The parking lot smelled of wet asphalt drying in patches, of exhaust from idling ambulances near the ER entrance.

White stopped on the passenger side, one hand resting on the roof. "She lied to us. Said she was working a multi-vehicle accident, but there wasn't one."

"And that nurse, Martinez, confirmed she wasn't even on shift."

"We'd have to get the official records from HR."

"If we need to. But she's already been caught in the lie," Hall said, watching a pair of paramedics wheeling an empty gurney back toward a waiting ambulance. "Question is why? Why construct a false alibi that's so easy to verify?"

"Panic," White suggested. "People don't think straight when they're covering something up."

Hall considered this. Rachel was nervous, certainly, but not panicked. There had been something calculated beneath the anxiety.

"What strikes me as weird," Hall said, "is that she said she was walking home through an alley at two in the morning. You know many women who will do that?"

A helicopter passed overhead, its blades chopping the air into segments of sound.

"Hell no," White said. "She was there for some other reason."

"And why leave right when help arrived?" she continued. "That's not normal behavior for a medical professional."

White's eyes narrowed. "You think she saw something? Maybe the actual killer?"

"Maybe. But if that's the case, why not tell us? Why lie about working?"

A young mother walked past them, pulling a toddler by the hand. White watched them pass before returning to the case at hand.

"What if she had more involvement than she's admitting to?" he asked, his voice dropping lower. "What if she's covering for whoever actually stabbed Lewis?"

The possibility hung between them, given weight by Rachel's confirmed lie. Hall had considered it from the moment they'd learned Rachel had fled the scene.

"Look, in seven years, how many times have we investigated a woman killing a man with a knife? Eight? Nine? And how many outside the home?" White asked.

"None."

"None. Every single one was an intimate partner, and in the house."

"So statistically, she didn't stab him?" Hall asked.

"No. But, how often do we find women covering up for some guy? At least ten a year where a woman lies for her man," White said.

"So we need to find the man in her life," Hall said, trying to hide the disappointment in her voice.

"Maybe they were in the alley, Lewis interfered with something," White suggested. "Sex. Drugs. Heat of the moment there's an argument, boyfriend stabs Lewis. Boyfriend runs, nurse Rachel tries to save the guy. Can't. She runs."

Hall remembered a case from five years back—a fight over a woman, one dead, the woman swearing she didn't know either man. Then she stuck by her man through the arrest and dumped him the day after conviction.

"I don't know," Hall said, her instincts pulling in multiple directions. "Something doesn't add up."

"What's our next move?" White asked, though they both knew the answer.

Hall sighed, finally unlocking the car with a press of the key fob. "We treat her as a possible suspect rather than just a witness. Check her background, find her boyfriend, track her movements last night, any connection to Lewis or the area where he was killed."

White nodded, opening his door. The familiar smell of their shared workspace—coffee and mint gum and the Blue Mist air freshener—drifted out. "I'll start with a warrant for her financials and phone records as soon as we get back to the station."

Hall slid into the driver's seat. As White settled beside her, she pushed the start button. On the radio, a news announcer mentioned a storm system moving in by evening.

"I will check her socials," Hall said, backing out of the space. "Find out if she really does live alone."

White adjusted his seat belt, grimacing as it pressed against his hip. "Time to hunt."

Hall guided the car toward the exit, glancing one last time at Mercy General in the rearview mirror—its clean lines and glass facade reflecting clouds and sky. Somewhere inside, Rachel Fenimore continued her shift, tending to the wounds of strangers while her own secrets festered beneath the surface.

"Prey," Hall agreed, pulling into traffic.

Chapter 6

The homicide division hummed with midday energy: a lull between the morning's fresh cases and whatever Happy Hour might bring. Hall unwrapped her sandwich at her desk, the waxed paper crackling between her fingers as she watched the precinct's life unfold around her. Across the room, someone's microwave lunch released the sharp stench of fish into the air, temporarily overwhelming the usual blend of sweat and machismo. The windows along the eastern wall admitted blocks of sunlight that cut across the worn floor, illuminating dust motes that danced in the still air like evidence of something no one had bothered to document.

Hall glanced at the clock on her computer screen: 1:17 P.M. White had disappeared fifteen minutes ago, muttering something about case files in the basement. The division was half-empty—detectives out interviewing witnesses, following leads, or simply escaping the confines of the office for their lunch hour. She took a bite of her sandwich and reached for the can of soda she'd pulled from the vending machine that morning. The aluminum was room temperature now, no longer offering even the illusion of refreshment.

She set the sandwich down and pulled Rachel Fenimore's file toward her. It wasn't much of a file yet—just the preliminary background check she'd run in the system. No warrants, no arrests, no calls-for-service. Clean record, no traffic stops, nursing license in good standing. A woman without obvious shadows, which in Hall's experience only meant the shadows were hidden better than most.

The lie about working last night changed things. It transformed Rachel from witness to suspect, from someone who might help solve Ira Lewis's murder to someone who might have been involved. Hall studied the phone number listed in the file, considering her approach. People lied for reasons. Understanding those reasons was the skeleton key that unlocked most cases.

She picked up her desk phone and dialed. The receiver was smooth against her ear, warm from the sunlight that had been hitting it all morning. Three rings passed before Rachel answered.

"Hello?" The voice on the other end sounded tentative, as if Rachel sensed who might be calling.

"Ms. Fenimore? This is Detective Hall." She kept her voice professional, neutral. "I hope I'm not catching you at a bad time."

A beat of silence stretched between them. In the background, Hall could hear the muted sounds of the hospital—voices on an intercom, the distant chime of a call button. "I'm on my break," Rachel said. "What can I do for you, Detective?"

Hall leaned back in her chair, the springs creaking beneath her weight. A detective two desks over laughed at something on his computer screen, the sound jarring against the serious tenor of her thoughts. "I was hoping you might be able to come down to the station tomorrow. There are a few more questions we'd like to ask about what you witnessed last night."

"I'm not sure what else I can tell you." Rachel's voice had taken on that careful quality people used when they thought they were being led into a trap. "I told you everything I could remember at the hospital."

"Sometimes details come back later," Hall said. "The hospital wasn't really the ideal environment for this kind of conversation. Too many interruptions, too much noise. We find people often remember more in a quieter setting."

Another pause. Hall could almost see Rachel weighing her options, calculating risks and rewards like compound interest. A phone rang at a nearby desk, going unanswered until it clicked over to voicemail. The detective who'd been laughing now unwrapped a sandwich, the smell of onion joining the fish in the office air.

"I don't think I can be more help," Rachel said at last. "It all happened so fast, and it was dark, and the rain—"

"Do you remember me?" Hall asked, cutting through Rachel's hesitation. "From when Detective White was in the hospital? I came to visit him nearly every day during his recovery."

The question seemed to catch Rachel off guard. "Yes," she said after a moment. "Yes, I remember you. You always brought those paperback novels. The ones with the spaceships on the covers." A smile crept into her voice. "I never forget a beautiful woman."

The comment hung in the air between them, unexpected and strange. Hall felt her eyebrows rise of their own accord. Was Rachel flirting with her? She glanced toward White's empty chair, almost expecting him to have materialized there to witness this bizarre turn in the conversation. The sunlight through the windows had shifted, casting new patterns on the floor. Someone walked past her desk, trailing the scent of an expensive cologne that didn't belong in a police precinct.

"See?" Hall said, recovering her professional footing. "You do have a good memory." She kept her tone light, letting a smile warm her voice. If Rachel was attempting to disarm her with flirtation, two could play at that game. "When can you come in? Tomorrow afternoon would be ideal."

"I suppose I could come in around two," Rachel conceded, her tone shifting back toward professional caution. "My shift ends at one-thirty."

"Two would be perfect." Hall made a note on the pad beside her keyboard. "We'll try not to take up too much of your time. Just a few follow-up questions to clarify your statement."

"My statement." Rachel's voice flattened on the words. "Of course."

Hall sensed the withdrawal, the mental doors closing. She needed to leave the conversation on a warmer note if she wanted Rachel to actually show up tomorrow rather than calling with an excuse. "I'm looking forward to seeing you again," she said, letting a touch of personal interest color the professional words. "Under better circumstances than a hospital room."

"Are police interrogations really better circumstances?" Rachel asked, but there was a hint of humor beneath the question.

"We'll have better coffee, at least." Hall smiled despite herself. "See you at two, Ms. Fenimore."

She hung up the phone and reached for her soda, taking a long swallow before grimacing. Warm and flat, with a metallic undertone that reminded her of blood. She set the can down and pushed it away, no longer interested in its dubious comfort. The conversation with Rachel lingered in her mind like the aftertaste of the soda. Unexpected, slightly off, but impossible to ignore.

What was Rachel's angle? The flirtation seemed calculated, a distraction technique perhaps. Hall had seen it before from suspects who thought they could charm their way out of trouble, who believed a smile or a suggestive comment might make a detective forget the inconsistencies in their stories. But Rachel didn't strike her as that type. Her deceptions were more deliberate, more complex.

The clock on her computer advanced to 1:32. White would be back soon, and they would need to strategize about tomorrow's interview. Hall made another note on her pad: "R.F.—FLIRTATIOUS? BOYFRIEND?" She underlined the question twice, a visual reminder to watch for this behavior tomorrow, to be alert to its purpose in Rachel's larger strategy.

From across the room came the sound of someone dropping a stack of files, papers scattering across the floor with a sound like birds taking flight. A murmur of sympathetic comments and suppressed laughter followed.

Hall double-clicked the Socials folder on her desktop, a digital archive meticulously curated over the years. She had long ago bookmarked all the important social media platforms—the ubiquitous giants alongside the smaller, local sites that sometimes held the most revealing truths. She moved through them alphabetically, a ritual of investigation that had become second nature.

The proliferation of "Rachel Fenimore" accounts surprised her. One in New Hanan. Only two in the entire state. She clicked through, her fingertips cool against the mouse. The accounts were private fortresses, but their avatars stood exposed like sentinels at the gate. And there she was. Rachel Fenimore. With another woman, their shoulders touching in a way that suggested intimacy rather than mere acquaintance.

She moved deeper into the digital terrain. Profile after profile revealed the same story—Rachel alone or with the same woman, their poses shifting but their connection constant. In one image, they were kissing, faces half-shadowed but unmistakable. No men. No boyfriend. The LED lights hummed above as Hall felt something shift inside her, like a key turning in a lock long rusted shut. So Rachel had flirted with her. And Rachel was likely not covering for a boyfriend-turned-killer.

Hall printed the pages, each one emerging warm from the machine. She gathered them quickly, not with the hurried panic of someone fearing discovery but with the careful precision of someone collecting fragments of a truth too precious to scatter. The pages disappeared into her folder, evidence of something she wasn't yet ready to name.

For Hall, queerness had always been a private room within the house of her professional life. At Kowalski's retirement party last year, twenty detectives had gathered at McGinty's, each orbited by wives, husbands, partners—constellations of belonging. Hall had nursed a beer alone at the bar, the amber liquid catching light as she swirled it. When asked, she'd offered the familiar words—"Not seeing anyone right now"—knowing the silence that followed contained relief rather than curiosity. They would accept a solitary woman far more readily than a lesbian. She had learned this long before she pinned on a badge.

The folder went into her drawer, and she pulled out Ira Lewis's file, to the photo of his body in the alley, rain-soaked and abandoned. Whatever game Rachel was playing, whatever secrets she was keeping, they were connected to this man's death. And Hall intended to find out how.

White returned to his desk with case files tucked under his arm and an expression on his face that Hall had seen directed at suspects but rarely at her. He settled into his chair, the aged leather releasing a soft sigh of compressed air, and stared at her across the battleground of their facing desks.

Hall leaned forward, closer to White, so she could tell him without being heard by others. "Rachel Fenimore's socials show her with a woman, not a man. She's probably not protecting a man."

White's eyes were narrowed, lips pressed into a thin line beneath his two-day stubble. He mouthed something—a single word that Hall couldn't quite make out—but the shape of it didn't look like congratulations.

Hall pretended not to notice, shuffling papers with studied concentration. The tension stretched between them like a tripwire, waiting for someone to make the wrong move. The office sounds continued around them—keyboards clicking, phones ringing, the soft murmur of detectives comparing notes on cases—but their shared space had gone silent and cold.

White finally broke the silence, but not in the way Hall had expected. "Any update on the Henderson case?" he asked, his voice deliberately casual. "The gas station shooting."

Henderson. The twenty-four-year-old night clerk shot during a robbery gone wrong three weeks ago. A case that had started hot and turned lukewarm as leads dried up and witnesses disappeared back into the city's shadows. Hall recognized the question for what it was—a professional lifeline thrown across the growing chasm between them.

"Nothing new," she said, accepting the olive branch with relief. "We're still waiting for the Fingerprint Unit to get back to us on the partial we lifted from the counter." She paused. "Jenkins thinks it's a dead end. Says the print was too smudged to be useful."

White grunted, a noncommittal sound that could have meant agreement or dismissal. He shifted in his seat, wincing as he adjusted his position. His hand moved to his right hip, pressing against it through the fabric of his slacks. The pain was worse today—the weather, maybe, or the extra hours they'd put in on the Lewis case. Hall had learned to read the signs over their years together, could track White's discomfort in the tightening around his eyes, the careful way he distributed his weight when sitting.

"Is there a problem, White?" The question came out more defensively than she'd intended. Outside, a car horn blared from the street below, a sound that cut through the air like an accusation. Hall felt herself tensing in response to both.

White looked at her then, his gaze steady and uncompromising. "No problem." His tone contradicted his words. "Just in a bad mood. Leg hurts." He reached into his pocket and extracted an orange prescription bottle, the rattle of pills inside like tiny bones being shaken in a cup. He tapped one white tablet into his palm, then recapped the bottle and returned it to his pocket.

Hall watched as White reached for his water bottle—one of those stainless steel things that kept drinks cold for hours, a gift from his sister last Christmas. He swallowed the pill with a long drink, his Adam's apple bobbing above his loosened tie. When he set the bottle down, water beaded on its surface like sweat on skin.

"You should keep it professional, Hall." The words landed between them like stones dropped from a height. "With Fenimore, I mean."

Something cold and hard formed in Hall's chest. "When have I ever not been professional?"

"That phone call just now? 'Looking forward to seeing you'?" White's imitation of her voice was unflattering, pitched higher than her actual tone. "The smile in your voice? I could hear it from across the room."

Where the hell had been listening from?

"It's called building rapport," Hall said, the cold thing in her chest spreading outward. "Making a witness comfortable. Getting them to trust you. Basic interviewing techniques, White. Nothing you haven't done a hundred times yourself."

"She's not just a witness," White countered. "She's a potential suspect who already lied to our faces once. And that thing about never forgetting a beautiful woman? What was that about?"

Hall felt heat rising to her face. "That was her, not me. I can't control what she says. How—"

"No, but you can control how you respond to it." White's voice had dropped lower, meant only for her ears despite the open floor plan around them. Another detective walked past, nodding at them both before continuing to the water cooler in the corner. "You sounded... receptive."

The implication hung in the air between them like cigarette smoke, acrid and impossible to wave away. Hall felt something shift between them, a recalibration of a partnership she'd thought was built on mutual respect. Had White always seen her this way—as someone whose professionalism could be compromised by a pretty face and a suggestive comment?

"It was strategy," Hall said, each word distinct and cold. "Getting her to come in voluntarily instead of having to track her down with a material witness warrant. Nothing more."

White held her gaze for a long moment before turning to his computer, the conversation apparently over as far as he was concerned. The dismissal stung worse than the accusation. Hall watched as he logged into the system, his fingers moving over the keyboard with force. His profile in the harsh light from the windows showed the lines that hadn't been there when they'd first partnered seven years ago—the creases around his eyes, the deepening furrow between his brows, the slight softening beneath his jaw.

They had grown older together in this job, witnessed each other's triumphs and failures, saved each other's lives in ways both literal and metaphorical. And now he thought she would compromise an investigation because a suspect—a woman—had called her beautiful?

Hall turned to her own computer, the screen swimming before her eyes. She blinked hard, forcing her vision to clear, and looked again at the case files on Ira Lewis. The photographs from the scene. The alley in harsh flash lighting, Lewis's body a dark shape beneath the white sheet, bloodstains diluted by rain but still visible on the concrete. She stared at the images, letting them cool the hurt and anger that pulsed beneath her skin.

White was wrong about her motivations. But what if he was right about Rachel? What if the flirtation had been calculated, a strategy to throw Hall off balance? It had worked on White, clearly—disturbed his perception of his partner's judgment. What else might Rachel be capable of manipulating?

Hall glanced at White, who was still focused on his screen, his shoulders rigid with unspoken disapproval. The afternoon stretched ahead of them, hours of shared space and silence before they could retreat to their separate lives. The precinct continued its rhythms around them—phones ringing, doors opening and closing, the soft symphony of a workplace dedicated to uncovering truths while its occupants buried their own.

Tomorrow at two, Rachel Fenimore would walk into this building, into an interview room, and Hall would need to be at her sharpest. No distractions, no personal feelings, nothing but the clear, cold pursuit of facts. White was wrong about her professionalism, and she would prove it—to him, to herself, and to the ghost of Ira Lewis, who deserved nothing less than the complete truth about his final moments in that rain-soaked alley.

Chapter 7

Hall studied her reflection in the washroom mirror, fingers working through her hair with the slow deliberation of someone performing a ritual rather than a routine. The harsh LED lights above the sink cast shadows beneath her eyes that hadn't been there two years ago when she first saw Rachel Fenimore. Now, she was beautiful. She frowned at the thought, at the vanity it revealed. Beautiful wasn't a word that belonged in homicide investigations, and yet here she was, brushing her hair for a murder suspect.

"You're a goddamn cliché," she told her reflection. The words bounced off the mint-green tiles, flat and honest in the empty room.

She tucked the brush back into her purse, then pulled it out again, dragging it through the ends of her hair one more time. The glass reflected a woman in her forties, neither young nor old, neither beautiful nor plain. Just a detective who had seen too many bodies and not enough justice. Two years older and wearier than when she'd sat beside White's hospital bed with those science fiction paperbacks, trying to distract him from the pain of a bullet wound that would never heal.

Hall tucked the brush away again, this time with finality. She straightened her blazer, squared her shoulders, and gave her reflection a curt nod of acceptance. Whatever Rachel Fenimore saw when she looked at her—beautiful woman, authority figure, potential ally or adversary—it didn't matter. What mattered was Ira Lewis, dead in an alley with a knife wound that had emptied his body of blood and his face of dignity.

The hallway outside was quiet, just the distant ring of a phone from Major Crimes two offices over. The air smelled faintly of someone's lunch—not fish today, but something with cumin and chili that made Hall's stomach growl a reminder of her own forgotten meal. She walked back toward the homicide division, heels clicking against the polished concrete floor in a rhythm that matched her heartbeat.

White was at his desk when she returned, his hand withdrawing from his mouth as he swallowed something. The orange prescription bottle sat on his desk blotter, lid off, a white tablet still visible inside. His face was pale, lips pressed tight against whatever pain had driven him to take a pill in the middle of the afternoon. When he saw her, he recapped the bottle and slipped it into his pocket.

"You okay?" Hall asked, sliding into her chair.

White nodded, a single dip of his chin that conveyed both affirmation and dismissal. "Fine," he said, the word clipped. "Hip's acting up. Weather change coming."

Hall glanced toward the windows where sunlight still streamed through, turning the dust in the air into tiny points of fire. No sign of the storm that had been promised, at least not yet. But White's hip never lied about rain. Two years of partnership before the shooting had made them colleagues; the bullet and its aftermath had made them something else—not quite friends, but people who had seen each other at their most vulnerable and chosen to continue the journey together.

"Rachel Fenimore's here," White said, changing the subject with the abruptness of someone slamming a door. "Showed up fifteen minutes early. She's waiting in Interview One."

Hall checked her watch—1:47. Rachel's shift had supposedly ended at 1:30, but Hall had expected her to go home first, change out of her scrubs, maybe prepare herself mentally. The early arrival suggested either eagerness or anxiety. Both were worth noting.

"I want you to take the lead on this." White's voice was flat, his eyes not quite meeting hers. "I'll sit in, take notes, but she's more likely to open up to you."

The words hung in the air between them, heavy with yesterday's accusation. Hall could read the subtext. White still thought Rachel might respond to her on a personal level, might say more to a "beautiful woman" than to a male detective with a cop's face and a war veteran's eyes. But she also knew that wasn't the whole truth. White's hip was giving him hell today, and sitting silent in a corner while Hall asked the questions would give him a chance to observe without the distraction of his own pain.

"Fine," she said, matching his curtness. She reached for her notebook—standard issue, faux black leather cover, the pages now filled with stories of human tragedy written in her precise hand. "You planning to contribute at all, or just sit there looking intimidating?"

A ghost of a smile touched White's lips. "I'll jump in if I see an opening. But she's your witness." He stood, wincing as he put weight on his right leg. "Let's not keep her waiting."

Hall rose, tucking the notebook under her arm and grabbing a pen from the cup on her desk. Her mind was already shifting, organizing the questions she wanted to ask, plotting the course of the interview. Rachel had lied about working the night of the murder. That was the thread Hall intended to pull, watching to see what unraveled.

They walked together through the homicide division, past desks where other detectives hunched over phones and computers, past the whiteboard where Ira Lewis's name was written in Hall's handwriting beside the date of his death. The smell of cumin faded, replaced by floor cleaner and the artificial pine scent someone had sprayed in a misguided attempt to freshen the air. A door opened somewhere ahead, releasing a burst of laughter that cut off abruptly as it closed again.

White moved beside her with the careful gait of a man who had learned to live with pain as a constant companion. Hall matched her pace to his, a courtesy neither of them acknowledged. They had done this dance a thousand times—walking to interview rooms, to crime scenes, to the cars that carried them from one human disaster to another. The choreography was so familiar that neither needed to think about the steps.

Interview Room One waited at the end of the corridor, its door a slab of institutional gray that revealed nothing about what waited on the other side. Hall paused before it, centering herself in the moment. Rachel Fenimore sat beyond that door. Rachel who had lied about working, who had flirted on the phone, who might have been the last person to see Ira Lewis alive—or the last person he ever saw.

Hall opened the door and stepped into the next chapter of the investigation, White a solid presence at her back.

Rachel Fenimore sat at the metal table, her back straight, hands folded before her like a student waiting for class to begin. When Hall pushed open the door, Rachel's face brightened with a smile that reached all the way to her eyes. But as White limped in behind Hall, that light dimmed, the smile faltering at its edges before settling into something more measured. The change was subtle—a fractional narrowing of the eyes, a slight tension at the corners of her mouth—but Hall had built a career on noticing these kinds of micro-expressions.

"Thank you for coming in, Ms. Fenimore," Hall said, settling into the chair across from Rachel. The metal legs scraped against the concrete floor, the sound sharp in the small room. Above them, the LED panels cast a shadowless light that flattened everyone's features into masks. The air hung still and cool, touched with the ghost of cleaning products and the faint scent of someone's perfume—Rachel's, Hall guessed, something with sandalwood notes that didn't quite match the hospital nurse image.

White positioned himself in the corner, arranging his body in the plastic chair with the careful movements of a man setting a broken bone. He placed his notebook on his knee, pen poised, his face arranged in the neutral expression he wore like armor at crime scenes and funerals.

Rachel's eyes tracked him, then returned to Hall. She wore civilian clothes now—dark jeans and a deep blue sweater that made her skin look paler than it had in her scrubs. Her hair was pulled back in a simple ponytail, revealing a face that seemed younger in this setting, more vulnerable without the professional context of the hospital.

"We'll be recording this conversation," Hall said, pointing at a camera in the corner of the ceiling. She stated the date, time, and names of those present, then looked at Rachel. "Why don't you tell us what happened that night? In your own words."

"Why are you recording? Am I under arrest?"

Hall smiled and shook her head. "No, you aren't under arrest. We record everything in this room. Standard procedure."

White cleared his throat. A sign that said, "But we don't normally point it out."

Rachel's fingers found the edge of the table, tracing its metal border in a gesture Hall recognized from the hospital. A self-soothing movement, unconscious and revealing.

"I had just finished my shift at work," Rachel began, her voice steady despite the nervous fingers. "It was late, after one in the morning. I was walking home, like I told you before. That's when I saw..." She paused, swallowed. "Someone in the alley."

Hall let the silence stretch for three beats. "You saw him from the street? In the dark?"

Rachel shifted in her chair, her gaze dropping to her hands for a moment before rising to meet Hall's again. "I might have heard something first. A sound. Something caught my attention." Her tongue darted out to wet her lips. "So I went in to check."

From the corner, White's voice cut through the room, measured but sharp as a blade. "Brave of you. A woman alone, heading into an alley at that hour."

Rachel's head turned toward him, her eyes narrowing. Something passed across her face—a shadow of an expression Hall couldn't quite name. "I guess I'm used to it, on a certain level," she said. "Working in emergency medicine, you develop instincts. When someone needs help, you don't think about danger. You just act."

Her voice had taken on the rehearsed quality of someone who had prepared their answers, anticipated the questions. Hall noted this, filed it away with other observations: the way Rachel's right foot tapped silently against the floor, the slight tremor in her fingers when she brushed a strand of hair from her face.

"Anyway," Rachel continued, "I saw him and tried to render aid, then called 911. I waited until the paramedics arrived, and I left."

Hall tilted her head, her face a mask of polite skepticism. "That's not quite right, though, is it? You left before the paramedics arrived."

Rachel blinked, a rapid flutter of eyelashes. "Well, you know what I mean. They were pretty much there. I could hear the sirens getting closer. They couldn't have been more than a block away."

"Why did you leave at all?" White asked from his corner, the pen motionless in his hand. The room felt smaller with his voice in it, the walls closer.

Rachel's fingers found her collar, tugging at it though it sat perfectly against her neck. "I didn't want to get in the way. Once the professionals arrived, I thought it best to step aside."

"But you are a professional," Hall pointed out. "Don't you think your skills as an ER nurse would have been helpful to the paramedics? You could have briefed them on what you'd observed, what measures you'd already taken."

Rachel's gaze settled somewhere past Hall's left shoulder. "I knew he wasn't going to make it," she said, her voice dropping. "The blood loss was too great. The wound...he was breathing out blood. Probably hit the lung. It needs immediate surgery."

The words were clinical, detached, a nurse's assessment. But something in Rachel's voice struck a false note, like an instrument out of tune. Hall couldn't place what felt wrong—the precision, perhaps, or the certainty.

"Did you get any blood on you while you rendered aid?" White's question cut through Hall's thoughts, direct and uncompromising.

Rachel's eyes widened, a flash of something—alarm? recognition?—crossing her face before she composed herself. "Oh god, so much," she said, her hands spreading before her as if the blood might still be visible.

Memory.

"It was everywhere. On my hands, my clothes. I had to throw out the sweatshirt I was wearing."

Hall leaned forward. "Did you see or hear anyone else in the alley? Any witnesses? Anyone running away?"

"No." Rachel shook her head, a single decisive movement. "No one. It was just me and him. The alley was empty."

White shifted in his chair, the plastic creaking beneath his weight. "Did you see the warehouse worker having a cigarette break?"

The question dropped into the room like a stone into still water, ripples of reaction spreading across Rachel's face. Her lips parted, eyes widening a fraction before she could master her expression. The tap of her foot against the floor stopped abruptly. Her hands, which had been in constant motion since she sat down, went still on the table.

For three heartbeats, no one spoke. The air conditioning hummed overhead, a sound so soft it had become invisible until the silence made it deafening. In that moment, Hall saw something shift in Rachel's eyes—a calculation, a decision being made. And she knew, with the bone-deep certainty that had solved more cases than forensic evidence ever had, that whatever Rachel said next would be a lie.

Chapter 8

"Warehouse worker?" Rachel's voice cracked on the question. Her eyes darted from White to Hall and back again, like a trapped animal seeking an escape route that didn't exist. The trembling in her fingers spread to her hands, then her arms. She pressed her palms flat against the table as if trying to force the shaking to stop through pressure alone. The interview room's temperature hadn't changed, but a flush crept up Rachel's neck, turning her pale skin blotchy pink beneath the collar of her blue sweater.

"Yes," White said, his voice neutral despite the spark of interest in his eyes. "Security supervisor at the storage facility next door. He was outside having a cigarette around the time of the incident."

Rachel swallowed, her throat working visibly. "I didn't know anyone else was there." Her voice had dropped to just above a whisper. "What—" She cleared her throat, tried again. "What did he see?"

Hall watched the calculation happening behind Rachel's eyes. The muscles in her jaw tightened, relaxed, tightened again. The LED lights overhead cast no shadows on her face, but Hall didn't need shadows to read the fear etched there.

"He said he saw a woman running from the direction of the alley," Hall said, keeping her tone conversational, as if they were discussing the weather rather than a murder. "Around 2:15 A.M."

A muscle jumped in Rachel's cheek. "Well, yes. I did leave. I told you that." She tugged at the sleeve of her sweater, a nervous gesture that exposed the face of her expensive watch. "After I called 911, I needed to get home. I was exhausted from my shift, and there was nothing more I could do for him."

Hall noted the repeated lie—the fictional shift at Mercy General that hospital records would disprove. She let the falsehood hang in the air between them, neither challenging nor accepting it. The room felt smaller now, the walls pressing in with Rachel's deception.

White leaned forward in his chair, the plastic creaking beneath his shift in weight. "Tell us again why you walked into that alley, Ms. Fenimore."

Rachel's fingernails scraped against the metal table, leaving no mark but filling the room with a sound like distant chalk on a blackboard. "I told you. I saw someone. I wanted to help." Her eyes fixed on a point past Hall's left shoulder. "It's what I do. It's who I am."

The phrase hung between them, hollow as a Christmas ornament. Hall thought of the man in the alley, Ira Lewis, whose life had drained away into the rain-washed concrete while Rachel Fenimore stood over him, hands bloody, then ran. Whoever Rachel was, whatever she believed about herself, that moment in the alley had revealed something else—something she was desperate to conceal.

"I think that's all we need for now," Hall said, closing her notebook with a soft snap that made Rachel flinch. "Thank you for coming in, Ms. Fenimore. You've been very helpful."

Relief washed across Rachel's face, so naked and profound that Hall almost felt sorry for her. Almost. The nurse gathered herself, smoothing her sweater, tucking a strand of hair behind her ear with a hand that still trembled.

"That's it?" Rachel asked, the question escaping before she could contain it.

"For today," White said, the qualifier hanging in the air like a promise—or a threat.

Hall stood, gathering her notebook and pen. "I'll walk you out."

The hallway outside felt vast after the confines of Interview Room One. The air smelled different too—someone's lunch lingering in the corridor, the sharp tang of mustard and onions from a sandwich unwrapped at a desk they passed. Rachel walked beside Hall, her steps measured and careful, as if she feared a misstep might betray her further.

"Thank you for coming in," Hall said as they approached the elevator. "I know it can be intimidating, talking to police in a formal setting like this."

Rachel's fingers found the sleeve of her sweater again, twisting the fabric. "I just want to help. If there's anything else I can do..."

The elevator doors slid open with a soft pneumatic hiss. They stepped inside, and Hall pressed the button for the lobby. In the enclosed space, Hall caught the scent of Rachel's perfume more clearly—sandalwood and something sharper beneath it, something that reminded her of hospitals despite Rachel's civilian clothes.

"Actually," Hall said as the elevator began its descent, "there is something you could clarify. You mentioned you were coming from work that night, from Mercy General?"

Rachel's spine stiffened, almost imperceptibly. "That's right."

"And your shift ended at what time?" Hall kept her voice light, conversational.

"Around one-thirty," Rachel said, the words automatic. "Maybe a bit later. We had a trauma case come in near the end of my shift."

Hall nodded, filing away the lie. The elevator reached the lobby, doors opening onto the precinct's public face—the front desk with its uniformed officers, the hard plastic chairs where citizens waited to file reports or speak with detectives. The air here smelled of floor cleaner and the faint, sour odor of too many bodies in too small a space.

They crossed the lobby together, Rachel's steps quickening as they neared the exit. Freedom waited beyond those doors—freedom from questions, from her lies, from whatever truth she was hiding. At least for now.

"We'll be in touch if we have any more questions," Hall said, the standard phrase that might mean everything or nothing.

Rachel pushed through the doors into the afternoon sunlight, her pace increasing with each step away from the precinct. Hall followed her outside, stopping at the top of the concrete steps that led down to the sidewalk. She watched as Rachel walked to a blue compact parked across the street, fumbled with her keys, dropped them once before managing to unlock the door.

The sun slipped behind a cloud, casting the street in sudden shadow. A gust of wind brought the smell of exhaust from a passing truck, the distant scent of rain still hours away. Hall stood motionless, observing as Rachel started her car, pulled away from the curb with too much speed, and disappeared around the corner.

In the moment before Rachel's car vanished from view, their eyes met across the distance. What Hall saw there wasn't relief or gratitude, but something darker and more complicated—the look of someone who knows the hunt is on.

The Homicide division stretched before Hall like a museum exhibit on the working life of detectives—six pairs of desks facing each other in perfect symmetry, case files stacked with varying degrees of order, computer screens glowing blue-white in the afternoon light that poured through the windows along the eastern wall. Hall's steps echoed on the worn floor as she made her way back to her desk, where White waited, his face set in the particular expression she had learned meant he had reached a conclusion he didn't like.

She glanced at the clock on her computer monitor: 3:04 P.M. The interview with Rachel had consumed a full hour, though it felt both longer and shorter—the way time behaved in rooms where truth and lies circled each other like wary predators. Hall settled into her chair, the springs protesting beneath her weight. The desk between them was a battlefield of folders, sticky notes, and half-empty water bottles.

"A full hour," Hall said, letting the words fall into the space between them like stones into still water. "Doesn't seem possible."

White grunted, his fingers drumming a rhythm on his thigh. "Time flies when you're being lied to."

The statement hung in the air, blunt and unvarnished. From across the room came the muffled conversation of two detectives comparing notes on a domestic gone wrong. Someone sneezed, followed by a chorus of mechanical "Bless you"s that had become the call-and-response of office life. Through it all, White's eyes remained fixed on Hall, waiting.

"Your thoughts?" she asked, though she already knew the shape they would take. Their partnership had lasted seven years—longer than most marriages. She could read White's conclusions in the set of his shoulders, the angle of his head, the way his fingers tapped against his leg in groups of three.

"A lie is almost as good as a confession," White said, each word precise as a surgical cut. "Said she was at work, walking home from a shift that never happened. After working on a trauma that never happened."

Hall nodded, watching dust motes dance in the shafts of sunlight that cut across their shared space. "She lied about why she was in the alley. 'I saw someone and wanted to help' doesn't track. That part of town, that time of night? Most people cross the street if they see someone in an alley."

"And she lied about why she left," White continued, shifting his weight to ease the pressure on his hip. The chair creaked beneath him, a sound so familiar to Hall she barely registered it anymore. "Said she didn't want to get in the way of the paramedics. But she's a nurse—her input would have been invaluable. No, she ran because she didn't want to be there when the police arrived."

Hall leaned back, letting her head rest against the chair. The ceiling above her desk had a water stain shaped like the state of Florida—a detail she noticed only when she needed to look anywhere but at the case in front of her. The air conditioning kicked on, sending a draft across her skin that smelled of dust and electronics.

"That's an awful lot of lies for someone who's innocent," she said, bringing her gaze back to White.

He nodded, his face grim. "Three lies that we know of. Probably more we haven't caught yet."

A detective from Narcotics walked past their desks, the smell of cigarettes clinging to his clothes like a second skin. He nodded to them both, his eyes bloodshot from too little sleep or too much of something else. The moment passed, and they were alone again in the public privacy that police work provided—surrounded by people but isolated in their shared focus.

"What bothers me most," Hall said, lowering her voice, "is that she stuck to the work story even after we asked and asked. Most people would have pivoted. Said they were wrong about which night. They find a new explanation. But she doubled down." She tapped her pen against her notebook. "That suggests either incredible stubbornness or..."

"Or she's practiced this story," White finished for her. "Rehearsed it enough times that she can't adapt when it falls apart."

His words settled over them both. From the far corner of the room came the sudden bark of laughter, sharp and out of place in the quiet murmur of the division. Someone had found humor in the darkness they all waded through daily—a rare gift in homicide.

"We need to confirm she wasn't at work," Hall said, though they both knew it was a formality at this point. "Get the official record from Mercy General's HR department."

White nodded, already reaching for his phone. "I'll call now. Better coming from me—I've got contacts there from my time as a patient."

"How is that official?"

"If they cooperate, no warrant required"

Hall watched as he dialed, his fingers moving with the ease of someone who had made thousands of such calls in his career. The sun shifted, casting new patterns on the floor beneath their desks. A beam of light caught the framed photo on White's desk—his nephew in a baseball uniform, frozen mid-swing in a moment of potential that would never change or fade.

"What do you think she was doing there?" Hall asked when White hung up. "In that alley, with Ira Lewis?"

White's expression darkened, the lines around his mouth deepening. "Slicing a man open."

The words settled between them, heavy with experience. They had seen countless lies unravel beneath the steady pressure of investigation. People lied for reasons—fear, shame, self-preservation. But most of all, people lied to hide the truth. And the truth Rachel Fenimore was hiding would cost her her freedom.

Hall turned to her computer, fingers poised above the keyboard. The case file for Ira Lewis waited on her screen—the medical examiner's report, the crime scene photos, the witness statements collected from the area around the alley. Somewhere in those documents lay the connections that would link Rachel Fenimore to Ira Lewis, that would explain why a nurse would abandon a dying man in an alley, that would reveal what had happened in those rain-soaked minutes before the 911 call.

As she began to type her interview notes, Hall thought of Rachel's eyes in that final moment before her car disappeared around the corner—not the eyes of someone relieved to be helping with a case, but the eyes of someone who knew the hunt had just begun. And she was the prey.

Chapter 9

The morning sun slanted through the windows of the Homicide Division, cutting the room into bright planes and shadowed corners. Hall stared at the photo of Ira Lewis on her desk—alive in his booking shot—public intoxication—looking sullen and tired. Nothing like the gray shell of a man they'd found in the alley. The phone on her desk rang, a harsh intrusion that startled her from her thoughts. She picked up, her "Detective Hall" clipped and professional despite the headache building behind her eyes.

"Detective, there's a Harper Langston here to see you," said the front desk officer. "Says it's about the Lewis case. Says it's important."

Hall straightened in her chair. The name meant nothing to her, but the Lewis case had become an itch she couldn't scratch. "I'll be right down."

She glanced at White's empty chair—he'd gone to collect the official employment records from Mercy General, proof that Rachel Fenimore had lied about working the night Ira Lewis died. Hall pushed back from her desk, the wheels of her chair catching on an errant paperclip. Three days into the investigation, and they had a witness who lied, a victim with no apparent connection to her, and nothing solid to explain why a nurse would flee the scene of a man dying in an alley.

The elevator hummed as it descended, the sound vibrating through the soles of Hall's shoes. She mentally rehearsed her opening questions for this Harper Langston. Was it a witness they'd missed in the canvas? Someone who'd seen something in that alley and only now found the courage to come forward?

The front desk area smelled of someone's breakfast—eggs and cheese from a sandwich half-eaten and abandoned on the counter. The desk officer nodded toward the waiting area, where a woman sat alone, back straight, hands clutching a leather tote bag in her lap.

The woman from Rachel's socials.

Harper Langston looked to be in her early thirties, her honey-blonde hair pulled back in a low ponytail that emphasized the sharp angles of her face. She wore the uniform of

New Hanan's creative class—black jeans, gray sweater, ankle boots that had cost more than Hall's entire outfit. Her knuckles were white where she gripped the bag, the only visible sign of her tension.

"Ms. Langston?" Hall approached, badge already in hand. "I'm Detective Hall. You wanted to speak with me about the Lewis case?"

Harper looked up, her green eyes red-rimmed from either lack of sleep or recent tears. Perhaps both. "Yes," she said, her voice steadier than her hands.

"Let's go somewhere private," Hall said, hand gesturing toward the innards of the building.

Hall led her through the security checkpoint and down the corridor to Interview Room 2—smaller than Room 1, with a round table instead of the institutional metal rectangle. The room was designed for cooperative witnesses rather than suspects, with cushioned chairs and a window that actually opened, though it looked out onto an air shaft rather than the street.

"Can I get you some water?" Hall asked, gesturing toward the chair facing the door.

Harper shook her head, settled into the seat. "I'm fine. Thank you." She set her tote bag on the floor beside her, then changed her mind and placed it on the table between them, like a barrier.

Hall took the seat opposite, noting the way Harper's eyes tracked the movement, the slight flinch as the chair legs scraped against the floor. "What can I tell you about the Lewis case, Ms. Langston?"

"Nothing." Harper's lips pressed together, a thin line of determination. "I'm here to tell you about Rachel Fenimore."

The name landed in the room like a stone dropped into still water. Hall kept her face neutral through long practice, but her mind accelerated from idle to full speed in an instant. "How do you know Rachel?"

"I'm her ex-girlfriend." Harper's fingers found the strap of her tote, twisting the leather. "We broke up two weeks ago, but we're still..." She paused, searching for the right words. "We still live together. Separate bedrooms. The lease isn't up until September, and neither of us can afford to break it."

Rachel had said she lived alone. Another lie.

Hall nodded, encouraging. "And you have information about Rachel in connection with the Lewis case?"

"Yes." Harper swallowed, her throat working visibly beneath the collar of her sweater. "I know she came home covered in blood that night. Around three in the morning."

The words hung in the air between them. Hall could almost see them, bright and sharp as glass shards. The image of Rachel Fenimore walking through her front door at 3 A.M., blood on her clothes, her hands, perhaps her face. The same Rachel who had told them she'd been working at the hospital, a lie that even now White was confirming with employment records.

"Tell me everything you remember about that night," Hall said, her voice gentle despite the hammering of her pulse.

Harper closed her eyes, as if gathering strength. When she opened them, they were clearer, more focused. "First, you need to know something about Rachel. She's been stealing painkillers from the hospital. For months."

"Stealing?" Hall repeated. "For herself, or to sell?"

"For herself, I think. At least at first." Harper's fingers abandoned the tote strap, found a loose thread on her sweater instead. "She has a prescription for her migraines, but it's never enough. And she developed a tolerance. She started taking more, needing more."

Hall thought of the orange prescription bottle White carried, the way his hand drifted to his hip when the weather changed. Pain changed people. Made them do things they'd never imagined themselves capable of. "Go on."

"She'd come home wired some nights, crashed others." Harper tugged at the thread, unraveling a tiny section of her sweater's cuff. "That night—the night the man died—she came home around three. I was up. Waiting for her."

"Why were you waiting?" Hall asked. "Was that unusual, for her to be out so late?"

Harper's eyes dropped to her hands. "She sleepwalks. Has since she was a child. Takes medication for it, but sometimes—especially when she's stressed—she still wanders. I woke up around one and noticed she was gone."

The pieces shifted in Hall's mind, rearranging themselves into a new pattern. Rachel Fenimore, sleepwalking through the streets of New Hanan. Finding herself in an alley with a homeless man who perhaps had what she wanted—painkillers, or money to buy them. A confrontation that ended with a knife in Ira Lewis's stomach and Rachel standing over him, bloody-handed and confused.

"What did you think when you saw the blood?" Hall kept her voice neutral, a collector of facts rather than a builder of cases.

"I didn't know what to think." Harper's voice dropped lower, almost to a whisper. "She was... not herself. Dazed. She said she was called into work for a car accident. Something like that. She's an ER nurse. But when she came home...." She trailed off, shaking her head. "She wasn't really there."

"You don't think she was working?"

Harper rearranged the bag on the table. "No. I checked the news. There we no major car accidents that night."

"And what do you think happened?" Hall asked. "What's your honest assessment?"

Harper looked up, her eyes meeting Hall's for the first time since they'd sat down. "I think she was sleepwalking. Ended up in that alley. Found that man already hurt, or dying. Tried to help, like she said. And then... I don't know. Panicked. Ran. Came home."

Hall considered this version of events. It was possible. Or a story from an ex who was trying to curry favor. But it didn't explain much at all. If she'd been sleepwalking, why not say so? Why construct an elaborate fiction instead?

"You said you woke up at one and found her gone," Hall said. "And you stayed up, worried about her sleepwalking. What made you particularly concerned that night?"

"She'd been a wreck all week," Harper said. "Ever since she almost got caught taking pills from the medication cabinet. One of the other nurses suspected something. Rachel was afraid she'd lose her job, her license." She tugged at the thread again, her fingers restless. "When I woke up and found her gone, I just... had a bad feeling."

"Did you think she would hurt herself?"

Harper nodded. "She's not the kind, but it just seemed so strange. I thought it was her blood at first."

Hall nodded, making a note in her small black notebook. The picture was becoming clearer—Rachel, desperate to keep her addiction secret, fearful of losing everything she'd worked for. Stress triggering her sleepwalking. And somewhere in the night, an encounter with Ira Lewis that ended with him bleeding out in the rain while Rachel fled, confused and afraid.

But there were still gaps, still questions. The knife, for one. If Rachel had stabbed Lewis, where was the weapon? And if she'd only found him already injured, who had wielded the blade that took his life?

"Did Rachel bring anything home with her that night?"

"Like what?" Harper asked. A crease furrowed her brow.

"Did Rachel have a knife?"

"No I—wait. You really think? No. I think the only thing she had was her phone. But she went into the shower. Clothes on. She wasn't okay when she got home," Harper said.

Hall made a note. "Thank you for coming forward," Hall said, writing in her notebook. "I know this wasn't easy."

Harper nodded, her shoulders slumping as if a weight had been lifted from them. "I loved her once," she said. "Still do, I guess. But this secret was too big to carry alone."

Hall understood. Some secrets were like that—too heavy for one person to bear, crushing you slowly until you had to set them down or be destroyed by their weight. She'd seen it before, would see it again. The human need to unburden, to share the load of knowledge that became too painful to carry in solitude.

And now she carried part of Harper's burden. The question was what she would do with it.

Hall leaned forward, her elbows on the table between them. The question had been forming in her mind since Harper first mentioned the blood, rising to the surface like a body in dark water. She needed to ask it, though she suspected she already knew the answer. "Has Rachel ever been violent? With you, or with anyone else that you know of?"

Harper's head jerked back, as if the question itself were a physical thing that had struck her. "No. Never." She shook her head for emphasis. "Rachel isn't... wasn't... like that." Her eyes found a spot on the wall behind Hall, focusing there. "She saves people. That's who she is."

"But she's been different since that night," Hall prompted. "You said she's been a wreck."

"Yes." Harper's fingers found the loose thread on her sweater again, worrying it. "She barely sleeps. When she does, she has nightmares. She's called in sick to work twice this month, and Rachel never calls in sick. Ever." She paused, swallowed. "And she keeps pretending nothing happened. But I know something did."

Hall made a note. This wasn't the behavior of a cold-blooded killer, but it wasn't necessarily the reaction of an innocent bystander either. It existed in that gray space between—the territory of someone who'd done something terrible without meaning to, or who'd witnessed something they couldn't process.

"The clothes she was wearing that night," Hall said. "Do you know where they are now?"

Harper blinked, as if the question had pulled her back from some distant place. "What? Oh, the clothes." She frowned, thinking. "As far as I know, they're still in the laundry basket. In the bathroom."

"She didn't wash them?" Hall kept her voice neutral, though her pulse quickened. Bloody clothes, still unwashed after three days—it was the kind of evidence that could break a case wide open. Perhaps a cut, if the knife slipped. Blood spatter patterns, something.

"No," Harper said. "She just... took them off and put them in the basket. I don't think she's done laundry since that night. Like I said, she's been a wreck."

Hall nodded, making another note. "And is this a bathroom you share?"

"Yes," Harper confirmed. "The apartment only has one. We've been on opposite schedules since the breakup, so it's not as awkward as it could be." A small, sad smile touched her lips, then vanished. "I use it at night, she uses it during the day. When she works evening shifts."

"Ms. Langston," Hall said, choosing her words. "Would you be willing to consent to letting us collect those clothes? As potential evidence?"

Harper didn't hesitate. "Yes. Of course."

"And would you be willing to come with us now? To give us access to the apartment?"

"Now?" Harper glanced at her watch, a simple gold band that caught the light. "I have a client meeting at one, but I can reschedule." She straightened her shoulders, a visible rallying of resolve. "Yes, I'll go with you now."

"Thank you." Hall stood. "I just need to speak with my partner for a moment. I'll be right back."

She left the interview room, closing the door softly behind her. The corridor felt cooler than the small room had been, the air flowing more freely. Hall took a deep breath, organizing her thoughts before seeking out White. The case had just shifted beneath her feet—not dramatically, but significantly. The clothes could prove whether Rachel had been in direct contact with Lewis as he died, might confirm or refute the story she'd told them about finding him already stabbed.

White was at his desk when she returned to the homicide division, his face set in the familiar lines of frustration that appeared when cases refused to move in straight lines. He looked up as she approached, something in her expression making him sit straighter.

"What is it?" he asked before she could speak.

"Rachel Fenimore's ex-girlfriend is in Interview Room Two," Hall said, keeping her voice low. "Harper Langston. They broke up two weeks ago but still live together." She paused, let the next part land with its full weight. "She says Rachel came home at three A.M. the night Lewis died, covered in blood."

White's expression sharpened, his eyes narrowing. "Covered in blood."

"And according to Langston, the clothes are still in the laundry basket in their shared bathroom." Hall leaned against the edge of his desk. "She's consented to let us collect them."

"Jesus." White stood, the chair rolling back behind him. "She's downstairs now? Ready to go?"

Hall nodded. "Says she'll take us to the apartment, let us in."

"Do we need a warrant?" White asked, already reaching for his jacket. The question wasn't about legality—they both knew the rules. With Harper's consent as a resident of the apartment, they could legally enter and seize evidence in plain sight in the common areas, including the shared bathroom. The question was about building a case that would hold up under the scrutiny of defense attorneys and judges.

"No," Hall said. "Langston's consent is sufficient for the common areas. The bathroom is shared. We're good." She paused. "But there's something else you should know. Langston says Rachel has been stealing painkillers from the hospital. And that she sleepwalks. Says she woke up at one A.M., found Rachel gone, and stayed up waiting for her."

White absorbed this, his face unreadable. "Sleepwalking. That's convenient."

"Maybe," Hall said. "Or maybe it's true." She pushed away from the desk. "Either way, those clothes could tell us a lot more than Rachel has."

White grabbed his coat, checking his pocket for the orange prescription bottle with a motion so habitual he probably didn't realize he was doing it. "Let's go."

They walked back to Interview Room Two together, their steps matched from years of moving through the world side by side. The corridor narrowed with White beside her, his bulk taking up space in a way that had once felt protective and now felt merely familiar.

Harper looked up when they entered, her eyes tracking from Hall to White and back again. She'd put away whatever vulnerability she'd shown earlier, her face now composed into the mask people wore when dealing with authority—polite, cooperative, but guarded.

"Ms. Langston, this is Detective White," Hall said. "He'll be accompanying us to your apartment."

Harper stood, smoothing her sweater over her hips. "Of course." She reached for her tote bag, slipping the strap over her shoulder. "My car is in the visitors' lot."

"We'll follow you," White said. His voice was neutral, but there was an undercurrent of tension that Hall recognized—the particular frequency that vibrated through him when a case was about to break. "You can direct us."

They moved through the precinct as a unit, White leading, Harper in the middle, Hall bringing up the rear. The front desk officer glanced up as they passed, his eyes lingering on Harper with the clinical assessment of someone who categorized every person who entered or left the building. A delivery person arrived with a stack of white paper bags—lunch orders for detectives too busy to leave their desks—releasing the smell of grilled meat and fried potatoes into the lobby air. The automatic doors parted before them, admitting a blast of midday sunlight that made Hall blink against its sudden intensity.

Outside, the city of New Hanan continued its business, unaware and unconcerned with the small drama unfolding among the three people descending the precinct steps. Cars passed, their windows reflecting fragments of sky. A couple argued on the corner, their voices rising and falling like waves against a shore. A child dropped an ice cream cone on the sidewalk across the street and began to wail, the sound carrying clear and sharp through the traffic noise.

And somewhere in that city, Rachel Fenimore moved through her day, unaware that the clothes she'd worn on the worst night of her life were about to be collected as evidence in a murder investigation. Unaware that the woman she'd once loved had just unlocked the door to whatever secrets those blood-stained garments might reveal.

Chapter 10

Harper Langston's apartment sat above Geller's Pawn, a second-floor walk-up accessed by a narrow staircase behind a glass door. Hall followed Harper up the steps, each footfall creating a hollow echo that announced their arrival. White brought up the rear, his breathing heavier than usual, the stairs challenging his damaged hip.

Harper fumbled with her keys, sorting through them with fingers that trembled. A dog barked somewhere down the block, the sound carrying clear in the still air. The lock clicked, and Harper pushed the door open, stepping aside to let the detectives enter first.

"It's not much," she said, her voice tight with what might have been embarrassment or tension. "And it's a bit of a mess right now."

Hall stepped inside, the cool air of the apartment washing over her skin like relief. The space opened immediately into a combined living and dining area, small but thoughtfully arranged. A bookshelf crammed with paperbacks dominated one wall, while a gray sectional sofa faced a modest television. The room bore the particular emptiness of a space recently divided—gaps on shelves where objects had been removed, hooks on walls where pictures once hung. The remnants of a relationship ended but not yet disentangled.

White moved past her, his eyes sweeping the apartment with professional assessment. "Which way to the bathroom?" he asked, his voice neutral.

Harper pointed down a short hallway. "Last door on the right. Rachel's bedroom is on the left, mine is the one straight ahead."

Hall noted the way Harper's voice changed when she said Rachel's name—a slight hardening, as if the syllables themselves had edges that could cut. The apartment smelled of someone's morning toast, the faint lingering scent of brewed coffee, and beneath that, the chemical sweetness of scented candles that had burned too long.

They moved down the hallway, their footsteps muffled by a runner carpet that had once been blue but had faded to a nondescript gray. A phone chirped from Harper's purse—a text message notification that she ignored. The bathroom door stood half-open, revealing a slice of white tile and the edge of a shower curtain patterned with geometric shapes.

"The hamper is under the sink," Harper said, hanging back in the hallway. "The clothes should be in there. I haven't done laundry since... since that night."

Hall pushed the door open. The bathroom was small but clean, with white tile and blue accents that gave it a vaguely nautical feel. A wicker hamper sat beside the pedestal sink, its lid slightly ajar. A toothbrush stood in a cup on the counter—just one, Hall noticed. Had one of them moved their personal items elsewhere since the breakup? The air smelled of mint toothpaste and some kind of lavender soap.

"Ms. Langston, would you mind stepping back?" Hall asked, glancing over her shoulder. "Detective White and I need to examine the space."

Harper nodded and took a step back, her shoulder brushing the wall. She crossed her arms over her chest, watching with eyes that seemed wider than they had been at the precinct. "You have to hurry, Rachel will be home soon."

Hall moved to the hamper, looking at what sat on top. Inside were several items of clothing—a pair of gray leggings, two towels, what looked like a cotton sleep shirt. She looked for anything with visible bloodstains. Nothing.

"I don't see anything that matches your description," Hall said, glancing back at Harper. "No bloody clothing."

White stepped into the doorway behind her, the small space becoming even smaller with his bulk added to it. His reflection in the mirror above the sink looked tired, lines deepening around his mouth.

"May I?" he asked, gesturing toward the hamper.

Hall stepped aside, allowing White to examine the contents. He leaned over, movements deliberate, his face set in concentration.

After a moment, he straightened up, wincing as his hip protested the change in position. "Nothing," he confirmed. "Ms. Langston, are you certain the clothes were placed in this hamper?"

Harper next to White in the bathroom. Three adults in a space meant for one. "Yes, I'm certain. I saw her put them in here. They have to be there."

Hall stepped out of the bathroom to give Harper room. The hallway felt suddenly confining, the walls too close. She could hear a neighbor's television through the thin walls, the indistinct murmur of a news broadcast or talk show.

"We don't see any blood-stained clothing in the hamper," Hall said, keeping her voice level. "Are you sure it wasn't disposed of elsewhere?"

Harper's face transformed, indignation replacing uncertainty. "I know what I saw. And I know where she put those clothes."

Hall and White retreated from the bathroom. Plain sight meant plain sight, and they could see nothing.

"What? No, where are you going?" Harper asked. She pushed past Hall into the hallway, then turned back with a look of determination. "Come with me."

She led them back to the living room, her steps quick and purposeful. Hall exchanged a glance with White, who shrugged almost imperceptibly. In the brighter light of the main room, Harper's face showed high spots of color on her cheeks, her jaw set.

"Maybe she moved them," Harper said, more to herself than to the detectives. Without warning, she strode back down the hall, returning moments later with the wicker hamper in her arms. "But I know what I saw."

With a swift, angry motion, Harper upended the hamper, spilling its contents across the living room floor. Towels, t-shirts, and underwear tumbled out in a jumble of cotton and terry cloth. And among them—unmistakable—a gray hoodie and jeans, both stiff with what could only be dried blood.

"There," Harper said, her voice a mixture of triumph and distress. "I told you."

The blood had dried to a dark brown, almost black in places. It covered the front of the hoodie in a wide splash pattern, as if Rachel had kneeled in front of Lewis as he bled out. The track pants bore less blood, but still showed significant staining around the knees.

Hall heard White's sharp intake of breath behind her. These weren't the clothes of someone who had simply tried to help a stabbing victim. These were the clothes of someone who had been present for a significant blood loss event—close enough to be covered in spray and splatter.

"Jesus," White muttered, reaching into his jacket pocket for his notebook. The pages rustled as he flipped to a clean sheet, his pen already in hand. "Ms. Langston, I need you to tell me when and where you saw Ms. Fenimore place these items in the hamper."

Hall couldn't take her eyes off the clothing. The blood pattern told a story that Rachel's words had not—a story of proximity, of presence, of involvement that went beyond finding a man already injured. The clothes looked like they belonged to someone who had been there when the knife went in, not after.

Harper sank onto the edge of the sofa, suddenly looking exhausted. "Not this hamper, the one in the bathroom. Three in the morning," she said. "The night that man was killed. I saw the blood even then. She came in, went straight to the bathroom. I heard the shower running. When she came out, she was wearing her robe. She put those clothes in the hamper."

White's pen moved across the page, recording Harper's statement. His face had gone hard, the way it did when a case shifted from ambiguity to clarity. "And you're absolutely certain of the time?"

"Yes," Harper said. "The clock on the microwave said 3:07. I remember looking at it when I heard her key in the lock."

Hall finally tore her gaze from the bloody clothes to look at Harper. The woman's earlier bravado had faded, leaving behind something fragile and uncertain. Whatever she had expected from this moment—closure, vindication, justice—the reality of it settling on her with unexpected weight.

"Thank you for showing us," Hall said. She turned to White, who was still writing. "We'll need to document this properly and get these items into evidence."

White nodded, his face grim. "I'll make the calls."

On the floor between them, Rachel Fenimore's bloody clothes lay exposed in the afternoon light, transforming from secret to evidence in the span of a single, revelatory moment.

Hall tore her eyes away from the bloodstained clothes and pulled her phone from her pocket. This was no longer just a witness interview or a casual collection of potential evidence. The sheer volume of blood crusted on the gray fabric transformed everything—this was now a murder investigation with physical evidence linking Rachel Fenimore to Ira Lewis's death. She pressed the speed dial for Gloria Townsend, the assistant district attorney who handled most of their homicide cases, and stepped toward the window for better reception.

The phone rang twice before Townsend answered, her voice crisp with the particular efficiency of someone perpetually juggling multiple crises. "Townsend speaking."

"Gloria, it's Detective Carolyn Hall." She turned her back to the room, looking out at the brick wall of the neighboring building. A pigeon landed on the narrow ledge outside, its head cocking as if listening to her call. "I need a telewarrant for clothing evidence in the Lewis homicide. We've got bloody clothes belonging to a person of interest, found in plain sight in her apartment."

White had already pulled out his phone and took a single photograph. Harper remained on the edge of the sofa, her face pale, hands clasped tightly in her lap.

"What are we talking about?" Townsend asked, the sound of shuffling papers coming through the line. "Give me details."

Hall turned back to look at the pile of clothing. "We have a woman, Rachel Fenimore, who was on scene of a stabbing, but claims she is a witness. We have in plain sight, one pair of jeans, one gray hooded sweatshirt, and what appears to be a dark t-shirt. All three items show significant bloodstaining consistent with close proximity to the victim during the stabbing. The clothing belongs to Ms. Fenimore, who we've confirmed was at the crime scene that night."

"How did you find the clothes?" Townsend's voice was neutral, but Hall could hear the underlying question: Is this legal?

"Fenimore's roommate has voluntarily shown them to us. Her roommate—ex-girlfriend—witnessed her placing the clothes in their shared bathroom hamper at approximately 3:07 A.M. the night of the murder."

The pigeon outside the window took flight, startled by something Hall couldn't see. The sudden movement drew her eye, a flash of gray wings against brick.

"Ms. Langston," Hall called over her shoulder, "can you please step back from the clothing? Just have a seat on the sofa and don't touch anything."

Harper, who had been leaning forward as if drawn toward the bloody evidence, straightened and settled back onto the couch cushions. She tucked her hands beneath her thighs, like a child being told not to touch something valuable.

"Is Langston willing to sign a statement?" Townsend asked in Hall's ear. The question was a formality; they both knew Harper's testimony about the timing and Rachel's behavior would be crucial.

"Yes," Hall said. "She's the one who showed us the clothes."

White was still moving around the pile. His face had taken on the intense focus that appeared when cases crystallized from possibilities into certainties. He kneeled, favoring his good leg, to get a close-up of what appeared to be a handprint in dried blood on one leg of the track pants.

"Alright," Townsend said. "I'm initiating the telewarrant process now. Judge Baxter is on call today, so this should move quickly. Stay on the line."

The apartment fell into a strange silence, broken only by the White's grunt as he rose, and the faint sounds of traffic rising from the street below. A door slammed somewhere in the building, followed by footsteps on the stairs—someone coming home, or leaving, their life continuing unchanged while in this apartment, three people stood frozen around evidence of a life that had ended.

Hall watched Harper, noting the way her eyes kept returning to the bloody clothes despite her obvious effort to look elsewhere. What would it be like, Hall wondered, to see physical proof that someone you had loved was capable of violence? To have your worst suspicions confirmed in such a visceral way?

"Hall?" Townsend's voice broke through her thoughts. "Judge Baxter has signed the warrant. You're good to collect the evidence. I'm sending the digital confirmation to your email now."

"Thank you," Hall said. "We'll get the clothes into evidence immediately."

She ended the call and turned to White, who had finished his notes in his small black notebook. "Warrant's been signed. I'm going to get an evidence bag from the car."

White nodded without looking up from his writing. "I'll stay with the scene."

Hall moved to the apartment door, pausing to look back at Harper. "Ms. Langston, I'll just be a moment. Please remain seated, okay?"

Harper nodded, her face set in lines of resignation that hadn't been there when they'd first arrived. The revelation of the bloody clothes drained something from her. She was turning over evidence—physical, real—that seemed to rule out innocence.

The staircase felt steeper going down than it had coming up, each step reverberating under Hall's feet. The street-level door opened onto heat and noise—a delivery truck idling at the curb, its diesel engine rumbling; two teenagers chatting in front of the convenience store across the street, their voices rising and falling in the cadence of minor grievances; somewhere nearby, the tinny sound of music playing through cheap speakers.

Hall moved to the unmarked car parked in the small lot beside the pawnshop. The sun had heated the vehicle to an oven-like temperature, the steering wheel too hot to touch comfortably. She popped the trunk and reached for one of the large paper evidence bags they kept for collecting clothing and other fabric items. The paper was brown and sturdy, designed to allow the evidence to breathe rather than creating a sealed environment that could promote mold growth on damp or bloody items.

She closed the trunk and made her way back up, the evidence bag tucked under her arm. Nothing had changed in the apartment during her brief absence—White still stood beside the pile of clothing, his notebook closed; Harper still sat perched on the edge of the sofa, her hands now fidgeting; the bloodstained clothes still lay exposed on the floor, their stains dark against the gray fabric.

From a pocket in her blazer, Hall withdrew a pair of latex gloves. The familiar snap as she pulled them over her hands was unnaturally loud in the quiet apartment. The latex clung to her skin, already growing damp with sweat in the apartment's stillness.

"Detective White, if you could open the evidence bag for me," she said, approaching the clothing.

White set his notebook aside and took the bag, holding it open with the top folded down to create a wide opening. His movements were routine evidence collection, as familiar to them both as breathing.

Hall kneeled beside the pile of clothes and began the careful process of transferring them to the bag. She started with the t-shirt, which had been partially hidden beneath the hoodie. The fabric was stiff with dried blood, making a faint crackling sound as she lifted it. The blood had soaked through in places, creating a mirror pattern on the inside of the garment.

Next came the jeans, the dried blood around the knees flaking as she lifted them. The pattern suggested Rachel had kneeled beside Lewis, perhaps in an attempt to help him as she'd claimed. But the sheer volume of blood contradicted her story about arriving after the stabbing. This much blood meant she was present when the artery was severed, not minutes later.

Finally, Hall lifted the hoodie—the most heavily stained item. The front was covered in several larger areas where blood had pooled and dried. This wasn't the clothing of someone who had rendered aid; this was the clothing of someone who had been inches away when life left a body.

She placed each item in the evidence bag, mindful not to disturb any potential trace evidence that might be caught in the dried blood. When all three pieces were inside, White folded the top of the bag down and sealed it with evidence tape, then used a pen to write the case number, date, time, and location on the designated area.

"Ms. Langston," Hall said, turning to Harper as she peeled off her gloves, "thank you for your assistance today. We'll need you to come to the station to make a formal statement about what you witnessed the night of the murder and today with the clothing."

Harper nodded, her eyes fixed on the now-sealed evidence bag. "What happens now?" she asked, her voice small in the quiet apartment.

"You come with us. Now we continue our investigation," White said, his tone neutral but firm.

"Give me a minute? I'll be down in just a minute."

Hall took the evidence bag, its contents lighter than she'd expected given what they represented. She followed White to the door, both of them pausing to look back at Harper, who hadn't moved from her perch on the sofa.

"Don't be long," Hall said.

Then they were back outside, descending the stairs with their burden of evidence and a growing certainty.

The parking lot behind Geller's Pawn still has three empty spots, creating a pocket of still air that smelled of hot asphalt. Hall placed the evidence bag in the trunk of their unmarked car, ensuring it sat flat rather than folded. The paper crinkled beneath her hands, the only sound besides the distant hum of traffic and White's measured breathing as he stood beside her, keys already in hand. They were about to leave when White's body stiffened, his attention caught by something over Hall's shoulder.

"Well, well, well," he said, his voice low. "Rachel's blue compact. Coming in from the street."

Hall froze, her hand still resting on the edge of the evidence bag. The trunk lid cast a shadow across her face, shielding her eyes from the afternoon sun. In that shadow, her thoughts crystallized with sudden, perfect clarity. "Rachel?"

White nodded once, a sharp dip of his chin. "Let her park. I'll intercept."

He moved away from the car with a casualness that belied the tension Hall felt radiating from him. His right hand drifted toward his hip.

Hall closed the trunk, the sound impossibly loud in her own ears. She turned slowly, careful not to make any sudden movements that might spook Rachel if she was watching. The blue car was pulling into a space near the stairs that led up to the apartment, its driver still hidden behind the glare of sunlight on the windshield.

White positioned himself beside a faded red pickup truck, one hand raised in a gesture that might have been mistaken for a neighborly greeting rather than a command to stop. "Ms. Fenimore," he called, his voice carrying across the small lot. "Could you hold up a moment?"

The car's engine cut off. For a heartbeat, nothing happened. Then the driver's door opened, and Rachel Fenimore emerged, her face shadowed beneath a baseball cap pulled low over her eyes. She wore scrubs—pale blue, the color of Mercy General's nursing staff—and carried a tote bag slung over one shoulder. She looked smaller than Hall remembered from the hospital and the interview room, her body seeming to fold in on itself as she recognized the two detectives.

"Detective White?" Rachel's voice wavered, uncertain. She glanced toward the stairs leading to her apartment, then back to White, then past him to where Hall now stood beside their car. "What are you doing here?"

Hall moved forward, closing the distance between them with measured steps. The asphalt was soft beneath her shoes, heated to the point where she could feel its give with each footfall. The smell from a dumpster grew stronger as the breeze shifted—old cooking oil and food scraps turning rancid in the heat. A car horn sounded from the street beyond the lot, a quick, irritated blast followed by the screech of tires.

"Rachel Fenimore," Hall said, her voice steady and formal. The words tasted like copper in her mouth, the familiar ritual of arrest made strange by the evidence bag now locked in their trunk. "You're under arrest for the murder of Ira Lewis."

Rachel's face went blank, as if the words had erased something vital from behind her eyes. Her lips parted, closed, parted again. "What? No, there's been a mistake. I didn't—I didn't kill anyone."

"Turn around, please," Hall said, moving closer. "Place your hands against the vehicle."

Rachel didn't move. Her tote bag slipped from her shoulder, landing on the asphalt with a soft thud. Inside, something shifted, the contents settling. "This is crazy," she said, her voice rising. "I helped him. I called 911. I tried to save him!"

White stepped forward, his presence solid and immovable. "Ms. Fenimore. Turn around."

Something in his tone—the absolute certainty, perhaps, or simply authority—broke through Rachel's shock. She turned slowly, placing her hands flat against the warm metal of her car. Her shoulders trembled beneath the thin fabric of her scrubs.

Hall moved in, her motions precise and practiced. She placed her hands on Rachel's shoulders first, then moved down her arms, her sides, her waist, her legs. The routine of it was almost soothing—a procedure performed hundreds of times throughout her career, the physical search for weapons or contraband that preceded every transport of a prisoner.

"Is there anything in your pockets I should know about?" Hall asked, her hands pausing at Rachel's hip. "Anything sharp, anything that might stick me?"

"No," Rachel whispered. "Just my keys. Right pocket."

Hall found them—a ring with three keys and a plastic fob for the hospital parking garage—and handed them to White, who placed them in an evidence bag he'd pulled from his jacket. The small, ordinary action—the securing of personal items—seemed to drive home the reality of what was happening. Rachel's breathing hitched, a sound that wasn't quite a sob but contained the seeds of one.

"I'm placing you in handcuffs now," Hall said, reaching for the cuffs on her belt. The metal was warm from being pressed against her body all day, almost hot to the touch. "I need you to keep your hands behind your back."

The cuffs closed around Rachel's wrists with twin clicks that echoed in the still air of the parking lot. Hall adjusted them, checking to ensure they weren't too tight, the professional courtesy that separated good arrests from bad ones. Rachel's skin was cool beneath her fingers despite the day's heat.

White stepped forward, his notebook open to the page where the Miranda warning was printed, though Hall knew he didn't need to read it. They both had the words memorized, embedded in their consciousness through years of use.

"Rachel Fenimore, you have the right to remain silent," White began, his voice clear and even. "Anything you say can and will be used against you in a court of law. You have the right to an attorney. If you cannot afford an attorney, one will be provided for you. Do you understand these rights as I have explained them to you?"

Rachel's chin dropped to her chest. "Yes," she said, the word barely audible.

Hall reached for her radio, pressing the transmit button. "Dispatch, this is Detective Hall. We need a patrol unit at Geller's Pawn on Waller Street for prisoner transport to Central Booking."

The radio crackled with the dispatcher's acknowledgment. "Unit en route, ETA five minutes."

Rachel's shoulders began to shake, small tremors that grew into the unmistakable movements of silent weeping. Tears dripped from her face onto the asphalt, dark spots that evaporated almost as soon as they formed. Hall recognized the particular quality of this crying—not the manipulative tears some suspects produced, but the genuine breakdown that came when reality finally shattered through denial.

"Let's have you sit down while we wait," Hall said, gentling her voice. She guided Rachel to the back of their car, opening the door and helping her settle into the seat. The handcuffs made the movement awkward, Rachel's body bending at an unnatural angle to accommodate her restrained arms.

White stepped away from the car, motioning for Hall to join him. They moved to the front of the vehicle, far enough that Rachel wouldn't overhear their conversation but close enough that they could keep her in sight. The sun beat down on them, White's face shining with sweat, the lines around his eyes deeper than usual.

"Good clean arrest," he said, his voice low. His gaze shifted to Rachel's huddled form in the backseat, then back to Hall. "Glad we got her before she could run."

"You arrested her?"

Harper approached, hands spread as if incredulous.

"Yes, Ms. Langston. We're going to have to ask you to come to the station on your own."

Harper looked at Rachel in the back seat, the detectives, the blue compact, and deflated. She nodded and retreated to her apartment.

Hall nodded, though something in her chest felt hollow. The evidence was clear—the bloody clothes, the lies, the flight from the scene. Rachel Fenimore had been present when Ira Lewis died, had likely been the one who plunged the knife into his abdomen. And yet Hall couldn't shake the image of Rachel kneeling beside Lewis in that rain-soaked alley, calling for help even as she knew it was too late.

"She'll be processed and interviewed again at Central," Hall said, keeping her voice professional. The satisfaction she'd expected to feel at closing the case was absent, replaced by something more complex. "We'll get a full confession."

White's eyes narrowed, reading something in her face that she hadn't intended to reveal. "You having doubts?"

"No," Hall said, and meant it. The evidence spoke for itself. But evidence told what, not why, and the why of Rachel Fenimore's actions remained as murky as the rainwater that had washed away so much of the crime scene that night. "Just thinking about what comes next."

The patrol unit pulled into the parking lot to take Rachel Fenimore from the free world into the system that would determine her fate.

Chapter 11

The interview room at Central Booking looked different from the one at the precinct—older, more worn, the table scarred with initials and crude drawings carved by generations of restless suspects. Hall had been waiting for twenty minutes while processing completed Rachel's intake, filling out the endless paperwork that transformed a person into a prisoner. The LED panels overhead glowed with an intensity just at the edge of too bright, a light that burrowed into the skull during long interviews.

The door opened, and a uniformed officer escorted Rachel inside. The orange jumpsuit hung loose on her frame, the county's standard issue designed to fit everyone and therefore fitting no one well. Her hair hung lank around her face, still damp with sweat.

The officer removed the handcuffs—standard procedure for cooperative suspects during formal interviews—and Rachel sank into the chair across from Hall, her movements slow and mechanical. Her wrists bore red marks where the cuffs had pressed, and she rubbed them absently, staring at the table's scarred surface. Without her watch, her expensive Tissot, she kept glancing at her bare wrist as if the absence of time itself disoriented her.

"Would you like some water?" Hall asked, gesturing to the bottle someone had left on the table.

Rachel nodded without speaking and reached for it. Her hands trembled as she raised it to her lips, the plastic crinkling in her grip.

Hall opened her notebook to a fresh page, the recorder's red light already pulsing its steady rhythm. "I need to ask you some more questions about that night, Rachel. About what really happened in that alley."

Rachel set the bottle down with careful precision, aligning it with a groove in the table. "I already told you everything."

"You told us you found Ira Lewis after he'd been stabbed," Hall said, keeping her voice neutral. "That you tried to help him and called 911. But we both know there's more to the story than that."

A muscle twitched in Rachel's jaw. She looked away, toward the blank wall, the one-way mirror that reflected her own image back at her. "What else is there to say?"

"The truth," Hall said. "We found your clothes, Rachel. The ones you were wearing that night. The blood pattern will tell us you were right there when his artery was severed. Not after—during."

"You talked to Harper, didn't you?"

Hall nodded. "You told us you lived alone."

"It's complicated."

"So is this, Rachel. Harper told us a lot about you."

Rachel's fingers found the water bottle again, turning it slowly on the table. The label was already peeling at the edges, revealing the adhesive underneath. "I was sleepwalking," she said, the words coming out flat, rehearsed. "I woke up next to him. He was already dying. There was so much blood, and I didn't know how I got there, or what happened before I woke up."

The explanation landed between them like something dead. Hall had heard it already from Harper, but hearing Rachel say it herself, with desperation wrapped in false certainty, changed its texture entirely.

"Why didn't you tell us this before?" Hall asked, though she already knew the answer.

Rachel's laugh was sharp and humorless. "Tell you I had no memory of how I got to an alley where a man was stabbed? That I woke up covered in his blood with no explanation?" She shook her head. "I know what that looks like."

Hall made a note, the scratch of her pen loud in the quiet room. Outside, someone's radio crackled with dispatch codes, the sound muffled by the walls but still audible. "So you lied about working that night. About walking home from the hospital."

"Yes." Rachel's voice had gone small, defeated. "I panicked."

Hall studied Rachel's face, looking for the seams where truth separated from fiction. The story was convenient—presence at the scene wrapped in absence of intent. "Have you sleepwalked this far from home before?"

Rachel shook her head. "Not usually. When I was a kid, my parents would find me in the yard, or the kitchen. As an adult..." She paused. "Once in the hallway outside our apartment. Once in the stairwell. Never blocks away. Never in an alley."

The admission hung in the air between them, its implications clear. Hall leaned forward. "Then why that night? Why that alley? Why Ira Lewis?"

Rachel's composure cracked, her face contorting as tears spilled over. "I don't know. I don't know what it means. But I swear, I would never hurt anyone. Never."

Hall waited, letting the moment stretch. She'd seen enough suspects cry to recognize the difference between performance and genuine distress. Rachel's breakdown had the messy, uncontrolled quality of real fear—the kind that came when a person confronted something they couldn't rationalize away.

A strand of hair had fallen across Rachel's face, sticking to her wet cheek. She pushed it back with trembling fingers, drawing several deep breaths. "Maybe I was there earlier. Maybe I was sleepwalking and saw something, or heard something, and that's why I went into the alley. But I didn't stab him. I couldn't have."

"Sleepwalking." Hall knew about the Toronto case: a man found not guilty for driving to his in-laws and killing one of them, because he was sleepwalking.

"Non-insane automatism. Then what did happen that night, Rachel?"

Rachel's gaze darted around the room as if searching for answers in the blank walls. "Non-insane? I don't know, but..." She leaned forward, her voice taking on a desperate edge. "Maybe Harper followed me. Maybe she saw me sleepwalking and followed me. Maybe she killed him to set me up."

The theory was so patently desperate that Hall had to work to keep her expression neutral. "You think Harper Langston followed you from your apartment as you sleepwalked several blocks, murdered a homeless man you had no connection to, then left you there to take the blame?"

Rachel flinched but pressed on. "You don't understand what our breakup was like. How angry she was. Harper wanted me out of the apartment, but I couldn't afford to break the lease." She leaned forward, eyes intent. "She hated me being there."

Hall made another note. "Does Harper hate you enough to commit murder?"

Rachel's certainty faltered. "Maybe. I don't know. Sometimes I felt like she did."

The water bottle tipped over as Rachel's gestures grew more agitated, spilling across the table. Rachel didn't seem to notice, even as water dripped onto her jumpsuit. Hall retrieved paper towels from the dispenser, mopping up the spill with efficient movements.

"Maybe someone tried to kill me," Rachel continued, the words tumbling out now, "and Ira stepped in to protect me. Maybe that's when I woke up, but by then the killer was gone."

The theory grew more elaborate with each sentence, built on maybes and what-ifs. Hall had heard plenty of such theories in this room over the years—complicated narratives constructed to explain away simple, brutal facts.

"Did you see anyone else in the alley?" Hall asked. "When you woke up, was there anyone else present?"

"No," Rachel admitted, her momentum deflating. "No one that I saw."

"And why would someone want to kill you, Rachel?"

Rachel's lips parted, the answer forming on her tongue, when the door swung open with particular abruptness. White stood in the doorway, his eyes fixed on Hall with an intensity that contained both warning and command.

"Detective Hall," he said, his voice neutral but his eyes anything but. "A word, please."

Hall felt the moment shatter, the careful pressure of questioning dissolving. What the hell did White think he was doing?

"I'll be right back," she said to Rachel, closing her notebook. She rose and followed White into the hallway.

He pulled the door shut behind her, the latch engaging with a definitive click. The hallway felt cavernous after the close confines of the interview room, the air cooler, tinged with the smell of someone's takeout from the break room down the corridor.

"What is it?" Hall asked, unable to keep the edge from her voice. "She was about to answer."

White took a step away from the door, gesturing for her to follow. When they were several feet away, he stopped, his face closed and hard. "This interview needs to end. We're deep into conspiracy theory territory now. First sleepwalking, then her ex-girlfriend framing her, now mysterious figures trying to kill her?" He shook his head. "It's a waste of time."

Hall felt heat rise to her face. "That's how these interviews work, White. They start with denial, move to implausible explanations, and eventually—if you keep pushing—you get to the truth."

"Process?" White's voice remained low but took on particular intensity. "She's making up stories as she goes. Next it'll be aliens."

A detective passed them in the hallway, nodding before continuing on. For a moment, neither spoke.

"We have her at the scene," White continued. "We have her clothes soaked in blood. We have her running from the scene, lying about where she was. We have an admission that she was there when it happened, even if she's wrapping it in this sleepwalking story." He adjusted his stance, easing weight off his bad hip. "We don't need elaborate conspiracy theories. We need her in a cell while we process the physical evidence."

Hall crossed her arms. "There are holes in her story. Big ones. But there are holes in our case too. The timeline is tight. The murder weapon is still missing. And we have no clear motive."

White's expression didn't change. "Those are details we can fill in later. Right now, she's spinning fairy tales, and you're encouraging it."

Hall stopped, took a breath. The argument was heading nowhere productive. In their partnership, this was the unspoken agreement—Hall led the interviews, White made the calls on when to end questioning, when to move a case forward.

She uncrossed her arms, a gesture of surrender without words. "Fine. We'll end it for now. But I want to go back to Harper Langston, dig deeper on their relationship."

White nodded, tension easing. "That's legitimate follow-up. She should be in later today."

The compromise settled between them, neither satisfied but both willing to move forward. Hall returned to the interview room alone, the door opening to reveal Rachel sitting as she'd left her, hands folded on the table, eyes fixed on the recorder.

"We're going to end here for today," Hall said, reaching for her notebook. "Someone will come to take you back to your cell in a few minutes."

Rachel's face tightened, her eyes widening. "But I was explaining—I was telling you why someone might want to—"

"We'll continue this conversation another time," Hall cut her off, her voice firm but not unkind. The notebook felt heavier than it should have as she picked it up, weighted with all the things Rachel hadn't said.

Hall moved to the door, pausing with her hand on the knob. Behind her, Rachel remained frozen in her chair, the orange jumpsuit bunched up around her shoulders, her face a mask of thwarted desperation. For a moment, Hall considered going back, asking the question one more time—why would someone want to kill you, Rachel?—but White was waiting in the hallway, and some instinct told her that whatever answer Rachel had been about to give, it wouldn't have been the truth. Not yet.

She stepped out, pulling the door shut behind her. The latch engaged with a click that sounded like the period at the end of an unfinished sentence.

Chapter 12

The Homicide Division existed in that strange early morning state where the world felt both empty and full of possibility. Hall sat alone at her desk, the only detective yet to arrive for the day shift. Morning light poured through the eastern windows, cutting across the room in sharp angles. The division smelled like the building's overnight cleaning—a harsh lemon that hadn't yet been overtaken by the scents that would accumulate as the day went on.

The phone on her desk rang, its sound startling in the empty room. Hall picked up on the second ring.

"Detective Hall."

"Detective, this is Officer Reyes from Central Booking." The voice was young, carrying that particular note of someone who hadn't been on the job long enough to lose the enthusiasm. "Rachel Fenimore is asking to speak with you. Says it's urgent."

Hall straightened in her chair. Rachel had been desperate to continue talking yesterday when White had cut the interview short. "Have her brought to Interview Room 2. I'll be there in ten minutes."

She hung up and gathered her notebook. White wouldn't be in for at least another hour. She had time. Whatever Rachel wanted to say, she wanted to say it without him present.

* * *

Inside Interview Room 2, Rachel sat at the small round table, hands folded, eyes fixed on the wall. The flip-flops she's been given were too large, and slipped easily off her feet. Without makeup, the circles beneath her eyes looked like bruises against her pale skin.

Rachel's gaze snapped to Hall as she entered, her body tensing, then relaxing. "Detective Hall." Her voice was hoarse. "Is Detective White with you?"

"No," Hall said, settling into the chair opposite. "He doesn't start this early. It's just me."

Relief washed over Rachel's face, a transformation so complete it was like watching a different person emerge. Her shoulders lowered, her hands unclenched.

"Good," she breathed. "That's good."

Hall opened her notebook to a fresh page. "Before we start, I want to make sure you understand your rights are still in effect. You have the right to have an attorney present."

Rachel shook her head. "I don't need a lawyer for this. I just need to tell you something—"

"And you are still being recorded."

Rachel paused, then shrugged. "I couldn't say this yesterday." She leaned forward, her voice dropping. "It's about that night. About what I saw in the alley. I think there was someone else there. Someone I was afraid to name."

Hall's pen hovered over the page. "That's a convenient memory to have overnight."

"I couldn't say anything before because—" Rachel's voice dropped to just above a whisper. "I think it was." The next words were mouthed: Detective White.

The pen stilled in Hall's hand. "Detective White? You're suggesting my partner was in that alley?"

"I know it sounds crazy, but listen to me. Two doctors who worked on Detective White's leg surgery have died in the past two years." The words came faster now, rehearsed. "Dr. Martin Fowler was murdered in what looked like a home invasion fourteen months ago. Dr. Victoria Strickland supposedly committed suicide six months ago. A surgical nurse named Sandra Kim died in a robbery eighteen months ago. And Jennifer Moss, another nurse on the surgical team, was supposedly killed by her boyfriend a year ago."

She'd kept her voice low, a hand over her mouth. The recording would, at best, be garbled and difficult to transcribe. Clever woman.

Hall wrote the names in her notebook, drawing a line beneath them. Four medical professionals, four deaths. "You're talking about a murder, a suicide, and two other deaths that were investigated and at least one was closed. And you're connecting them because they all worked on Detective White's surgery?"

Rachel nodded, eyes fever-bright. "Four people who worked on his surgery, all dead within two years. That can't be a coincidence."

"People die, Rachel. Medical professionals aren't immune to tragedy." Hall kept her tone measured. "Did you know all these people personally?"

"Not all of them. I knew Sandra and Jennifer. We worked some of the same shifts. I heard about the doctors through hospital gossip."

"So you're connecting deaths you only heard about secondhand." Hall made another note. "That's not compelling evidence."

"Don't you see? What if Detective White was going to kill me that night? What if Ira Lewis somehow stopped it, and it cost him his life?"

Hall studied Rachel's face—the dark circles, the tension, the flush in her cheeks. Genuine fear, or desperate invention? "Let me understand this theory. You believe Detective White, a twenty-year veteran with an exemplary record, has been systematically killing members of his surgical team. And Ira Lewis—a homeless man with no known connection to you or Detective White—intervened and was killed instead."

When spoken aloud, the theory collapsed under its own weight.

"I know how it sounds." Embarrassment colored Rachel's words. "But the coincidences, the timing—"

"Were you on the surgical team?"

Rachel looked at her hands. "No."

"And you said you were in the alley after sleepwalking? That you'd left home in the middle of the night, asleep, and walked six blocks to an alley, still asleep, only to have Detective White...what? Follow you from your home? Choose the alley to kill you only to discover it was not empty, so instead of killing you, or both of you, he killed Mr. Lewis?"

Rachel sat back. Defeated.

"Rachel." Hall closed her notebook with a snap that made Rachel flinch. "You're facing murder charges. The physical evidence against you is substantial. Now you're accusing a decorated detective of multiple homicides based on nothing more than hospital gossip and paranoia and a theory that should not include you at all."

Rachel's shoulders slumped. "You don't believe me."

"No," Hall said. "I don't."

"Officer," Hall called, raising her voice. The door opened immediately. "Please take Ms. Fenimore back to Central Booking. We're finished here."

Rachel stood, her movements slow and resigned. As the officer took her arm, she turned to Hall one last time. "Just look into it. Please."

"No." She watched as Rachel was led from the room, the orange jumpsuit bright against the institutional gray beyond.

When they were gone, Hall remained standing in the empty interview room, the closed notebook heavy in her hand. Four medical professionals who had worked on White's surgery, all dead within two years. And Rachel, not part of the surgery and with no apparent foreknowledge of this theory, was on the list.

It was one of the better conspiracy theories she'd heard. Better than Adderly's claims that the President had killed the little girl and framed him. Better than Trevino's theory that his sister had dressed up like him and stolen his DNA to frame him for killing his wife.

Hall returned to the Homicide Division, shaking her head. The accused could sometimes go to great lengths to deny their involvement. It was not unusual at all to invent a shadowy figure who actually did the killing. But to out and out accuse the detective investigating you? That was a new one.

The office had filled while she'd been in the interview—detectives settling at desks with coffee and conversation, someone microwaving something with onions. The normalcy of it felt surreal against the weight of the four names in her notebook.

White sat at his desk across from hers, logging into his computer. He'd arrived at 8:45. His coffee, black, no sugar, was already positioned within reach.

"Morning," he said without looking up.

"You're here early."

"Yep."

Hall settled into her chair, sliding the notebook to the edge of her desk. "Rachel Fenimore wanted to talk again. Asked for me specifically."

White's fingers paused over his keyboard. "When?"

"This morning, around seven. I was already here, so I took it."

"Should've waited for me." His voice carried a note of irritation. "What'd she want?"

"More of that conspiracy theory she started yesterday. She thinks someone else was in that alley." Hall kept her tone dismissive, professional.

White looked up, eyes meeting hers. "Harper Langston?"

"Yeah. She's got a whole narrative built up now. How she might have been lured there, how maybe Lewis saved her from this mystery attacker. Maybe Harper, maybe some unknown Black Ops assassin," Hall spread her hands. "Standard stuff. Desperate people grab at desperate explanations."

White nodded, his expression unchanged. "Warehouse guy didn't mention seeing anyone else."

"That's what I thought," Hall said. "But I wanted to double-check. Did he say anything about another person that didn't make it into the report?"

White reached for the case file, flipping through pages with efficient precision. "No. Just what's in the report. 'Small woman, running from the direction of the alley.' Time-stamp 2:14 A.M. No mention of anyone else."

Hall watched his hands as he closed the file. Steady, methodical. "You know how suspects get," White said. "Once they're locked up, they start making shit up. Throwing everything at the wall to see what sticks."

"Yeah." Hall let resignation enter her voice. "I've seen it before." She paused, as if the thought had just occurred to her. "I don't suppose we've found any connection between Rachel and Ira yet? Something that explains why she'd target him specifically?"

White took a sip of his coffee. "Nothing concrete. Different worlds. He was homeless, she's middle-class. He was an addict, she's clean as far as we know."

"Harper said Rachel was taking medication from the hospital. Maybe an addict," Hall offered. "Maybe meeting her dealer?"

The division hummed around them—phones ringing, conversations overlapping. Someone walked past trailing the scent of cinnamon gum.

"I'll call the shelter where Lewis was staying," White said, reaching for his phone. "Find out if Rachel ever volunteered there, if they ever crossed paths. Find out if Ira was dealing."

Hall nodded and turned to her computer, pretending to focus on the screen while keeping White in her peripheral vision. He dialed, the beeps of the numbers audible in the small space between their desks. Then he raised the handset to his ear.

"Yes, this is Detective White from New Hanan PD, Homicide Division. I'm calling about a former resident of yours, Ira Lewis."

Hall's eyes flicked to White's desk phone. The base had three lines, each with a button that lit up when in use.

All dark. No connection. No call.

What the hell was he up to?

White continued his one-sided conversation, asking questions, pausing as if listening to answers, jotting notes on a pad beside his keyboard. His performance was flawless—the slight changes in expression as he "received" information, the professional tone, even the way he thanked the non-existent person before hanging up.

Hall felt something cold settle in her stomach.

"Shelter has no record of Rachel volunteering or visiting," White said, turning to her. "Lewis was only there a few weeks before he died. Kept to himself, according to the manager. Not a dealer, as far as they know."

Hall forced her expression to remain neutral. "Makes sense. Most of these cases, the perpetrator and victim know each other. But sometimes it's just wrong place, wrong time."

"Exactly." White reached for his coffee again. "Rachel was there, Lewis was there. Something happened between them. The rest is just noise."

Noise. The word hung in the air between them.

Hall turned back to her computer, her mind racing. White had faked a phone call. A small deception, perhaps, but deliberate. A lie. As good as a confession. But to what?

She opened a search window and typed "Fowler, Martin" into the database. The case file loaded. She and White had worked it together fourteen months ago. An elegant townhouse on the east side, Fowler found in his study with a single gunshot wound to the chest. Home invasion gone wrong. Thomas Pryor had confessed three weeks later.

The case summary, incident report and crime scene documentation were exactly what she remembered. Hall lingered, looking at the study where Fowler had died. Nothing out of the ordinary.

The administrative section was next. Hall scrolled through the digital file, looking for the Statement of Disclosure form. Every detective was required to fill one out if they discovered a personal connection to a victim or suspect. The form ensured transparency, prevented conflicts of interest.

There was no form. No disclosure from White that Fowler had been his surgeon.

White was meticulous, a stickler for procedure. In seven years, she had never known him to skip a step, to miss filing a form. If he hadn't disclosed his connection to Fowler, it was a deliberate choice.

Hall frowned and moved on to the evidence log. In Fowler's home, she had found the crowbar Pryor had used to break in. Projectile, casing.

Click.

Evidence from Pryor's home. Bullets similar to the ones at the scene. She stopped at the entry for the jewelry. Found in Pryor's bedroom closet, packaged in a cloth bag. White had found it during the secondary search, after Hall had already cleared that room. She remembered the moment: White emerging with the evidence bag, his expression carefully neutral. "It was in the back corner, behind some shoes," he'd said. "Easy to miss."

She'd felt embarrassed then.

Sloppy.

Now she felt something else entirely.

Hall glanced across at White. He was reviewing case notes, being the same man he had always been. Her partner. Her friend.

Except now she wasn't sure who he really was.

The four names in her notebook pulsed beneath her hand: Fowler, Strickland, Kim, Moss. Four medical professionals connected to White's surgery. One fake phone call. One missing disclosure form.

She couldn't be sure they were all dead. She couldn't be sure of anything. Or anyone.

Rachel's words echoed in her mind: *Just look into it. Please.*

Hall closed the Fowler file and returned to her regular work, going through the motions while her thoughts churned. The afternoon bled into evening, shadows growing longer across the division. Detectives finished their shifts and drifted away.

White stood, gathering his jacket. "Calling it a day. You coming?"

Hall kept her voice casual. "Got a few things to look at on Henderson. Thought I'd stay a bit longer."

White nodded. "See you tomorrow."

She watched him walk away, his gait measured and careful. When he reached the door, he paused, half-turned back—a habit from years of partnership, a final check-in before parting ways. Hall raised her hand in a small wave.

And then he was gone.

Hall sat motionless, counting her heartbeats. Thirty seconds. A minute. Two minutes. Enough time for White to reach the elevator, descend to the parking level, drive away.

Only when she was certain he was gone did she turn back to her computer.

She had work to do, and it would take hours.

The division stood empty around her, the desks bare of their usual occupants, chairs tucked in or pushed back at odd angles. The silence pressed against her ears, broken only by the distant hum of air conditioning and the soft glow of LED lights overhead.

Hall opened her browser and typed "Victoria Strickland New Hanan" into the search bar. Looking at the official case file on a suicide would trigger an alert—she couldn't risk that. But a web search was safe, innocuous. Just a detective doing background research.

The results loaded: obituaries, medical journal citations, a profile from Mercy General's website. Strickland had been Chief of Orthopedic Surgery, specialized in trauma cases. The articles called her death "a shocking tragedy," colleagues expressing disbelief that someone so accomplished, so vital, would take her own life.

Hall clicked through methodically. Strickland's professional life was well-document-ed—board certifications, research papers, a teaching position at New Hanan Medical School. Her personal life remained more obscure. Divorced five years ago, no children, lived alone in an upscale neighborhood on the east side.

Nothing unusual. Nothing that explained why she would commit suicide six months ago.

Hall clicked on a local news article about Strickland's funeral. The piece was brief, respectful, noting the hundreds who had gathered to mourn. Former patients, medical students, colleagues from Mercy General. She scrolled down to the accompanying pho-tographs.

The first showed the church. St. Catherine's on Maple Street, its stone facade solemn against a cloudless sky. The second captured the casket being carried by pallbearers in dark suits. The third showed mourners filing out after the service.

Hall's breath caught.

In the background, partially obscured by other attendees but unmistakable to someone who knew him well, stood White. His face was somber, his posture rigid in a dark suit she'd never seen before. He stood apart from the crowd, watching, a solitary figure among the mourners.

She enlarged the photo, her fingers clumsy on the keyboard. White's face grew larger, pixelated but still recognizable. He wasn't speaking to anyone, wasn't part of any group. Just standing there, observing.

Hall sat back, the chair springs protesting. From the break room came the sound of the night janitor emptying trash bins, the rustle of plastic bags a counterpoint to the thunder of her pulse.

White had never mentioned attending Strickland's funeral. Never mentioned knowing her beyond the professional capacity of surgeon and patient.

It could be innocent. Gratitude could explain his presence—Strickland had rebuilt his shattered hip, had given him back the ability to walk. Respect for the woman who had saved his career.

That's all it was. That's all it could be.

Hall minimized the photo and stared at her notebook and opened a new Internet search: "Sandra Kim New Hanan nurse." The results came quickly. A brief mention in the obituaries, a news article about her death. Killed in a robbery outside Mercy General eighteen months ago. The case had been handled by the eighth precinct's homicide team, not theirs. Not White. Just another street crime in a city full of them.

Hall searched the public case details but found little. No arrests, no suspects named. The investigation had gone cold within weeks. But White was not mentioned anywhere.

Another search: "Jennifer Moss New Hanan." More results this time. Moss had been strangled by her boyfriend, Kevin Parrish, a year ago. Parrish was serving twenty-five to life at New Hanan Correctional. Open and shut—the boyfriend had a history of violence, neighbors had heard them fighting the night she died, physical evidence had tied him to the scene.

Four deaths. Four different circumstances. A home invasion, a suicide, a robbery, a domestic murder. Nothing connected them except one thing: they had all worked on White's surgery.

Hall pulled up the Fowler case file again, the one she had the most access to. She read through the investigation notes with fresh eyes, looking for anything she might have missed. Thomas Pryor's confession had been thorough, detailed. He'd known things about the crime scene that hadn't been released to the public—the exact position of Fowler's body, the caliber of the weapon, the point of entry, the angle of the wound.

Remarkably observant for someone who'd committed a panicked murder.

White had conducted that interview alone. Hall had been in court that day. She'd never watched the interview video.

Why would she? White was a great detective.

Hall opened the interview records tab. The mouse pointer turned from white to black as she hovered over the video file. Then white again. She knew if she opened the video, it would trigger an alert. Black. White. Black.

White.

Hall opened the transcript instead. No alerts. Safer.

DETECTIVE WHITE: When did you first enter the residence?

PRYOR: Around eleven. Maybe eleven-thirty. I don't know, I wasn't checking my watch.

DETECTIVE WHITE: And you entered through which door?

PRYOR: The back. Through the kitchen. Window was unlocked.

Hall leaned back and stretched. She'd been at it for hours. The Pryor interview was three and a half hours long, and it was getting late. She knew she was close to the end. She knew she had to power through.

DETECTIVE WHITE: When you saw Dr. Fowler in the study, where exactly was he positioned?

PRYOR: What do you mean?

DETECTIVE WHITE: Was he standing? Sitting? Behind the desk or in front of it?

PRYOR: He was... he was behind the desk. In his chair, I think. Yeah, in the chair.

DETECTIVE WHITE: And the wound. You fired from what distance?

PRYOR: I don't know, man. Few feet? It happened fast.

DETECTIVE WHITE: But you remember the angle. The bullet entered at a downward trajectory, didn't it? Like you were standing and he was seated.

PRYOR: Yeah. Yeah, that's right. I was standing, he was in the chair.

DETECTIVE WHITE: And the surgical scar on his chest, the recent one, still pink, you noticed that when you shot him?

PRYOR: I... yeah. I saw it. There was a scar.

DETECTIVE WHITE: A vertical scar. About six inches long, just left of center.

PRYOR: Right. Vertical. I remember now.

Hall closed her eyes, pressing her fingertips against her eyelids until she saw bursts of color. The case had never felt wrong at the time. Pryor was a career criminal with a string of B&Es. He'd confessed. The evidence had supported his confession. She'd testified at his trial without hesitation, watched him sentenced without doubt.

Hall read it again. Pink scar. Pink scar. She remembered Fowler's body. Shot in the chest. Through his shirt. She scratched her head, then opened the crime scene photos.

Fowler was wearing a white shirt, buttoned almost to the neck. In his chair, shirt soaked with blood. The shirt in evidence, cataloged. She zoomed in. No incision.

Hall cleared her throat and tried to click the autopsy photos, but missed, hitting the administrative tab by mistake. Click, click, and the autopsy report covered the screen.

Healed surgical incision, vertical orientation, approximately 15cm in length, located 3cm left of midline sternum. Consistent with recent cardiac surgery.

Pryor knew about a scar he never saw.

Or someone told him about it.

From down the hall came the sound of the janitor's cart moving closer, metal wheels on linoleum. Hall glanced at the clock—nearly 9 P.M. She'd been here for over twelve hours.

She needed to decide. Right now, sitting alone in this empty division with the evidence of White's deceptions spread across her screen, she needed to choose a path forward.

She could close these windows, lock her notebook in her desk, and return tomorrow morning as if nothing had changed. Continue being White's partner, working cases, maintaining the fiction that everything was normal. Ignore Rachel's accusations and the questions that now gnawed at her.

Or she could keep digging. Follow this thread wherever it led, even if it meant unraveling everything, destroying the career of a decorated detective, betraying the man who had saved her life.

The choice sat before her like a chasm. Once she stepped across, there would be no return.

Hall opened a new document and began typing. Four names at the top: Fowler, Strickland, Kim, Moss. Below each, she listed the details she'd found—dates of death, circumstances, connections to White. The missing disclosure form. The scar. The fake phone call. The funeral photo.

When she finished, she saved the document to a thumb drive, then deleted the automatic backup from her computer and cleared her browser history. She ejected the drive and slipped it into her pocket, a small weight against her hip.

The janitor appeared in the doorway, pushing his cart. He nodded at Hall, unsurprised to find a detective working late. She nodded back and gathered her things. Coat, bag. The notebook she locked in her desk drawer.

At the door, she paused and looked back at the two desks she shared with White. In the LED light, they looked ordinary. Just furniture, just workspace. Nothing to suggest the fracture that had opened between the partners who occupied them.

Hall switched off the lights and stepped into the hallway.

She knew what she had to do next. Tomorrow morning, before White arrived, she would go to Internal Affairs. She would show them the names, the missing disclosure, the pattern she'd uncovered. Let them investigate properly, with subpoena power and official authority.

It would end her partnership with White. It would end the friendship, the trust, everything. But if he was killing people—if Rachel was right and White had murdered four people and tried for a fifth—then Hall had no choice.

She needed the night. She needed to not think. She needed to feel something else.

She walked through the empty precinct, her footsteps echoing in the quiet corridors. The building felt different at night. Colder, more honest somehow.

Outside, the August air hit her face like a slap. Hall stood on the precinct steps, looking out at the city she'd sworn to protect. Somewhere in those lights was White, going about his evening, unaware that his partner had just decided to investigate him.

Or maybe he knew. Maybe he'd been waiting for this moment since Rachel first opened her mouth. Maybe he'd seen it in Hall's face when she watched him fake that phone call, when she'd stayed late without a real reason.

Hall descended the steps and walked to her car. The thumb drive pressed against her hip like a brand, marking her as a traitor or a hero depending on what the investigation revealed.

She wouldn't know which until it was too late to change course.

Chapter 13

The morning light carved harsh angles across the Homicide Division, slicing between the blinds to lay bright strips on the floor. Hall sat at her desk, her eyes gritty from too little sleep and her tongue coated with the memory of bourbon. She had returned to the precinct wearing yesterday's clothes, the fabric holding the ghost of cigarette smoke and perfume that wasn't her own.

She could not bring herself to go to IA, to risk everything, ruin everything.

Her notebook lay open before her, the four names staring up at her with accusatory clarity: Fowler, Strickland, Kim, Moss. Four deaths, one connection. White.

The division hummed with morning activity—phones ringing, keyboards clicking, the low murmur of detectives comparing notes on cases that had nothing to do with medical professionals who had died after working on her partner's hip. Someone had brought in donuts; the sweet, doughy smell drifted across the room, mingling with the sharp tang of someone's aftershave. Hall closed her notebook as the elevator dinged at the far end of the room.

White arrived at 9:32 A.M. As unpredictable as ever. His timing was as imprecise as everything else about him was precise—his pressed shirts, his organized desk, his methodical approach to interrogation. He moved toward their shared space with his characteristic measured gait, favoring his right leg just enough to remind Hall. The bullet that had brought him under the care of four medical professionals who were now dead.

"Morning," White said, settling into his chair with a slight wince. He glanced at Hall, his eyes tracking over her rumpled shirt, the same black blazer she'd worn yesterday. His expression changed, so subtle that anyone who hadn't worked with him for years might have missed it. "Same clothes as yesterday."

Hall's hand moved to smooth her hair, a reflexive gesture she caught halfway through. "I didn't notice."

"Must've been a memorable night." White turned to his computer, tapping the keyboard to wake the screen.

The words hung between them, sharp-edged and unexpected.

"Excuse me?" Hall's voice came out colder than she'd intended.

White glanced up, his face showing mild surprise at her tone. "What?"

"Memorable?" The word felt vulgar in her mouth, like something that belonged to someone else. "What the hell does that mean?"

Hall drew a deep breath.

"It doesn't mean anything." White shrugged, his shoulders rising and falling beneath his gray suit jacket. "Just an expression. You're wearing yesterday's clothes. You look tired. I made an assumption." He turned back to his computer, as if the exchange was over.

But it wasn't over. Not for Hall. The comment lingered like cigarette smoke, impossible to wave away. This wasn't White—not the White she knew. Or thought she knew. The White whose behavior she'd never questioned. Until Rachel Fenimore.

"It's not 'just an expression' coming from you," Hall pressed. "In seven years, I've never heard you talk like that to me."

White's jaw tightened, a muscle jumping beneath the skin. He kept his eyes on his screen, fingers tapping keys with more force than necessary. "Jesus, Hall, it was a joke."

Hall studied his profile, searching for signs of the partner she trusted with her life, the man who had taken a bullet meant for her. She found only a stranger wearing White's face.

"White—"

He held up his hand, the gesture silencing her as effectively as a shout. "Fine. Forgettable night. Feel better now, snowflake?" His desk phone rang, and he picked it up immediately, turning away from her. His voice shifted into his professional register, all business, no trace of the tension that had charged the air moments before.

The words sliced through the air between them, cutting deeper than he could have known. Or did he know how they would land?

Hall watched him, her heartbeat loud in her ears. The division continued its morning rhythm around them—a detective laughed across the room, someone dropped a file folder, the elevator dinged again. Normal sounds, normal day. Except nothing felt normal anymore.

White's one-sided conversation continued, his voice low, his back half-turned to Hall. She couldn't tell when he was faking a phone call, and when he was really on one. The realization sent a chill through her that had nothing to do with the building's aggressive air conditioning.

She was pissed off.

She turned to her computer. While White was occupied with his call—real or pretended—she would see who investigated the Sandra Kim case.

Hall called up the database, entering her credentials with ease. The search field blinked expectantly. She typed "Sandra Kim," clicked the Homicide checkbox, and pressed enter. Her eyes flicked constantly toward White, monitoring his posture, the angle of his head, the hand that gestured occasionally as he spoke. He was ignoring her, as if their exchange had never happened.

The search results appeared: one case file. Hall clicked to open it, her pulse quickening as the summary loaded on her screen. Sandra Kim, 33, found dead in the parking garage of her apartment building eighteen months ago. Cause of death: blunt force trauma. The case was assigned to Detectives Carpenter and Robbins from the eighth precinct, both younger detectives Hall knew only by reputation.

She scrolled through the file, scanning for White's name. Nothing in the initial report. Nothing in the witness statements. Nothing in the crime scene photos. She was beginning to think she was wrong.

Doubt.

One more click, and she reached the supplementary notes.

There it was, on page twelve: "Det. White provided review of recovered items and suggested follow-up leads; logged in case file." A consultation. Not unusual in itself—senior detectives often consulted on complex cases.

Click. Administrative section. No disclosure form. White had never mentioned knowing Sandra Kim. Never disclosed that she had been on his surgical team.

Hall's fingers moved to a new search: "Aubrie Thomas," the name of the man arrested for Kim's murder. The system responded with links to the case file, court records, and current status. Aubrie had pleaded not guilty but was convicted on the strength of DNA evidence found on a watch pawned three days after the murder. The judge had handed down a sentence of life plus 30 years. The case was currently under appeal.

Hall leaned back in her chair, the springs creaking beneath her weight. White was still on his call, his voice a steady murmur that provided cover for her investigation.

She wondered if she had enough evidence to...what?

What the hell was she doing?

White cleared his throat, the sound like gravel under tires. Hall's finger stabbed at the keyboard shortcut to close the window, the motion as instinctual as drawing her weapon at the sound of gunfire. The Sandra Kim case file vanished from her screen, replaced by the blank blue of the department's home page. She turned to face White, her heart hammering against her ribs, certain he had seen what she was looking at, certain he knew she was investigating him.

But his expression showed nothing—just the usual mask of professional detachment. He leaned back in his chair, the leather creaking beneath his weight. "Heading out for lunch with the guys. You want in?"

Hall forced her features into a neutral arrangement, though her pulse still raced. "Who's going?"

"Rossi, Terrence, Velázquez." White adjusted his tie, a simple blue one today, not the striped one he usually wore on Wednesdays. Another small deviation from his patterns. "That sandwich place on Madison."

The thought of sitting at a table with White and three other male detectives, ignoring her as they always did, talking over her, dismissing her, made Hall's stomach clench. She needed space, needed time alone to think, to investigate.

"Thanks, but I'm waiting on a call from Forensics," she lied. "About the clothing from the Lewis case."

White's eyes narrowed. "I thought they weren't processing that until tomorrow."

Hall kept her face still, though something cold settled in her stomach. She hadn't known that. Hadn't checked the processing schedule before inventing her excuse. "The tech said they might fit it in today if they clear their backlog."

For a moment, White said nothing, his gaze steady on her face. Hall met his eyes, refusing to look away though every instinct screamed at her to break contact. In that moment, something passed between them—an acknowledgment, perhaps, that the ground between them had shifted. That the partnership built on seven years of trust now stood on uncertain foundation.

"Suit yourself." White pushed away from his desk and stood, his movements carrying the careful precision of someone living with chronic pain.

"Next time," she said.

Hall watched as he crossed the division to where Rossi and Terrence waited by the elevator, Velázquez joining them from the break room. The four men stepped into the elevator together, White turning just before the doors closed to look back at Hall. His expression remained unreadable, his eyes hidden by the reflection of light on his glasses.

When they were gone, Hall released a breath she hadn't realized she was holding. The division had emptied for lunch, most of the detectives gone to nearby restaurants or the cafeteria on the ground floor. Only Alvarez remained at her desk across the room, headphones on, typing steadily, oblivious to Hall's presence.

Hall turned back to her computer, opening a fresh search window. Her fingers hesitated over the keys for a moment before she typed "Jennifer Moss homicide." The fourth name. The last on her list.

The system processed her request, then returned a single result. Hall clicked to open the file, her eyes scanning the initial details. Jennifer Moss, 29, found dead in her apartment one year ago. Cause of death: strangulation. Boyfriend—ex-boyfriend, the report clarified—arrested at the scene, clothing covered in the victim's blood from defensive wounds she had inflicted.

Their precinct. Hall didn't remember this case at all.

She scrolled down, looking for the assigned detectives. The name that appeared sent a jolt through her system: Detective Robert White, primary. Detective Thomas Velázquez, secondary.

White had been the primary detective on Jennifer Moss's murder.

Hall sat back, her chair rolling a few inches from the force of her movement. That wasn't possible. She would have known if White had worked a case involving someone from his surgery. She would have remembered.

Unless she hadn't been there.

She checked the date of the murder: June 18th, last year. Hall had been on vacation that week, a rare ten days off to visit her sister in Seattle. She remembered the trip clearly—the constant rain, the coffee shops on every corner, her sister's children grown so much since she'd last seen them. While she'd been there, White had caught this case. Had investigated the death of a woman who had been part of the surgical team that saved his career.

And he had never mentioned it. Not when she returned. Not in the year since.

Hall leaned closer to her screen, scrolling through the case notes. White's documentation was extensive—every interview detailed, every piece of evidence cataloged with meticulous precision, every step of the investigation recorded in his distinctive, methodical prose. The thoroughness itself was suspicious.

White was a good detective, but he wasn't obsessive about documentation. He recorded what was necessary, what would hold up in court, not every small action and decision.

Why the deviation for this case? Why document this death with such exhaustive detail? Why another case with no disclosure form?

The boyfriend, Kevin Parrish, had confessed after sixteen hours of interrogation. White had conducted most of the questioning, with Velázquez stepping in only briefly. The confession was recorded, transcribed, airtight. Parrish took an Alford plea, accepting a deal for twenty-five to life instead of risking trial and a potential death penalty.

Case closed. Justice served.

Hall closed the file, her chest tight with something that felt like fear but ran deeper. The empty division stretched around her, the other desks vacant, the air still and silent except for the soft glow of the LED lights overhead. In that silence, the truth she had been circling for days settled over her like a shroud.

Four medical professionals who had worked on White's surgery.

Four deaths in two years.

Three cases where White had been involved without disclosing his connection to the victims.

Her partner, the man who had saved her life, the man she would have trusted with anything—might be a serial killer.

How could she go to Internal Affairs with that?

Chapter 14

The dry cleaning tag clung to her sleeve like a forgotten promise, the suit so fresh its newness felt like an accusation. Hall plucked it off and dropped it into the trash bin beside her desk, watching it spiral down among yesterday's coffee cups and discarded memos. The charcoal gray fabric stood at attention against her skin, its crisp edges and perfect seams a kind of armor she hadn't worn in months. She'd spent twenty minutes that morning before her closet's open door, rejecting outfit after outfit until her fingers found this suit—cleaned, pressed, waiting. Anything to avoid White's eyes lingering on her clothes, measuring the hours between yesterday and today.

The Homicide Division breathed around her, half-empty in the early morning light. Most detectives were still navigating the city's arteries or pausing at the corner deli where Manny greeted them by name, remembered their orders, asked after children and spouses whose faces he'd never seen. Hall's desk offered no such familiarity—just the blank computer screen and the ghost-print of yesterday's conversation with White, invisible but indelible.

She pressed the power button. The computer's soft whir rose to meet her, a sound so woven into the fabric of her days she rarely noticed it. This morning, each noise arrived with surgical precision—the elevator's distant chime, a chair's complaint across the room, the low conspiracy of uniforms by the water cooler. Their words indistinct but their posture familiar: bodies angled together, information passing between them like currency.

Her mouth tasted of too little sleep and too many thoughts. The break room waited twenty steps away, its fluorescent promise of caffeine and momentary blindness to the weight settling between her shoulder blades.

Burned popcorn hung in the air, night shift's legacy clinging to the walls despite the window someone had cracked against department policy. Hall pulled the refrigerator door open and wrapped her fingers around a cola. The cold metal anchored her to something solid while her thoughts circled like carrion birds. Detective Alvarez stood at the coffee machine, stirring cream into her "World's Okayest Detective" mug—last year's Secret Santa offering from Rodriguez or maybe Stark.

"Morning, Hall." Alvarez's voice carried sleep's sandpaper edge. "You look like hell."

"Thanks." The soda tab surrendered with a hiss, carbonation rising like tiny accusations. "Just what every woman wants to hear at eight-thirty."

Alvarez shrugged, unrepentant in her assessment. "White's looking for you. Something about Lewis."

The Lewis case. The beginning of everything—Rachel Fenimore, blood-soaked clothing, the arrest that should have been routine. Four names spoken in an interrogation room, now burning behind Hall's eyes whenever she closed them. She took a long swallow of soda, sweetness coating her tongue, caffeine a false prophet of clarity.

"Thanks," she said, turning toward the door. "I'll find him."

He had beaten her in. Unpredictable.

Hall drifted toward White's desk, her eyes scanning its surface with casualness. She wasn't sure what she hoped to find—a note about the Lewis case, something about Rachel, any fragment that might confirm or dispel the unease coiling in her gut. She shifted a memo about updated evidence protocols, nudged aside a departmental bulletin. White maintained his workspace with the same military precision he brought to everything else—each pen aligned, no confidential papers, the surface wiped clean of coffee rings or fingerprints. Nothing. She lifted a folder, found only blank requisition forms beneath. When she glanced up, Alvarez stood motionless in the coffee room doorway, mug suspended halfway to her lips, her gaze fixed squarely on her.

Hall sat down at her own desk, logged in, hoped for an email from White. Instead, her computer screen glowed with an alert from the case management system, the blue notification box stark against departmental gray.

Hall set down her soda and clicked.

"Defendant Rachel Fenimore granted bail. Released 22:47 last night."

The words remained unchanged no matter how many times she read them. Rachel Fenimore—the woman they'd found with blood-saturated clothing and a story thin as tissue paper about sleepwalking—was free less than 72 hours after being charged with murder. First-degree murder charges rarely saw bail, especially with evidence that spoke so clearly of guilt.

Hall's finger traced the information on the screen. Judge Franklin Harrison. Bail set at $750,000. Bondsman Eric Levin. Everything according to procedure, everything within the letter of the law, everything wrong.

She leaned back in her chair. Rachel Fenimore was free—free to disappear, free to scrub away whatever evidence they hadn't yet found, free to craft something more convincing than sleepwalking. And free, if White was indeed the target of her accusations rather than their architect, to continue weaving suspicion around Hall's partner like a spider spinning silk around prey.

Maybe the judge had been swayed by those wide blue eyes, that vulnerable tremble in Rachel's lower lip. Men in positions of power had made worse decisions for less compelling women. Harrison was pushing seventy, a man whose courtroom reputation had calcified over decades—granite-faced with violent offenders but occasionally yielding to emotional appeals from certain defendants. And Rachel, with her nurse's scrubs and her tale of trying to help a dying man, fit some archetype he couldn't resist.

The notebook in Hall's desk drawer called to her. Its presence radiated through metal and wood, a physical weight she felt in her fingertips before she even touched the handle. She glanced across the division—morning quiet still held, detectives just settling into chairs with steam rising from coffee mugs—then pulled open the drawer and extracted the small black book.

Four names stared up at her from yesterday's page. Not just deaths but question marks, each one a thread pulled loose from what she thought she knew about White.

Hall traced the names with her fingertip. The ink had smudged where sweat transferred from her hand to paper, names blurring at their edges like memories losing definition.

The thought that had been forming in her mind for two days crystallized, ice-sharp and cold. If Rachel was right—if White had somehow been involved in these deaths—then the murder that landed Rachel in jail might be connected. What if Ira Lewis wasn't simply homeless and unlucky? What if he had witnessed something, known something about one of the other deaths?

And what if Rachel truly had been trying to help him?

Her desk phone rang, the sound fracturing the quiet. Hall closed her notebook and lifted the receiver.

"Detective Hall," she answered, the words coming out brittle.

"Detective." A voice thick with tears, female, trembling. Hall needed a moment to place it. "It's Rachel Fenimore."

Hall straightened, her free hand reaching instinctively for a pen. "Ms. Fenimore. I just saw the notification about your bail. Congratulations."

"Someone tried to kill me." The words tumbled raw with fear. "I need your help. Please, you have to believe me."

"Slow down," Hall said, keeping her voice steady though her pulse had quickened. "What happened?"

"A car—it came straight at me. Outside my apartment." Rachel's words broke against sharp intakes of breath, the sound of someone trying not to shatter. "Please, can you come? I don't know who else to call."

"What about 911?"

The words escaped before Hall could catch them. She felt the mistake in her throat.

"Sorry, yes. Text me your address," Hall said, decision already made. "Go inside. I'll be there in twenty minutes." There was nothing wrong with talking to a suspect who called you.

Right?

She hung up and stood. Her new suit suddenly felt like armor fitted for someone else's body, constricting across her shoulders. She caught sight of White entering the office, his face set in lines she once would have read as professional concentration but now saw as a mask—the careful arrangement of features hiding something darker beneath.

He raised a hand in greeting. Hall was already moving toward the exit.

The parking lot behind Geller's Pawn trapped heat like a convection oven. Blacktop radiated warmth despite the early hour, the air shimmering above cracked asphalt. Hall parked beside a small blue compact, next to a faded green dumpster. Broken furniture spilled over its edges, the metal exterior layered with graffiti tags that had long since stopped being legible, one generation of marks obscuring another.

Rachel Fenimore sat huddled in the open doorway of her apartment. Her body curled forward as if trying to disappear into itself, arms wrapped around drawn-up knees, face streaked with tears that had dried in tracks down her cheeks.

Hall walked slowly. Her footsteps carried across the empty lot, announcing her arrival to anyone watching from surrounding buildings with their drawn blinds and silent windows. Rachel looked up. Her eyes were red-rimmed and swollen, hair falling in tangled strands around her face like a curtain she'd given up trying to close.

"You came," Rachel said. Relief broke her voice into fragments. She rose unsteadily, one hand bracing against the doorframe, fingers splayed white against peeling paint. She wore what must be her arrest clothes—jeans and a gray T-shirt, both wrinkled and stained dark across the front. "I didn't know if you would."

"I'm here," Hall said, voice neutral as water. She stopped a few feet from Rachel, maintaining the distance that separated detective from witness, questioner from questioned. "Tell me what happened."

Rachel wiped at her face with the back of her hand, leaving a smear of tears like a watermark across her cheek. "I got home late last night. The bondsman dropped me off." Her words came in uneven bursts, fragments of thought that refused to assemble themselves into anything coherent. "I slept maybe two hours. This morning I went for coffee—there's this little place around the corner with the blue awning—and when I came back, crossing toward the lot, this car—" Her voice caught, frayed at the edges, fresh tears welling but not quite spilling over.

"Take your time," Hall said, though patience had never been her particular gift. Behind her stretched the half-empty parking lot, a patchwork of oil stains and cracked asphalt, cars belonging to residents who lived in the tired apartments above storefronts that had seen better decades.

Rachel drew a breath that snagged halfway through. "This car appeared—a black sedan, tinted windows—it turned into the lot and came straight for me." Her hands moved in her lap, fingers knotting together until the knuckles bloomed white. "Like it knew me. Like it was hunting. I jumped sideways and it swerved at the last second, missed me by inches, then tore out of the lot." She looked up, her eyes wide and glassy. "If I hadn't moved when I did—" She didn't finish the thought.

"Did you recognize the driver? Get a plate number?" Hall scanned the perimeter of the lot again, noting the conspicuous absence of security cameras on the building's facade. Typical for this part of New Hanan, where landlords calculated precisely how little they could spend on tenant safety without inviting lawsuits.

Rachel shook her head. "It happened so fast. A blur of motion and sound. I think it was a man driving, but—" She wrapped her arms around herself, a protective shell, shivering despite heat that rose in visible waves from the pavement. "It wasn't an accident. They were trying to kill me."

"Let me see your car." Hall gestured toward the dusty blue Corolla parked at an angle near the building's shadow. "Were you near it when this happened?"

"Almost to it." Rachel followed Hall through the lot, each step measured, her gaze darting toward the entrance as if expecting the black car to materialize again from the hazy street beyond. "I was going to drive to the store. Get some groceries."

"Going upstairs or going to your car?" Hall asked, squinting down the empty street where heat shimmered above the pavement.

"To the car," Rachel said, her voice small. "For groceries."

Hall circled Rachel's vehicle, examining it for damage—a scrape, a dent, any evidence that another car had come close enough to leave its signature. Nothing. The paint was dirty but intact, the bumpers unscratched. If a car had swerved toward Rachel with murderous intent, it had been precise enough to leave no physical trace of the encounter.

"Is there security footage?" Hall straightened, feeling sweat gather at the base of her spine. "A superintendent's office? Anyone who might have seen something?"

Rachel pointed toward a small office at the corner of the lot. Its window was plastered with yellowed announcements and faded lease information, like archaeological layers of neglect. "Mr. Geller owns the building. His office is there, but I knocked earlier. No answer."

They crossed to the office, their footsteps crunching on loose gravel and cigarette butts. A handwritten sign taped to the metal door read "Out until 11. Emergencies call 555-0198." Hall rapped her knuckles against it anyway, the sound hollow and final in the empty lot. Silence answered.

"Figures," Rachel said, her shoulders collapsing inward. "No cameras either. Harper complained about that when we moved in. Said it wasn't safe."

Hall peered through the grimy office window, making out only a cluttered desk and an ancient swivel chair, its vinyl cracked and peeling like a molting skin. "Any other witnesses? Did you see anyone else in the lot when it happened?"

"No one." The word seemed to cost Rachel something vital. "But you believe me, right? It wasn't just some random driver. They were aiming for me."

The question hung between them, dense as the summer humidity, weighted with implications Hall wasn't prepared to address. Before she could formulate a response, the sound of an approaching engine drew her attention to the lot entrance. A familiar sedan pulled in—unmarked, but unmistakable to anyone who knew what to look for.

He parked near Hall's vehicle and emerged, his movements deliberate, almost ceremonial. His face remained unreadable behind dark sunglasses, his shirt crisp and white against the suit that seemed to absorb rather than reflect the punishing sunlight. Hall felt her body respond before her mind could intervene—muscles tensing, pulse quickening—a physical memory she couldn't override.

"What's he doing here?" Rachel whispered, shrinking back toward the office door as if seeking shelter in its shadow. "Did you call him?"

"No," Hall said, the word bitter on her tongue, like something that had spoiled in the heat. She hadn't called White. Hadn't told anyone where she was going. Yet here he was, materializing as if summoned by some darker necessity than mere coincidence.

White approached them with the measured cadence of someone who expected the world to wait. "Detective Hall," he said, a single nod acknowledging her presence. His gaze drifted past her to Rachel, something hardening in the corners of his eyes. "Ms. Fenimore. I heard there was an incident."

"How did you know we were here?" The question left Hall's mouth sharper than she'd intended, betraying an unease she hadn't meant to reveal.

White removed his sunglasses with deliberate precision, each movement as calibrated as his words. He folded them closed and tucked them into his breast pocket, a small ritual that seemed designed to reclaim control of the moment. "Dispatch got a call about a disturbance at this address. System flagged it, sent me a notification. I recognized it from the Fenimore arrest." His eyes found Hall's, steady and unreadable. "Thought I'd check it out."

The explanation hung between them, reasonable in its particulars yet somehow incomplete. Hall felt something cold settle in her stomach, a familiar weight she'd come to associate with instincts she couldn't yet articulate. "Rachel says someone tried to run her down. A black car."

White shifted his attention to Rachel, his features arranging themselves into that particular blankness Hall had witnessed countless times—the careful emptiness that preceded judgment. "Is that right? You saw the vehicle clearly?"

"Yes," Rachel said. Something in White's presence seemed to transform her fear into something harder, more brittle. "It was deliberate. They swerved right at me."

"No witnesses?" White's gaze returned to Hall, each question falling into the space between them like pebbles into still water. "No damage to her vehicle? No injuries?" The ripples of his skepticism spread outward, invisible but unmistakable.

"We were just looking for security footage," Hall said. "The building owner isn't here."

White nodded, his silence more eloquent than words could have been about what he thought of their efforts. "Road rage, most likely. Or—" he paused, his gaze sliding back to

Rachel with the careful precision of a scalpel, "—given the stress Ms. Fenimore is under with the murder charges, possibly some paranoia. Not uncommon in defendants awaiting trial."

Color rose in Rachel's cheeks, anger bringing a flush to her skin that reminded Hall of fever. "I'm not paranoid. Someone tried to kill me. In a car a lot like—"

"Let's take a walk," Hall said, stepping between them. The heat of the morning pressed against her skin, insistent as doubt. "Show me exactly where you were standing when this happened."

They moved across the lot toward Rachel's car, the asphalt softening beneath their feet, releasing yesterday's heat back into the air. White followed at a distance that allowed him to observe without participating—a habit Hall recognized from a hundred crime scenes, the careful positioning of a man who preferred to watch rather than be watched. A truck rumbled past on the street beyond, its noise momentarily drowning the sound of their footsteps and the questions Hall couldn't bring herself to ask.

Hall approached the car, scanning it again. Nothing had changed, and yet—

"Look," White said.

She did.

There was something in the back seat. A white cloth. Hall frowned, certain it had not been there during her earlier inspection. Or had it? The heat wavered between certainty and doubt, making the world shimmer at its edges, making her question what she knew.

"This is where I was," Rachel said, stopping a few feet from her car. "I had my keys out, was about to unlock the door, when the car came at me from that direction." She pointed toward the lot entrance, her finger trembling slightly, as if the memory itself carried physical weight.

Hall nodded, only half-listening. Her attention remained fixed on the back door of Rachel's car, on that narrow gap that seemed to beckon her closer, promising answers to questions she hadn't yet formed but could feel taking shape within her.

"So you were on this side, getting into the driver's side?" White asked, his gaze tracking back to the entrance.

"I know what happened." Rachel's voice had the brittle edge of someone who has repeated herself too many times.

"I'm just trying to picture it. Your car is parked here. Presumably Hall's was not parked next to it."

"No."

"Okay, and then a car came this way," White said, his hand cutting through the air in a gesture that seemed to divide the world into before and after, "and almost hit you, where? Next to the car?"

Rachel crossed her arms, a shield made of flesh. "Not at the car, about here," she said, pointing to the middle of the aisle.

"So you did not get to your car?" Hall asked, the question emerging from some instinct deeper than conscious thought.

"No."

"Do you keep your car's security system on?" Hall stepped closer to the vehicle, cupping her hand against the glass to block the sun's glare. The interior revealed itself slowly, like a secret reluctantly surrendered.

Rachel let out a sound too hollow to be called a laugh. "I don't even bother locking it. I just wish it would get—"

Hall turned to her. "Get what?"

"Nothing. Just a joke," she said, her gaze dropping to her hands as if they might hold some answer she couldn't otherwise express.

Hall glanced at White, who stood with his hands in his pockets, watching. His face betrayed nothing—a canvas carefully blank, waiting. He tilted his head as if to say, 'Look.'

Hall looked into the car again. The shadowed interior of Rachel's back seat, and there, in the mesh organizer behind the driver's seat, was the dark handle of a knife. Although it was partially wrapped in a white cloth, Hall knew what she was seeing.

For a moment, she didn't move, didn't breathe. The world narrowed to that single object, its presence so unexpected and yet somehow inevitable. Was this the knife that killed Ira Lewis? The missing piece of their case against Rachel Fenimore? Found in Rachel's car? The questions formed and dissolved, like the heat rising from the asphalt—present but impossible to grasp.

Hall looked at White. He did not seem surprised. Hall shook her head, cast her doubt aside.

"Rachel," Hall said, her voice reaching her own ears as if across a vast distance. "Step away from the vehicle."

Rachel's confusion sharpened into fear, her features rearranging themselves like pieces of a puzzle being hastily reassembled. "What? Did someone damage—"

White extended his arm, creating a barrier between Rachel and the car. "The detective said back up."

Hall straightened, protocols and procedures cascading through her mind like water over smooth stones. "Turn around, please. Hands behind your back."

"No." Rachel retreated, each step uncertain. "No, no, no. What's going on?"

White advanced with the measured patience of a predator, his right hand drifting toward his holster—not drawing his weapon, but acknowledging its presence in the conversation. "You heard Detective Hall. Turn around."

Something in his tone—that particular note of certainty—sent ice water trickling down Hall's spine. She reached for her handcuffs, the metal warm against her fingertips, heated by proximity to her body.

"Rachel Fenimore," Hall said, the words rising from some automated part of her consciousness, "you're under arrest for the murder of Ira Lewis."

She closed the distance between them.

"Turn around."

Rachel's resistance dissolved like sugar in rain. Her shoulders curved inward, her eyes dulling as if someone had switched off the light behind them. She turned, placing her hands behind her back with the slow resignation of someone who had always expected this moment to arrive.

The cuffs closed around her wrists with twin clicks that hung in the still air.

"It's not mine," Rachel whispered as Hall guided her toward the unmarked car. "Someone's framing me. It's happening just like I said."

Hall recited the Miranda rights, each familiar word suddenly foreign on her tongue. She helped Rachel into the back seat, watching as tears carved silent paths down her pale cheeks, her gaze fixed on some invisible point in the middle distance.

"I'll call the ADA and CSU," White said, extracting his phone. His mouth had settled into a hard line of satisfaction. "Get them to process the knife, the car."

Hall nodded, though suspicion uncoiled in her gut like a snake testing the air.

She saw it all now.

Evidence discovered after the car had already been processed during Rachel's initial arrest.

No fingerprints because the killer wore medical gloves.

White materializing—in a black car—at precisely the right moment to witness the discovery, despite having no legitimate reason to be here.

Rachel never kept her car locked.

The entire tableau unfolding within spitting distance of her perhaps-vengeful ex-lover.

Hall pressed her palm against her car to steady herself. To remember that she had navigated complex cases before this one. She would navigate complex cases after.

With a breath that filled her lungs but did nothing to clear her head, she moved toward White, who had completed his calls and now stood beside Rachel's vehicle. He gazed at the knife through the window, his posture loose, his face showing only professional interest—as if this were merely another piece in another puzzle, nothing personal, nothing extraordinary.

"CSU will be here in fifteen minutes," White said without looking up. "They'll photograph everything in place, then bag the knife for transport to the lab."

"Fifteen minutes," Hall echoed. "About how long it took me to drive here from the precinct."

White's eyes shifted to her face, his expression unchanged. "Traffic was light. That's how I got here so quickly after the call came in."

"The call," Hall said, each word placed with the precision of someone crossing thin ice. "From dispatch. About a disturbance at this address."

White nodded, his attention returning to the knife. "That's right."

Morning sun pressed down on them, drawing beads of sweat along Hall's hairline. A delivery truck rumbled past on the street beyond the lot, momentarily drowning out the sound of her heart pounding against her ribs.

"Who reported the disturbance?" Hall asked, her voice deliberately casual despite the tension wiring her muscles tight. "Rachel just got out on bail last night. No one knows she's here except the bondsman."

"And her ex-girlfriend, I suppose." White straightened, a slight wince crossing his features. "Anonymous call. Burner phone. Heard shouting, maybe. Or someone driving by. Or Rachel herself."

"There was no shouting," Hall said. "Rachel was alone until I got here."

Something flickered in White's eyes—irritation, perhaps, or a deeper emotion Hall couldn't name. But his voice remained even, unbothered. "How do you know there was no shouting? You weren't here. Does shouting matter? We're here now, and we've found the murder weapon she tried to hide. This strengthens our case significantly."

Our case. As if they were still partners in the old sense, still a unit bound by trust and shared purpose. As if she hadn't spent hours excavating his past, unearthing connections that shouldn't exist, searching for answers to questions that should never have needed asking.

The approaching engines cut through the morning air—a sound that once signaled routine, now carrying undertones of finality. The CSU van and two patrol cars grew louder as they turned onto the street leading to the lot. White lifted his hand in acknowledgment, his gesture familiar yet suddenly foreign.

"Perfect timing," he said, his voice carrying the casual authority she had once found reassuring. "Let's get this processed and get back to the station."

Hall watched the vehicles pull into the lot. Uniformed officers emerged with that crisp efficiency born of repetition—the choreographed movements of people who had done this countless times before. Except nothing about this was routine. Not with White beside her, a perfect simulacrum of her partner but hollow where trust should be. Not with evidence materializing like apparitions at a séance. Not with four names smoldering in her consciousness, refusing to cool into mere facts in a case file.

She returned to her car. Rachel sat in the back seat, body curved inward as if attempting to collapse the space she occupied in the world—a world that seemed determined to consume her.

"One of the uniforms will take you in," Hall said, opening the door. The words felt scripted, detached from the uncertainty churning beneath her professional veneer. "Officer Kelly will read you your rights again and process your booking."

Rachel looked up. In her eyes, Hall found unexpected clarity—a window suddenly wiped clean after days of fog.

"He did this," she whispered, her voice barely audible above the ambient noise of the crime scene. "White. He put the knife there. He's framing me." A pause, then: "And he'll kill me next, just like the others."

Hall held Rachel's gaze. She neither confirmed nor denied, neither believed nor dismissed. The moment stretched between them—taut with unspoken questions, with possibilities too dangerous to articulate.

"Officers," Hall finally called, breaking the fragile connection. "Please escort Ms. Fenimore to Central Booking. Keep your body cams on."

She stepped back as a young officer helped Rachel from the car, reciting Miranda in a voice that seemed borrowed from someone older, someone who had earned the right to such solemn pronouncements. Hall watched Rachel's diminishing form as they placed her in the patrol car, the cage between seats casting thin shadows across her face.

The car pulled away, carrying Rachel back to the cell she'd vacated less than twelve hours ago. Hall remained standing in the lot, surrounded by the methodical disassembly of a crime scene—evidence tagged, photographed, bagged—all of it orbiting a knife that had appeared like an answer to a question no one had asked.

Four names. Four deaths. And now a fifth: Rachel Fenimore. Victim or suspect. Or both.

The heat of the morning pressed against Hall's skin as she walked toward White. He directed the CSU technicians with the easy confidence that had once made her proud to be his partner. His movements betrayed nothing of the strain that had colored their interactions over the past two days. He looked, for all the world, exactly what he had always claimed to be: a decorated officer, a dedicated detective.

Her partner.

One of the CSU techs approached White with a clipboard. "So you and Detective Hall spotted the weapon when you first arrived on scene together?"

White nodded without hesitation. "That's right. Soon as we arrived, we walked up to the vehicle, we both saw it through the window."

Hall stopped in her tracks. The lie settled in her stomach like something cold and dense. She retreated to her car, leaning against the hood. The metal radiated heat into her back—a counterpoint to the chill spreading through her chest. She watched the techs catalog the visible evidence, their movements precise and unhurried.

The car would be towed. White kept talking to the tech with the clipboard, his voice carrying across the lot—familiar cadences now rendered strange by what she knew, or thought she knew.

Why would he lie about that? She had already examined the vehicle—cursory, yes, but she would have noticed the white cloth practically luminous against the dark upholstery. He was the one who had pointed it out. And now he was rewriting their timeline, erasing those minutes when they'd been separated, when she couldn't account for his actions.

In that moment, she knew with bone-deep certainty that Rachel Fenimore had been telling the truth.

Chapter 15

The legality barely registered against the weight of necessity.

Hall sat motionless in her car across from White's building, the leather beneath her thighs retaining heat despite the air conditioning's mechanical sigh. She counted windows up the brick facade to the fifth floor where White's apartment faced the street. The spare keys pressed against her leg through fabric, a small, insistent burn.

Some thresholds, once crossed, could never be uncrossed.

She told herself this was verification only—a way to silence Rachel Fenimore's wild accusations, to prove her own judgment remained unclouded. That perhaps she should surrender the case to White after all, wash her hands of it.

Her watch read 1:07 P.M. White would remain at the precinct until evening. The imagined expression on his face should he discover her betrayal twisted something deep in her abdomen. But the knife in Rachel's car—appearing without explanation, as if summoned from darkness—refused to fade from memory. Four names in her notebook whispered without ceasing.

Hall stepped from the car into midday heat that enveloped her like a shroud. Her suit clung damply as she crossed the street, passing cars exhaling hot fumes that stung her eyes. Or perhaps the moisture gathering there had another source entirely.

The four keys had resided in her desk drawer for two years, pressed into her palm by White after his shooting with a solemnity that had surprised her. "Just in case," he'd said. She'd watered his plant, collected his mail. Never this.

The lobby door yielded to the second key. White's building carried the scent of fresh paint mingled with abandoned Thai food lingering in the recycled air. The elevator's polished doors reflected a woman Hall barely recognized—drawn, tense, her eyes holding knowledge they shouldn't possess.

A soft chime announced the elevator's arrival. She stepped inside, pressed five, watched the doors seal shut on her final opportunity for retreat.

White's apartment waited at the corridor's end, 5F. Hall paused, listening for any sound that might indicate presence. Confirmation.

The key slid home with a precision that felt like perfidy. The door swung inward without sound.

She entered, closing it behind her with a click that seemed to echo in the stillness. The apartment carried White's essence—faint aftershave, gun oil from his service weapon, the absence of scent in his preferred detergent. Its familiarity deepened her hesitation.

"This is wrong," she whispered to emptiness. The words hung suspended, neither absolving nor deterring.

The living room stood as she remembered—meticulously ordered bookshelves, uncluttered coffee table. The mantel photographs remained unchanged: White in Army uniform; White with parents at his police academy graduation; White and Hall at a department softball game six years past, both smiling, her arm draped across his shoulders.

She turned from the image, from evidence of a friendship that might already lie beyond recovery.

"Just making sure," she murmured, the words hollow even to her own ears.

She wouldn't search through drawers or pry at floorboards. Only examine what White had left visible, accessible. If nothing revealed itself, she would depart, perhaps find some way to rebuild what her suspicions had begun to dismantle.

The kitchen gleamed with a sterile calm, counters bare save for a coffee maker and a small bowl of fruit. No notes magnetized to the refrigerator, no calendar with suspicious dates circled in red. Just the ascetic space of a man who found sanctuary in order.

Hall drifted to the bathroom. White's medications sat in the cabinet above the sink—prescription bottles arranged in a precise line, each bearing his name and dosage in pharmacy print. She counted them with her fingertip, noting the consistency between dates and pill counts. No desperation in these orange bottles, no evidence of a man drowning his pain in pharmaceutical excess.

The bedroom door stood half-open. Hall paused, her hand hovering over the knob. A bedroom held intimacies that other rooms concealed—the vulnerable space where defenses fell away in sleep, where nightmares and desires played out beyond public scrutiny.

She turned away and moved toward the home office.

White's workspace mirrored the austerity of his apartment—standing desk with a five-wheel chair, the blue fabric arms worn unevenly, just slightly asymmetrical. Like at work, where his left elbow had polished one armrest to a subtle sheen.

The desk held a laptop with its screen locked in digital slumber, a USB charger, and a framed photograph of a woman Hall didn't recognize—someone from before their partnership, perhaps. A ghost from his past. To the left stood a lamp, its light cold and directional, a half-empty glass of water, and a neat stack of papers.

She kept her distance from the laptop. White was the type who would have security protocols sending alerts to his phone whenever someone attempted access. Probably with photographic evidence.

Hall instinctively stepped beyond the camera's sightline. Beside the desk stood a two-drawer filing cabinet, its silver lock button depressed. Sealed tight against intrusion.

She stared at it, remembering the small silver key on White's ring—the one she'd never needed, had never questioned.

Until now.

The keys made a soft, metallic whisper as she extracted them from her pocket, isolating the silver one between her fingers and slipping it into the cabinet lock.

It fit perfectly.

She gazed down at the cabinet, understanding that to turn this key would cross a boundary that concern for a partner could no longer justify. Looking through White's living spaces could be explained by worry, by the strange behavior he'd exhibited lately. But deliberately unlocking what he had chosen to keep hidden—that was a violation that admitted no defense.

The four names in her notebook seemed to pulse with accusation: Fowler, Strickland, Kim, Moss. Four medical professionals. Four deaths. One connection.

Hall turned the key and felt the lock release with a soft click. She would start with the top drawer. Drawing her hand into her jacket sleeve, she used the fabric as a barrier between her fingerprints and the metal handle.

She pulled.

Inside lay the ordered mind of her partner—file folder after file folder, each labeled with meticulous precision. Bank Statements. Insurance (Car). Medical. Phone.

Her eyes traced the row three times before settling on what she sought. Within the Medical folder, a brown leather spine caught the light.

A journal.

The leather felt cool at first touch, then warmed quickly as if remembering the heat of White's hands. Its weight surprised her—denser than its dimensions suggested. She drew a breath that emptied more than just her lungs and opened to the first page.

The handwriting was unmistakably White's—precise, angular, each character formed with the discipline of someone who believed penmanship revealed character. The date at the top corresponded to the day after his surgery.

And beneath it, in those careful letters that never wavered, began a chronicle of suffering that froze the blood in her veins.

The first entry opened with three words that caught in Hall's throat: "They failed me." Below, White had documented his pain level: 9/10. "Unbearable without medication. Strickland says this is normal. Normal? How would she know? She walks without pain." The next day's entry began similarly, but the pain had intensified: 10/10. "Medication insufficient. Nurses (S.K., J.M.) refuse to increase dosage. Following 'doctor's orders.' As if Fowler and Strickland understand anything about this kind of pain."

Hall's fingers trembled slightly as she turned the page. She needed evidence, something tangible she could take back, something that couldn't be dismissed as coincidence or misunderstanding. She retrieved her phone and opened the camera app, positioning it above the journal. The first click of the shutter seemed to echo through the silent apartment, though she knew it was merely her heightened awareness transforming ordinary sounds into accusations.

She photographed the pages with methodical precision, each image capturing White's handwriting—unfailingly neat, controlled, the letters marching across the page with military discipline. His words, however, betrayed what his penmanship concealed. He had devised a pain registry of clinical exactitude: numerical scales, time-stamped medication logs, effects charted with decimal points, sensations catalogued like specimens ("glass shards grinding between femur and tibia," "a slow acid burn from sacrum to knee"). A scientist documenting his own vivisection.

Between these cold records lay veins of molten fury. "Fowler smiled today. SMILED. Said I was making 'exceptional progress' while sweat soaked through my shirt from the simple indignity of crossing ten feet of linoleum. What could he possibly comprehend of exceptionalism? Of suffering? Of requiring a nurse's hands to lower you onto a toilet seat like a child?"

Something shifted in Hall's perception as she read. The White she thought she knew—the man who had returned to the department after eight months of recovery, who bore his injury as stoically as a veteran might carry shrapnel, who never spoke of pain—seemed now like a carefully constructed facade. Here on these pages lived another White entirely, one hollowed out by suffering, filled instead with a bitterness that had crystallized into something harder, something with edges.

She turned another page. The format changed.

A photograph of Dr. Martin Fowler—clearly printed from the hospital website—had been affixed to the page with perfect alignment. Beneath it, White had recorded Fowler's home address, his work schedule, observations of his movements. "Exits hospital 7:30 P.M. Tuesdays, Thursdays. Parks: Section C, Level 2. Wife absent Thursday through Saturday (sister's house, Montclair)."

The next page held Dr. Victoria Strickland's life, similarly dissected. Then Sandra Kim. Then Jennifer Moss. Each with their photograph. Each with their habits and patterns laid bare. Each reduced to a set of predictable coordinates in time and space.

Her fingertips had gone cold. She rested the phone against the nightstand to steady it, the camera's soft click marking each damning page. The bedroom air seemed to thin around her, as if the oxygen were being slowly extracted.

The next section contained drawings. Not the technical sketches of a trained artist but something more primitive—stick figures rendered with an unsettling intensity. Bodies twisted in agony, mouths stretched into black holes. In some, looming figures stood above them wielding instruments. In others, the figures lay broken, darkness pooling around them like spilled ink.

Several pages contained nothing but violent black scrawls, the pen having torn through paper in places where pressure had been applied with particular force. As if language itself had failed him, leaving only this raw expression of something beyond words.

And then she found it.

December 4, 2026. A baseball bat, drawn with the same precision he once brought to crime scene sketches. A single word: Mercy. The day Sandra Kim's skull was crushed.

March 17, 2027. A bullet. Mercy. Fowler's execution.

June 18, 2027. A diamond ring. Mercy. Moss strangled with her own jewelry.

October 31, 2027. A pill. Mercy. Strickland's apparent overdose.

Hall stared at the evidence before her, unable to reconcile it with the man who had sat across from her at countless crime scenes, who had methodically documented other people's violence. White had planned these deaths, had executed them with the same meticulous attention he brought to every aspect of his professional life. And he had labeled them "mercy"—as if these killings were acts of compassion rather than the systematic elimination of those who had failed to alleviate his suffering.

The final completed page revealed Rachel Fenimore's name. Her hospital ID photo smiled up from the paper, innocent of its context. Below it: her address, schedule, habits. All the familiar cartography of planned murder.

And four dates:

~~January 1, 2028~~

~~May 5, 2028~~

~~August 10, 2028~~

August 13, 2028

Ira Lewis died August 10. Rachel nearly struck by a car today. Four attempts. Four failures.

The journal trembled in her hands—or perhaps her hands trembled around the journal. The distinction no longer seemed important.

Hall's breath caught in her throat like a bird against glass. White had intended to kill Rachel in that alley, but something had gone wrong. Ira Lewis—wrong place, wrong time, or perhaps exactly where fate needed him to be—had somehow intervened. Had saved Rachel without knowing what he was saving her from.

She photographed the page with trembling fingers, then scrolled through her phone to check the images. Each one captured White's meticulous handwriting, his diagrams, his plans. Not evidence for a court perhaps, but enough for Internal Affairs to begin unraveling the truth. The journal lay open before her, its pages filled with the methodical documentation of a man whose pain had transformed him into something she could no longer recognize.

A sound from outside—metal against metal, a car door perhaps—made her start. Her pulse quickened as though White himself had materialized in the doorway, watching her betray him. But the apartment remained still, indifferent to her discovery, to the slow dissolution of everything she had believed.

She took one final photo of the "Mercy" page, ensuring the date stood in sharp relief, the connection to Ira Lewis's death unmistakable.

When she closed the journal, her fingers lingered on the worn leather cover. Something about its texture felt intimate, obscene. The words inside had rewritten her world, had taken the partnership she had valued above almost everything and revealed it as fiction.

White wasn't the man she had thought. He was a stranger who had walked beside her for years, his darkness pressed against her like a weapon she never felt.

Rachel waited in a cell at Central Booking, framed for a murder White had orchestrated. The knife appearing in her car, the timing of White's arrival—a plan constructed with the precision of a man who believed himself beyond suspicion.

And Hall had been his unwitting accomplice. Had snapped the cuffs around Rachel's wrists, had dismissed her story as desperate fabrication. This knowledge settled in her stomach not like lead but like broken glass, sharp-edged and impossible to ignore.

She replaced the journal exactly as she had found it, its position on the desk a silent promise to return. Her phone felt heavier now, weighted with pixels that could free one woman and destroy one man.

If she had the courage to use them.

The clock on White's wall measured seconds with soft, relentless clicks. She couldn't remain suspended in this apartment forever, caught between what she had been and what she might become. Soon White would finish his shift. Soon she would have to decide.

At the door, she paused. The apartment seemed to hold its breath, waiting for her choice. Then she stepped out, pulling the door shut behind her, the lock engaging with a sound like a single gunshot in an empty room.

The elevator descended with excruciating slowness, each floor a station in her private purgatory. Hall kept her eyes fixed on the illuminated numbers: 5, 4, 3, 2, 1. When the doors parted, she moved into the lobby on legs that felt borrowed from someone else.

Outside, afternoon had aged into early evening, shadows stretching like accusations across the street. Her car waited where she had left it, a reminder that beyond this moment, beyond White's journal, the world continued its indifferent rotation. She slid into the driver's seat, the leather warm against her back, a sensation so ordinary it seemed impossible.

She drove without destination until she found herself in a mall parking lot, engine silent, staring at her phone. Image after image of White's handwriting filled the screen, each swipe of her finger revealing another piece of his calculated madness. Evidence that could liberate Rachel and condemn White. Evidence she had obtained without warrant, without probable cause—fruit of a poisoned tree that might wither before a judge, leaving Rachel imprisoned and Hall stripped of the badge that had defined her.

The drive back toward the precinct felt longer than the actual distance, her discovery pressing against her shoulders, bending her spine. With each mile marker, with each traffic light, the question repeated itself: what kind of detective—what kind of person—did she wish to become?

Chapter 16

The Internal Affairs division occupied the eighth floor of the New Hanan Police Department—a space most officers avoided with the instinctive wariness reserved for contamination zones. Hall had been there exactly twice before today. The first time, she'd given a statement about a fellow officer's drinking problem; the second, she'd testified against a sergeant who falsified evidence. Each visit had left an invisible residue on her skin, as if the act of crossing that particular threshold altered something fundamental in her cellular structure. Now, sitting in the waiting area outside Lieutenant Barnes's office, she found herself counting the minutes until she could leave, wondering if there existed enough soap in the world to wash away what she was about to do.

The decision had crystallized during her drive back from White's apartment, the weight of her phone heavy against her thigh, evidence burning there like a coal. By the time she'd descended into the concrete hollow of the precinct garage, the path forward had narrowed to a single, inevitable choice. Some boundaries, once crossed, erased themselves behind you.

The air in the waiting area carried the lingering ghost of someone's lunch—tuna salad with too much onion, the smell clinging to the institutional furniture. A wall clock measured out her wait with mechanical indifference, each tick a small accusation. The chair beneath her, molded plastic in a shade of gray that existed nowhere in nature, pressed against her spine with deliberate discomfort. She kept her back straight, hands folded over her phone as if guarding a wound.

A door opened down the corridor. The sound traveled through the empty space, followed by footsteps—measured, unhurried. Lieutenant Barnes emerged first, tall and spare with the shaved head and wire-rimmed glasses that made him look more like a philosophy professor than a cop. Behind him came Sergeant Rocha, compact and solid, his salt-and-pepper hair cropped close, perpetual shadow darkening his jaw where his beard fought a daily losing battle against his razor. They approached with the careful rhythm of men accustomed to controlling rooms by controlling time—the power in making others wait, in withholding attention until precisely the moment they chose to bestow it.

"Detective Hall." Barnes extended his hand. His grip was dry, firm without the need to prove anything. "Thank you for waiting. Let's talk in my office."

The space beyond the door revealed itself as sparse but not quite barren—a desk, three chairs, filing cabinets arranged with mathematical precision, a window framing a slice of city skyline. No family photos interrupted the clean lines. No personal touches softened the edges except a single framed diploma on the wall: Harvard Law. The message required no translation: this was a workspace, not a confessional. Nothing here could be used to form judgments about the man who occupied it.

Hall lowered herself into one of the visitors' chairs. Rocha took the other. Barnes settled behind his desk, folded his hands on its polished surface, and fixed her with a gaze calibrated to reveal nothing while extracting everything.

"You said you had concerns about Detective Robert White," he said, his voice neutral as untinted glass. "Let's hear it."

Hall removed the thumb drive from her pocket and placed it on the desk between them. The small plastic rectangle looked almost childish against the dark wood, incongruously bright for what it contained.

"I have received anonymous photographs that lead me to believe Detective White is responsible for the deaths of four medical professionals who worked on his surgery two years ago, and that he attempted to kill a fifth—Rachel Fenimore—three nights ago in the alley where Ira Lewis was stabbed."

Barnes's expression remained unchanged, a masterpiece of professional neutrality. Beside her, Rocha leaned forward slightly—the only acknowledgment that her words had landed in the room.

"That's a serious accusation, Detective," Barnes said, the pause before "Detective" almost imperceptible. "What evidence are you basing it on?"

"The photographs on that drive," she said, nudging it forward with one finger, a small act of distancing herself from what it contained. Barnes picked it up while Rocha rose and rounded the desk. The click of the computer mouse seemed unnaturally loud in the silent room. Then nothing—both men gone quiet as images filled the screen.

"The journal documents White's pain after his surgery," Hall continued into their silence, "his anger toward his surgical team, and what appears to be surveillance notes on each of the four medical professionals who later died."

"Where did you get the drive?" Barnes asked without looking away from the screen. Rocha remained a silent presence behind him, his breathing the only indication he was still there.

"It was on my desk yesterday, when I returned from a call," she lied. The falsehood tasted metallic on her tongue. If she admitted to taking the photos herself, the investigation would turn inward, focusing on her rather than White.

"Did you check the logs to see who might have dropped it off?" Rocha asked, his voice rougher than Barnes's, eyes still fixed on whatever image held his attention.

"No sir. I would leave that up to IA." True, but incomplete—a lie of omission that felt heavier than the outright fabrication. "It took me a while to understand what I was looking at."

"Once I cross-referenced the dates and names, well, you can see why I brought them in." Her voice remained steady despite the tremor building beneath her sternum. "The page with the dates, toward the end? The ones marked 'mercy'? They correspond to the dates each person associated with Detective White's surgery died." She paused, watching their faces for any reaction. "And there's a page with Rachel Fenimore's information, marked with multiple dates crossed out. It includes the night Ira Lewis was killed."

Barnes's gaze fixed on Hall, his eyes like twin scalpels behind his glasses. "How did you obtain these photographs, Detective?"

"They came anonymously," she said, the words hanging between them like something fragile. She paused, feeling the weight of his scrutiny. "On a thumb drive, left on my desk."

Barnes studied her, his silence stretching until it seemed to fill the room. "Why would White target these specific medical professionals? What's the thread here?"

"Pain," Hall said softly. The word felt inadequate, too small for what she meant. "The kind that burrows beneath the skin and never leaves. His surgery promised relief that never came. You've seen his limp, how his body betrays him on the right side. The journal speaks of betrayal—how they 'failed him' when they promised healing."

"And Rachel Fenimore? Where does she fit in this constellation? This Ira Lewis?"

Hall's fingers pressed against her thigh, steadying herself. "She was his rehabilitation nurse. Three days ago, White and I arrested her for Lewis's murder." She gestured toward the calendar. "You see that date crossed out? And then today, when Ms. Fenimore made bail, someone tried to run her down. Today's date—also marked for elimination. Two failed attempts on her life."

"She killed someone?" Barnes's voice sharpened.

Hall exhaled slowly, tasting the complexity of truth. "The evidence against her... it has edges that don't align. I doubt it would survive a trial."

"Did you and White investigate these other deaths?" Rocha asked, breaking his silence.

Hall's throat tightened. She measured her response, calculating disclosure like medicine. "Fowler's, yes. Though I wasn't present when the suspect confessed."

"And you had no concerns then?"

"Not at the time," she said. The truth felt like ash in her mouth.

Rocha leaned forward, his voice carrying the textured rasp of a man who had once loved cigarettes too well. "Let me understand what you're suggesting. Your partner—twenty years on the force, decorated, respected—decides to systematically murder his surgical team because of persistent pain. He somehow keeps this hidden. Then he repeatedly attempts to kill this woman, fails, and simply... tries again? That's your theory?"

Hall met his gaze, unflinching. "Yes."

"Have you confronted White with any of this?"

"No." The single syllable fell between them. "If I'm right, he's like a cornered animal. If I'm wrong..." She let the thought dissolve. "I needed you to see this first."

"Why not investigate more thoroughly before bringing this to us?" Barnes asked, his tone softening almost imperceptibly.

Hall drew a breath that didn't quite fill her lungs. "Because it's your jurisdiction to investigate another officer. And if I'm reading the pattern correctly—the crossed-out date for today—Ms. Fenimore remains in immediate danger. He's planning these attacks. He's escalating."

Barnes's eyes narrowed, focusing on something beyond the surface of her words. "Rachel Fenimore. The woman you arrested for Ira Lewis's murder. The case you're actively working."

"Yes."

"And what exactly is the nature of your relationship with Ms. Fenimore?"

The question struck like cold water. Hall felt heat rise beneath her collar. "Excuse me?"

"It's straightforward enough, Detective. What's the nature of your relationship with Rachel Fenimore?"

"She's a suspect in an active investigation." Hall's voice sounded distant to her own ears.

"Nothing more? No personal entanglement?"

The flush spread to Hall's face, betraying what her words would not. "No. There's no personal connection."

Barnes exchanged a glance with Rocha—a silent current passing between them, the kind of wordless communication that partners develop over years. Rocha nodded, a gesture so slight it barely disturbed the air.

"Knowledge of these photographs," Rocha said, tapping Barnes's monitor with one blunt finger, "can't enter any official record. They're questionable evidence, but..." He leaned forward, elbows braced on his knees. "Worth pursuing."

Relief flooded through Hall—not a wave but a tide, pulling at something deep within her. She closed her eyes against its force. When she opened them, Barnes was watching her, his expression softened by the barest measure.

"Meanwhile," he said, "you return to work. Act normal. Give White no reason to suspect you've spoken with us."

"He's my partner," Hall said, the word suddenly strange on her tongue. "He knows me better than anyone. He'll see the change."

"Then become someone else," Barnes replied. "Because if your suspicions prove correct and he senses you know, you become a liability. White isn't just your partner anymore. He's potentially a killer who's planned multiple homicides. Remember that distinction."

Hall nodded, the weight of her actions—past and still to come—settling around her like something cold and metallic. She stood, retrieved her phone, and moved toward the door. Her hand was on the handle when Rocha spoke.

"Detective Hall."

She turned.

"If you're right about White," he said, his face carved with shadows, "you may have saved Rachel Fenimore's life. Carry that with you too."

* * *

Three days passed like a fever dream. Hall performed the rituals of normalcy—filling out paperwork, interviewing witnesses on the Henderson case, eating lunch at her desk—all while carrying the knowledge of White's journal like a bomb strapped to her chest, its ticking audible only to her. She maintained distance without making it obvious, offering case-related comments but letting die the small talk that had once flowed between them like an easy current. If White noticed the change, he gave no sign. Until today.

The Homicide Division hummed with Tuesday morning's particular energy—phones ringing at staggered intervals, keyboards tapping in arrhythmic concert, the soft whir of the printer in the corner birthing reports nobody wanted to read. Someone had brought in pastries; the sweet smell of icing and cinnamon hung suspended in the air, mingling with the brewing coffee from the break room. These ordinary comforts felt like artifacts from another life. Hall sat reviewing witness statements from a convenience store shooting, forcing herself to focus on details that seemed impossibly trivial compared to what occupied her thoughts, like studying pebbles while an avalanche builds.

When the elevator doors opened and White stepped out, Hall felt him before she saw him. The division's ambient noise seemed to dim, as if the room itself recognized a disturbance. Even from across the floor, she could see the tension coiled in his body, the rigid set of his shoulders beneath his dark suit jacket. His eyes swept the room, settling on Hall with an intensity that made her stomach clench. Something had shifted. The careful equilibrium of their mutual pretense had fractured.

White moved toward their shared desk space, his usual measured gait replaced by something harder, each footfall landing with deliberate weight. Detectives glanced up from their work, conversations faltering mid-sentence. The room quieted like a forest when a predator passes through, all smaller creatures holding their breath.

"You," White said when he reached her desk, his voice low but carrying an edge sharp enough to draw blood and attention from nearby colleagues. "Outside. Now."

Hall stood, her legs feeling hollow beneath her. She followed White to the small corridor that led to the fire stairs, a space neither public nor private enough for whatever was about to unfold. The smell of his aftershave—the same brand he'd worn for as long as she'd known him—reached her before his words did, familiar and now somehow threatening.

"Internal Affairs," White said the moment they were out of direct sight, his voice tight with a control that threatened to snap with each syllable. "They're investigating me. What the hell did you do?"

The question hit Hall like a physical blow. Had Barnes or Rocha been careless? Had they left breadcrumbs that led back to her? The corridor narrowed around her, the walls seeming to inch closer.

"What are you talking about?" she managed, her voice steadier than she felt. "I haven't done anything."

White's laugh was harsh, brittle, nothing like the rare chuckle she'd heard from him over the years. "Don't lie to me. They're asking questions about the Fowler case, about Kim's case." His eyes searched hers, looking for the betrayal he already believed he'd found.

"White, I don't—"

"Stop." He stepped closer, the space between them evaporating. "You went into my past, dug around in cases that were closed. Why? What made you suddenly decide your partner needed to be investigated?"

Hall's mind raced through possibilities like fingers searching for a light switch in darkness. Should she admit it? Deny everything? The air between them felt charged, dangerous. Before she could decide, White turned and walked back into the division, his movement sharp with purpose. Hall followed, dread pooling cold and heavy in her chest.

White stopped in the center of the room. "I want everyone to hear this," he announced, his voice carrying to every corner. Detectives froze, pens hovering over reports, phones held against shoulders. "I'm being investigated by Internal Affairs." He jabbed a finger into his own chest. "Me." The word hung in the air, both accusation and disbelief.

The silence that followed was absolute, broken only by the distant ring of a phone several floors away, the sound floating up like a call from another world. White turned, fixing his gaze on Hall.

"And I think Detective Hall is the one who went to them."

Hall felt the blood drain from her face as every eye in the division turned to her. This was professional suicide—White's for making such an accusation publicly, and hers if it was true. Or even if it wasn't. The weight of collective judgment pressed against her skin.

"That's not true," Hall said, her voice stronger than she felt, rising from some reserve of self-preservation she hadn't known she possessed. "I didn't go to IA about you."

"Then how do they know to look into the Fowler case?" White's voice rose with each word, control slipping away like water through cupped hands. "We worked that case together. Now suddenly they're asking why I didn't file a disclosure form."

"A form? They are asking you about a goddamned form?" Hall shouted back, her anger flaring genuine though her words were not. "How dare you accuse me of going to IA about a damned form!"

White closed the distance between them in three strides, each one erasing years of partnership, trust, shared coffees at midnight. "We were partners," he said, and the past tense cut deeper than Hall expected, a blade sliding between ribs. "Seven years."

Hall's anger refused to dissipate, even as she registered the audience surrounding them, the career dissolving like sugar in rain. "You bastard," she said, her voice lower than she intended, the words falling between them like small, hard stones. "What makes you think I'm tracking your paperwork?"

"You know what? Save it." White's voice dropped to something measured and final, the controlled tone more damning than any shout. "Whatever you think you know, whatever you think you found, you're wrong. And going behind my back instead of talking to me?" A pause, during which Hall could almost hear the severing of whatever had connected them. "That tells me everything I need to know about what our partnership meant to you."

He turned away, his limp more pronounced than usual, as if betrayal had settled into the damaged joint alongside the old injury. The elevator doors parted for him with perfect timing, and White stepped inside without a backward glance. When they closed, the silence in the division stretched taut, vibrating with unasked questions.

Alvarez broke it first. "What the hell was that about?"

Hall couldn't answer. She returned to her desk, aware of a strange disconnect between intention and movement, as if she were piloting her body from a distance. Around her, the division reassembled itself in fragments—someone coughed, a phone rang and was answered, a drawer slid shut—but beneath these familiar sounds ran an undercurrent that hadn't existed before.

"A form," Peterson whispered to Krueger, his voice carrying just far enough. "Wonder what else she's reported."

The implication settled over the room. If Hall had gone to Internal Affairs about White, who else might be next? What other perceived infractions had she secretly documented? The truth—that she hadn't gone to IA at all—seemed suddenly irrelevant. The seed was planted, taking root in the fertile soil of departmental paranoia. A rat was a rat.

Hall opened her computer file and stared at the screen. Words blurred before her. Denial would sound hollow; confirmation would be professional suicide. And if IA's investigation found nothing—if White's journal contained only the private thoughts of a man in pain—she would become the detective who destroyed her partner's reputation on circumstantial evidence and suspicion.

She was alone now. White had ensured it with his public accusation. She felt the distance growing already: conversations that would stop when she approached, case details that wouldn't be shared, the invisible line being drawn around everyone except her.

For twenty minutes, Hall performed the rituals of work. She clicked through files without reading them, typed fragments of reports she would never complete, lifted her phone receiver only to replace it. Her mind kept returning to White's words, examining them from different angles like a suspect's statement, searching for the inconsistency that would unravel everything. There was none.

A message appeared on her screen: "Meeting in my office. Now. -Rocha."

Hall closed her document and shut down her computer. She locked her desk drawer where her notebook still contained the four names that had started all this, then stood. As she moved toward the exit, she felt the weight of unmet gazes, the deliberate shifting of bodies away from her path. The division had already rendered its verdict.

The stairwell door closed behind her with a soft click that echoed upward through the empty space. Each step she climbed took her further from the life she had built and closer to whatever waited above. The sound of her footsteps accompanied her, a solitary rhythm marking her ascent.

The Internal Affairs corridor stretched before her, antiseptically bright. No shadows fell here; the overhead lights eliminated all ambiguity, all nuance. Hall moved toward Rocha's office, her pace slowing as she approached. The door stood open. Inside, the sergeant hunched over his desk, the salt-and-pepper in his hair catching the light from his lamp. Hall paused at the threshold, suddenly aware that crossing it would finalize something that until now had existed only in accusation.

She knocked on the door frame. The sound seemed to travel through the quiet of the eighth floor and return to her, altered. Rocha looked up, recognition settling into the lines of his face.

"Detective Hall," he said, gesturing to the chair across from his desk. "Come in."

Hall stepped inside. The carpet absorbed her footsteps, creating a strange sensation of floating. Unlike Barnes's sterile office, Rocha had made this space his own—framed photos tilted slightly on the desk, a worn baseball resting on a wooden stand, a degree from New Hanan State hanging at an angle that suggested it had been straightened and had slowly migrated back to its preferred position. The air carried the faint scent of peppermint gum, a detail Hall had noticed during their previous meeting and now registered again, a small continuity in a day where everything else had changed.

Hall entered Rocha's office with White's accusation still ringing in her ears. The fluorescent lights hummed overhead, casting a pallid glow that made the institutional beige walls appear sickly. She dropped into the chair across from his desk without greeting, the vinyl seat cool against her thighs.

"White knows," she said. "He confronted me in the middle of the division. Made sure everyone heard that he's being investigated and thinks I'm the one who reported him. For a disclosure form."

Rocha's expression remained neutral, but Hall caught the subtle shift in his body—a tightening around the shoulders, a recalculation happening behind his eyes like the silent clicking of tumblers in a lock.

"That's not surprising," he said.

"Not surprising?" The words caught in her throat. Hall leaned forward, her fingertips pressing into the edge of his desk until they whitened. "You told me he wouldn't find out. You said the investigation would be discreet."

"We try," Rocha said. He reached for his desk phone, the movement deliberate, unhurried. "But departments leak. People talk." He pressed a button and spoke into the receiver, his voice low. The words themselves mattered less than their tone—a quiet urgency.

Outside the window, New Hanan's perpetual gray pressed against the glass. Hall watched a raindrop trace its way down the pane, remembering how White's face had transformed when he'd confronted her—the familiar lines of her partner's face rearranging themselves into something foreign.

"Barnes will be here in a minute," Rocha said. "Tell me what White said. How he said it."

Hall recounted the confrontation—White's anger burning cold rather than hot, his accusation hanging in the squad room air, the way the other detectives had fallen silent, their gazes sliding away from hers. As she spoke, Lieutenant Barnes appeared in the doorway. He studied the scene without expression, then closed the door behind him. The soft click of the latch felt like a period at the end of a sentence she hadn't finished writing.

"White knows," Rocha said to Barnes. "Made a scene in Homicide."

Barnes crossed to the window, his tall frame cutting a dark shape against the muted light. He stood with his back to them, hands clasped behind him, watching the city below.

"What did he say about the investigation?" Barnes asked without turning. "What details?"

Hall swallowed. "That you're looking into the Fowler case, asking about his paperwork. That you wanted to know why he didn't file a disclosure form about his connection to Fowler."

Barnes and Rocha exchanged a look that passed between them like a current. Hall felt its charge but couldn't decipher its meaning.

"We haven't asked about disclosure forms yet," Barnes said, his reflection ghostly in the window glass. "We haven't even pulled the Fowler case files."

A chill spread through Hall's chest, radiating outward to her fingertips. The office seemed suddenly colder.

"Then how did he know that's what you'd be looking for?"

"Because that's what he'd be worried about," Rocha murmured, leaning back until his chair creaked. "The missing disclosure forms. It's the thread that could unravel everything."

Barnes moved away from the window, settling into the chair beside Hall. She caught the faint scent of coffee and aftershave as he lowered himself into the seat. His presence felt both reassuring and intrusive.

"Someone tipped him off," Barnes said. "Not about specifics, just that IA was asking questions about past cases."

"Who?" Hall asked, though she already knew the answer would be unsatisfying.

"Could be anyone." Rocha's fingers drummed once on his blotter. "The desk sergeant who processed the initial paperwork. The evidence clerk who pulled White's personnel file. The janitor who emptied my trash and saw a note with White's name on it." A small shrug. "Like I said, departments leak."

Hall stared at the space between them, at the dust motes drifting in a shaft of weak light. "He thinks I betrayed him," she said finally. The words tasted metallic. "Seven years of partnership, and now everyone in Homicide thinks I'm a rat."

"That concerns you more than the possibility that your partner has killed four people?" Barnes's tone held no judgment, which somehow made the question sharper.

"No," Hall said. She looked up, meeting his gaze directly. "What concerns me is that he knows I suspect him. And if he's what I think he is, that makes me a loose end."

Rocha nodded, his face grave. "We've thought about that. You could be in danger."

"I can request protection—" Hall began.

"Visible protection would tip our hand," Barnes interrupted. A radiator beneath the window clanked to life, punctuating his words. "Let White know we're taking this seriously. He'd either go to ground or accelerate his plans."

"His plans?" Something cold settled in Hall's stomach, a weight that seemed to pull her deeper into the chair. "You think he's still planning to go after Rachel?"

"If your theory is correct, yes," Rocha said. His voice had softened, as if speaking to someone in mourning. "He's only eliminated four of the five medical professionals on his list. The journal you found suggests he's not done."

Barnes leaned forward, elbows on his knees. The fluorescent light caught the silver at his temples. "We need more. The journal photos are enough to justify an investigation, but not enough for a warrant to search his home, his car, his office. We need something solid—physical evidence, witness testimony, an admission."

Hall knew what was coming before he said it. She could see it forming in the lines around Barnes's mouth, in the careful way he watched her reaction.

"What are you suggesting?" she asked.

"We want you to wear a wire. Next time White approaches you, next time he wants to talk about the investigation or Rachel or any of the cases, we need it recorded. Properly, legally, admissibly."

Hall shook her head. The motion felt distant, as if performed by someone else. "No. I can still come back from this."

"You've already crossed that line," Barnes said. His voice was gentle but unyielding. "Your reputation in Homicide is shot. Whether you're right or wrong about White, those detectives downstairs have already decided what you are."

"And backing down now won't change that," Rocha added. The ceiling light reflected in his glasses, momentarily obscuring his eyes. "All it will do is make it possible that White won't be properly investigated. That Rachel Fenimore will go to prison for a murder she didn't commit. Or that White will complete his 'mercy' mission."

Hall looked at her hands, surprised to find them steady when everything inside her trembled.

Hall's gaze drifted to the worn baseball on Rocha's desk—not just an object but a talisman from some cleaner time, when victories were measured in innings and not bodies, when loyalties weren't compromised by suspicion. She studied its scuffed surface, the faded stitching that held together what was coming apart in her own world.

"Think about it," Barnes said, his voice cutting through her thoughts. "If White is innocent, the wire confirms it. You'll hear nothing, and this ends. But if he's guilty—if he's taken four lives and tried to take Fenimore's—don't you need certainty? Don't you owe yourself that?"

The question expanded between them like smoke, impossible to wave away. Hall thought of the journal with its meticulous script, White's pain and rage documented in the precise handwriting of a man who cataloged everything, perhaps even his vengeance. She thought of Rachel in her cell at Central Booking, framed and abandoned. She thought of the dead—Fowler, Strickland, Kim, Moss—their lives ended because something in Robert White had never been mended, or perhaps because it had never been whole.

And White himself—her partner, who had pulled her from darkness more than once, whose steadiness she had mistaken for virtue. The man whose silences she had never properly read.

"I need time," she said, her voice seeming to come from somewhere outside herself, as if she were already separating from this moment, this choice.

"There isn't any," Barnes countered. "White knows we're looking. If he's what Rachel claims, he's erasing proof, covering tracks. And if she's right about the rest—if killing her was always the plan—he might decide to finish it before we can intervene."

"You're asking me to betray him," Hall said, the words scraping her throat raw.

"No," Rocha said, his voice softening in a way that made her distrust it more. "If he's guilty, the betrayal was his. The moment he decided murder was justice, he betrayed you. Betrayed that badge. Betrayed himself."

Hall sat in silence, the weight of their expectations pressing against her skin. Behind her closed eyes, she saw White as she had always known him—reliable, unflinching, the partner who had stood between her and harm without hesitation. And she saw him as he might truly be—patient, calculating, a killer who had walked beside her while she remained blind to what Rachel Fenimore had finally forced her to see: that monsters sometimes wore the faces of those we trusted most.

Chapter 17

Time had become a weight Hall carried, measured in the ticking of her watch and the slow revolution of the division around her. Four times in twenty minutes she had checked: 9:47 A.M. The text to White requesting a ten o'clock meeting hung in digital limbo between them, a thin thread connecting her present moment to whatever would follow. He would arrive soon, sliding into his chair with that familiar grunt—a sound that had once been as unremarkable as breathing until yesterday, when his arrival had fractured everything she thought she knew about their partnership.

The homicide division flowed around her desk like water around a stone worn smooth by years of current. Detectives who had once paused to share case notes or weekend plans now navigated wide arcs to avoid her space. Conversations ebbed as bodies approached, then swelled again once safely beyond her hearing. The wire taped against her ribs reminded her with every breath of her decision, its plastic edge damp with perspiration, a foreign appendage broadcasting betrayal to the men waiting on the eighth floor. She shifted, feeling the adhesive pull against her skin.

Alvarez passed by, the same woman who had stretched across their desks just two days ago, offering spearmint gum from a silver wrapper. Now she clutched her coffee mug with white knuckles, as though Hall might reach for it, might contaminate it with the same hands that had reached for the wire, for the recording device, for the button that would end careers. The division had rendered its verdict without trial. The rat. The one who had broken the unwritten code that bound them together against everyone else.

When the elevator chimed from the corridor, Hall's stomach contracted like a fist. She straightened a stack of papers that already stood at perfect right angles, opened a manila folder whose contents she could not have named if asked at gunpoint. The wire's slight movement against her skin seemed to scrape like sandpaper, though she knew the sound existed only in her mind. Barnes and Rocha were the only ones who could hear the rasp of her blouse against the device, the shallow breaths she tried and failed to regulate, the thundering of her pulse in her ears.

White stepped off the elevator at precisely 9:52, his military punctuality intact even now. He paused in the doorway as he had every morning for five years, scanning the room—locating exits, cataloging faces, a habit carried from desert patrols to fluorescent-lit bureaucracy. When his gaze found her, something in his expression shifted, subtle as a shadow moving with the sun. His walk toward their shared desk was measured, each step deliberate, his limp more pronounced than usual, as though the weight he carried had grown heavier overnight.

Hall kept her eyes fixed on her computer screen, where words blurred and reformed like creatures seen through murky water. The wire seemed to burn hotter now, a brand marking her as something other than what she had been yesterday. Her loose blouse—chosen after careful consideration in the gray light of dawn—revealed nothing of the device beneath, yet she was certain White would see it. He had always seen everything.

"Hall." His voice came softer than she expected, nothing like the thunderous accusation that had silenced the division yesterday. The springs of his chair complained as he lowered himself, a sound so familiar she could have identified him blindfolded by that creak alone. "I need to talk to you."

"Let's go to Interview 1," she said, rising from her desk, the chair rolling back too quickly, betraying her eagerness to contain whatever might follow.

"No. Here."

She looked up then, meeting his eyes for the first time since he had named her informant before witnesses who had once been friends. "What?"

"Yesterday." White's sigh seemed to carry more than air; it carried years, cases, bodies found and killers caught, drinks after shifts and silent car rides to crime scenes. "I was out of line. Some of the guys were asking questions—weird questions about old cases, about Fowler, about other stuff. They said Internal Affairs was looking into it. I jumped to conclusions."

Hall's mouth felt like cotton, her tongue thick and useless. Every word they exchanged traveled through the wire to Barnes and Rocha, who would be leaning toward speakers, coffee growing cold as they waited for the confession that would justify months of surveillance.

"Can we talk about this privately?" She needed walls around them, a space where words might be contained, where she might guide him toward or away from the precipice they approached.

"No," White said, his voice suddenly loud enough to turn heads. "Hey, everyone!" he shouted, and the division froze like a photograph. "I was an asshole yesterday. New pain medication got me a little loopy. Hall did nothing, she never talked to IA."

Hall sat back, the chair catching her weight as her muscles went slack with surprise. The wire pressed against her ribs, recording the moment, preserving it for men who would later replay it, dissect it, search for the lie within the public absolution.

"I'm sorry, Carolyn."

"It's fine," she said, the words hollow as a promise made without intention. "It was..." She could not bring herself to complete the sentence, to offer him the alibi that might later become his defense: I never meant to kill anyone, it was the medication talking.

White leaned forward, elbows on his knees, narrowing the space between them until she could smell the coffee on his breath, see the red vessels mapping sleeplessness across his eyes. "No, it's not fine. I accused you in front of everyone. Made you a target." His gaze swept the room, taking in the detectives who watched them from peripheral vision, pretending to work while straining to hear. "I should have talked to you first. Asked you directly."

"What would you have asked?" The question escaped before she could contain it, sharp-edged and dangerous, too close to the truth they circled like predators around wounded prey.

"If you went to IA." White's eyes held hers, searching for something in their depths—forgiveness, perhaps, or the confirmation of suspicions he couldn't quite articulate. "If you thought I had done something bad."

Bad.

Not wrong. Not sloppy paperwork.

Bad.

The division continued its mechanical life around them—phones chirping, keyboards clicking, someone laughing with forced brightness by the coffee machine. Hall felt sweat gathering at the base of her spine where the transmitter was secured, a small betrayal of moisture that might loosen the tape, might expose everything. "I didn't go to IA about you."

The lie fell from her mouth like a stone, landing between them with almost physical weight. White searched her face for a long moment, then nodded once, having found whatever he sought.

"I believe you." His shoulders loosened, the fabric of his shirt shifting as tension drained away. "Seven years as partners. Too much history. That night in the warehouse on Thurman Street. I got hit and you were there. That night and after. That kind of trust doesn't just vanish."

Hall remembered Thurman Street—mildew and old motor oil hanging in the air, gunfire cracking through darkness, White's shout as he fell. The bullet that had nearly ended his career, that left pain etched into every movement of his body. Pain that Rachel believed had driven him to murder.

"I know," Hall said, her voice steadier than her pulse. "I haven't forgotten."

"Partners trust each other," White murmured. "When everything else falls apart, that has to stand. Otherwise what's the point?"

The question settled between them, heavy with years of shared danger and triumph and loss. Hall thought of the journal hidden in White's apartment, four names written in his meticulous hand, dates marked "Mercy." Thought of Rachel, framed for a crime she hadn't committed. And beneath her blouse, the wire against her skin, transmitting every syllable to men who believed her partner was a killer.

"We should talk about that form. The Fowler case," she said, steering away from dangerous waters.

"I said I was sorry." His voice tightened at the edges.

"Yes. Sorry too," she replied, wondering if Barnes and Rocha could hear the hairline fracture running through each word.

White smiled then, his face transforming into something closer to the man she'd known before Rachel Fenimore spoke four names and altered everything. "Thank you for believing in me."

Before she could answer, footsteps approached from behind White—heavy, deliberate. Detective Matthews stopped at their desk, his broad hand descending onto White's shoulder, fingers digging into the fabric. His gaze fixed on Hall, hard as river stones.

"Everything okay here?" The question aimed at White though Matthews' eyes never left Hall's face.

White nodded, only a slight tightening of his jaw betraying that Matthews' grip might be too firm. "We're good. I was an asshole yesterday. Leg was killing me. Took it out on my partner. Should've known Hall would never go against me."

Matthews' fingers eased their grip, but his eyes remained cold. "Good. We don't want rats in our squad." He lingered on the word, lips curling slightly, then turned away, leaving the threat suspended in the air like cigarette smoke.

Hall watched him retreat through the bullpen, the wire burning against her skin, recording everything, betraying everything. Across their shared desk, White's eyes held nothing but trust, reflecting back at her like light from a blade's edge.

The phone rang, sharp against the murmured backdrop of the division. White sorted files with deliberate movements, each paper aligned with precision. Hall watched his hands, the wire a constant presence against her ribs.

"We're good?" she asked, fingers hovering above the receiver.

White glanced up, surprise flickering across his face. "Yeah, we're good. Answer your phone, Hall."

She lifted the receiver, tucking it between ear and shoulder, conscious of every gesture that might travel through the wire to Barnes and Rocha. "Detective Hall."

"It's Rachel," came the voice, thin and frightened. "Rachel Fenimore."

Hall's stomach contracted. Rachel Fenimore calling while she wore a wire feeding straight to Internal Affairs—a wire meant to catch White, not expose her contact with the woman he'd allegedly tried to kill. She swallowed, mind racing for words that wouldn't reveal too much.

"Yes, hello," Hall said, voice neutral as still water. "What can I do for you?"

"I've been released on bail again," Rachel said.

"How—" Hall caught herself. "How?"

"Overcrowded jails, and I've got no priors. Apparently some people still trust nurses," she replied, words tumbling out. "But when I got home, Harper had changed the locks. Left all my stuff in boxes outside. I don't have anywhere to go, and I'm scared to stay in a motel after what happened last time."

Hall glanced at White, catching his gaze fixed on her face. Something in her carefully measured tone had snagged his attention. The division seemed to contract around them, the air growing thin as tissue paper. Each breath she drew, each syllable she formed, traveled invisibly upward to the eighth floor, captured by the wire against her skin.

"I understand," she said, coating the words with a veneer of professionalism that felt like lacquer over rot. "Yes, that should be possible." Rachel's name remained trapped behind her teeth, the mention of bail locked in her throat—any acknowledgment would telegraph to Barnes and Rocha exactly who breathed on the other end of this line.

"Can you help me? Please?" Rachel's voice fractured, a hairline crack spreading through glass. "I don't know who else to call. I can't go to the hospital—they've suspended me pending the investigation. I can't go to friends—everyone thinks I'm a murderer."

The wire pressed against Hall's ribs with each inhalation, a constant reminder of its hungry presence. White sat too close, his attention a tangible weight. Barnes and Rocha listened somewhere above, disembodied ears. Rachel waited alone, her fear palpable through the receiver. Hall stood at the center of these converging forces, pulled in three directions at once.

"Lunch sounds great," she said, infusing artificial brightness into her voice. "Meet you there at noon."

Silence stretched across the line, confusion crackling through it like static. "Lunch? What are you talking about? Where?"

The question hung unanswerable. White's eyes never left her face. The wire recorded every breath, every hesitation. Hall's screen remained stubbornly blank, no bail notification illuminating its surface. Had Rachel fabricated her release? Was this some elaborate snare?

"Yes, that's right," Hall continued, aware of how her words must sound, how Rachel couldn't possibly decipher their meaning. "Noon works perfectly for me."

"Carolyn, I don't—" Frustration bled through Rachel's fear, her voice rising. "Where am I supposed to meet you? I need help now."

"I understand completely." Hall tapped her pen against her desk calendar where "12:00" sat printed in austere black type. "I'll see you at noon."

White's focus narrowed, his eyes tightening at the corners. His attention pressed against her skin like fingertips.

"Look, I don't know what's going on," Rachel whispered, her voice dropping so low Hall had to strain to hear. "But I'm scared. After what's happened—the knife, the setup—I think he's still trying to kill me. Please help me."

A chime from Hall's computer echoed a heartbeat later from White's desk. The screen illuminated with words that changed everything: "Defendant Rachel Fenimore granted bail. Released 10:37 A.M. today."

White's expression darkened as he read the same message on his own screen. His hand curled into a fist against the dark wood of his desk, knuckles bleaching bloodless. "Son of a bitch," he muttered—too soft to reach across the division but clear enough for Hall and the wire to capture.

"Wait," Hall whispered into the phone, watching White from her peripheral vision.

His fist crashed against the desk. Heads turned throughout the division. He stood abruptly, his chair rolling backward to collide with the desk behind him. "They granted her bail again," he said, voice tight as a wire. "After we found the knife. After everything."

Hall nodded, observing as White's hand disappeared into his pocket and emerged clutching a small orange bottle. "Do you know why? Is there a problem with the evidence?" The question felt hollow; she already knew the answer.

"How the hell would I know?" The words snapped from him like breaking branches. He turned toward the bathroom, his gait measured and deliberate—the walk of a man outpacing pain, the pill bottle clutched like salvation.

The moment he vanished around the corner, Hall brought the receiver to her lips. "Starlight Motel," she breathed, the words barely disturbing the air between her mouth and the plastic. "On Seventh. Give that to the courts as your address. I'll come." She replaced the receiver before Rachel could respond, before the wire could drink in anything more damning.

She sat motionless, staring at the phone. The decision crystallized in that moment—to meet Rachel, to help her, to follow this labyrinth to whatever waited at its center. White would return soon, his pain dulled by whatever prescription rattled in that familiar bottle, his anger perhaps tempered with it.

The bail notification glowed on her screen like a blue-white accusation. White had reacted as any dedicated detective might upon learning a murder suspect had slipped the system's grasp—with frustration, with righteous anger. But he had also reacted exactly as Rachel had predicted: like a man whose intended victim had just escaped his reach once more.

The wire bit into Hall's ribs with each breath, a sliver of metal against flesh recording every inhalation, every word, transmitting her betrayal in real time to men who waited eight floors above. She needed to know if they'd heard everything—needed and dreaded in equal measure.

She slipped into the stairwell, the door thudding shut behind her with a finality that sealed her off from the Homicide Division. The sound of that closure lingered in the concrete space, a soft punctuation mark at the end of one life, before the beginning of another. Her first few steps echoed between walls painted the color of surrender decades ago, a beige that had absorbed the whispers of a thousand other betrayals before hers.

Her fingers curled around the metal railing, cool and solid against her palm. She began to climb, each footfall deliberate as a confession.

The wire shifted against her skin as she moved, no longer an object but a presence, something alive and feeding on her. It pressed into the hollow beneath her ribs where doubt had made its home, a constant reminder of what she had become. Not detective, not partner, but informant. The word itself felt dirty in her mind, like something she couldn't wash away.

Eight flights between deception and revelation. Eight flights between the woman who had entered the building that morning and whoever would emerge when this was finished.

By the third floor, her body betrayed her in a different way. Her breath came faster, her legs burned with effort. She welcomed this simpler pain, this honest discomfort that asked nothing of her conscience. Physical exhaustion was clean compared to what churned inside her—the betrayal of White, the fear that clung to thoughts of Rachel, the knowledge that doors were closing behind her with every step upward.

Sweat gathered at her temples by the sixth floor, trickling down with the slow inevitability of choices narrowing. The transmitter shifted against her spine, cold despite her exertion. She had reached that invisible line where decisions calcify into fate. If she continued wearing the wire, continued gathering evidence against White, their partnership was already a ghost—regardless of what they found. If she removed it, she chose a different path, one that led to Rachel Fenimore waiting in that sad little motel room with its buzzing neon and thin walls.

The eighth floor arrived with the suddenness of consequences. Hall paused, hand on the door marked "Internal Affairs Division," feeling the last moment of choice slip away. Then she pushed through.

The corridor beyond received her with a hush thick enough to swallow secrets. Unlike Homicide with its perpetual motion and noise, IA maintained the weighted silence of a confessional. Her footsteps disappeared into the carpet as she moved toward Barnes's office, leaving no trace, as if she had already begun to disappear.

Barnes stood waiting, tall against the window that framed the city below, a city continuing its day, oblivious to the small betrayals playing out in rooms like this. He turned at her approach. Light caught his wire-rimmed glasses, obscuring his eyes for a moment, his face composed into professional detachment that revealed nothing of the man beneath.

"Detective Hall." His voice was neutral as lake water. He gestured her inside with long fingers that had never known the grip of a service weapon. "We were just listening to your conversation with White. That reaction to Fenimore's bail was... interesting."

Hall closed the door. The soft click of the latch felt like the sound of something valuable being locked away.

"I need you to remove the wire," she said.

Something flickered across Barnes's face—surprise, perhaps, or disappointment—before control reasserted itself. "Remove it? We're just getting started. His reaction to the bail notification shows promise, but we need more. Something explicit. Something we can use."

"I can't," Hall said, the words emerging with unexpected ease, as if they'd been waiting. "It's making me—" She stopped, unwilling to name the feeling as nervousness. "He'll notice. You know White. He doesn't miss details."

Apparently, they did.

The air conditioning hummed, a mechanical breath in the silence between them. Hall thought of White downstairs, returning to find her gone. Thought of Rachel waiting at Starlight Motel, alone with her fear. Thought of the four names in her notebook, a constellation of dead stars.

"I'll wear it again," she said, meeting Barnes's gaze. "But not today."

The lie settled between them, comfortable as an old friend.

"Nothing happening today will get White talking. Just paperwork. Routine."

Barnes studied her face. His stillness was its own accusation. "You know something you're not telling me."

It wasn't a question. Hall didn't treat it as one.

She reached beneath her blouse, feeling for the edge of the tape that held the wire against her skin. The adhesive pulled as she began to peel it back. That small pain cleared her mind like rain on a window.

"White trusts me again," she said, continuing to work the tape free. Each small tug was a decision reaffirmed. "If I keep acting strange, keep avoiding normal conversation, he'll wonder why."

The wire came free with one final pull. The skin beneath felt new, sensitive to air and possibility. She held the small microphone in her palm, its trailing black cord curled like something that had died there. She felt lighter somehow, though what waited for her downstairs still pressed on her shoulders with the weight of inevitability.

"Here," she said, offering the device. "You were listening live. You heard everything he's going to say to me right now."

She didn't add that it was enough. They both knew it wasn't.

Barnes took the wire, careful to avoid Hall's fingers during the exchange. Something had shifted in his face—a hardening, as if professional distance had calcified into something colder, more calculating. The transmitter lay between them now, a small black thing, innocuous in appearance but heavy with implication.

"A start isn't enough," he said, placing the device on his desk with deliberate precision. "Not with four people dead and a fifth in danger. You understand what's at stake here."

It wasn't a question. Hall nodded once, already turning toward the door, feeling the ghost-sensation of the wire still pressed against her skin. "I do. Better than anyone."

She left without waiting for his response, without looking back to see what judgment might have settled on his face. The corridor stretched before her, empty and silent, the institutional beige of the walls seeming to absorb sound, memory, intention. How many officers had walked this same path, carrying similar burdens of divided loyalty? The stairwell door waited at the end—a threshold between versions of herself.

Hall pushed through, began to descend. Each step felt lighter without the wire's weight against her skin, each breath easier without the knowledge that it was being recorded, transmitted, judged. The absence of surveillance was its own kind of vertigo. She had chosen her path now—not with White, not with Internal Affairs, but somewhere in the liminal space between, with Rachel Fenimore waiting at the far end of her decision.

The Starlight Motel. The thought steadied her as she continued down the stairs, back toward a division that had already decided what she was, toward a partner who might be a killer, toward a truth that waited to be uncovered. One painful step at a time, like pulling adhesive from tender skin.

Chapter 18

White had returned to his desk fifteen minutes ago, his movements carrying the underwater quality of someone fighting medication. His eyes held that particular glassy distance she recognized from previous injuries—the look of someone present but not entirely there. She hadn't asked where he was going or where he'd been. Once, she would have known without asking. Now it was none of her business.

He settled back into his chair with the careful concentration of a drunk trying to appear sober, focusing on his computer screen with exaggerated attention. Hall checked her watch—11:23 A.M.—and began gathering her things with small, measured movements. Thirty-seven minutes until she was supposed to meet Rachel at the Starlight Motel. Barely enough time to cross town in midday traffic, when the city congealed into a slow-moving mass of metal and frustration.

The division around her had settled into a tentative normalcy, detectives moving through their routines while stealing occasional glances in her direction. They didn't speak the accusation aloud, but their silence carried it just the same. Traitor. The word seemed to hover in the air between desks, unspoken but palpable.

Hall slipped her notebook into her jacket pocket and reached for her purse. Almost free. Almost—

Her desk phone rang, the sound sharp and sudden in the quiet division. She froze, hand suspended above the receiver, watching the display illuminate with a single word: Starlight. A small cold knot formed beneath her ribs.

She picked up. "Detective Hall."

"He's here." Rachel's voice came through breathless, pitched high with terror. "Someone threw a rock through my window. At the Starlight Motel. Room 108."

Hall felt the blood drain from her face, leaving a chill that spread from her temples down her neck. Her eyes flicked to White, but he remained unfocused, lost in whatever pharmaceutical haze had claimed him. "Yes?"

She turned away from him, lowering her voice. "Hurt?"

"No." The word caught in Rachel's throat like fabric on a nail. "But I could have been. The rock almost hit me. I was sitting on the bed, and it crashed through the window. Glass everywhere." A pause, filled with quick, shallow breathing that reminded Hall of a trapped animal. "Please come. I'm scared."

"I'll be there in fifteen minutes," she said, ignoring White's curious gaze now fixed on her profile. "Lock the door. Don't let anyone in until I get there."

"Hurry," Rachel whispered, and the line went dead.

Hall replaced the receiver and grabbed her purse, movements quick with purpose now. White watched her, his face a mask she could no longer read. Had he always been so inscrutable, or was this new opacity something she'd earned with her suspicion?

"Something up?" he asked, the words slurred at the edges. His fingers drummed a slow, irregular pattern against his desk—a habit from before, when he'd been trying to quit smoking. Now it seemed less deliberate, more like a nervous system misfiring.

"Follow-up with a witness," Hall said, the lie coming easier now that she'd had practice. Strange how deception could become familiar so quickly, like a foreign language suddenly unlocked. "Shouldn't take long."

White nodded, his attention already drifting back to his computer. The medication had dulled his edge, made him less observant than usual. Hall felt a stab of something like pity. The pill bottle in his pocket was both his salvation and his prison—relief from pain that came at the cost of the alertness that had once made him exceptional.

She stepped into the elevator and pressed the button for the parking garage. The doors slid closed, cutting her off from the division, from White, from the weight that now felt like a stone around her neck. As the elevator descended, she pulled out her phone and entered "Starlight Motel" into the GPS.

She could make it in nine minutes if the lights were with her. Nine minutes to decide who she would be when she arrived.

The parking garage trapped summer between concrete walls, exhaust and hot asphalt creating an atmosphere as oppressive as Hall's urgency. She slid behind the wheel, ignited the engine. The air conditioning labored, pushing warm air until the system could catch its breath. Hall pulled into New Hanan traffic with the precision of someone who had long ago stopped believing in the luxury of hesitation, cutting across three lanes for a left turn that earned her an indignant horn.

Nine minutes if traffic cooperated. The difference between Rachel breathing and Rachel not.

Hall watched a yellow light bleed to red and accelerated through it anyway. She needed to be faster than fear, faster than White—White, who shouldn't have known where Rachel was hiding. The question pulsed with each thrum of the engine: how had he found her?

The GPS directed her onto the expressway where Hall pushed her sedan to eighty, weaving between vehicles with the muscle memory of pursuit driving, reading gaps in traffic like a language she'd learned in another life. Her shield rested on the dash—not protection so much as a talisman against delay. Nine minutes. She had made this drive in less under different circumstances, with different stakes.

The Starlight exit appeared ahead, a reprieve from highway monotony. Hall cut across two lanes, trailing a chorus of horns in her wake as she took the ramp. The motel materialized two blocks later, a horseshoe of faded ambition surrounding a parking lot where three vehicles sat surrendering to midday heat. The sign promised COLOR TV and AIR CONDITIONING in letters bleached by decades of sun, artifacts from an era when such things might have been luxuries worth advertising.

Hall pulled in beside a patrol car that had no business being there. Nine minutes from the precinct, nine minutes with her driving, yet somehow uniforms had materialized before her. She stepped from her car into heat that pressed against her skin like an unwelcome confession. The smell of tar and exhaust filled her lungs, familiar and suffocating.

And there, outside Room 108 with its shattered window, stood White.

Something cold crystallized in Hall's stomach, a sensation at odds with the relentless heat. White, who had been at his desk when she'd left. White, dulled by pain medication, eyes unfocused as he'd stared at his computer screen. White, who had somehow arrived at the Starlight before her, standing now in perfect clarity.

She crossed the parking lot with measured steps, her face composed into professional detachment that masked the dread building beneath her ribs. White turned as she approached, his expression showing only mild surprise—the look of a man who has anticipated every move in a game his opponent doesn't realize they're playing.

"Hall," he said, voice sharper than it had been at the precinct, eyes clear as cut glass. "Funny running into you here."

"What are you doing here?" The question escaped her with more edge than she'd intended. Around them, the motel parking lot shimmered, air rising in visible waves from fractured asphalt. White stood in the thin mercy of shade cast by the concrete overhang, one shoulder against the wall in a posture of casual authority. He bore no resemblance to the man she'd left at the precinct—no trace of medication's fog, no hint of the pain that had necessitated those pills.

"I was in the area," White said with indifference. "Following up on the Henderson case. Witness lives two blocks over." He gestured vaguely eastward, the movement dismissive, almost bored. "Heard the call come over the radio. Rock through a window at the Starlight Motel." His mouth curved into something that resembled a smile only in the technical arrangement of muscles. "Imagine my surprise when dispatch said the room was registered to Rachel Fenimore."

He came here for a rock?

Hall maintained her neutral expression though her heart hammered a warning against her ribs. The call had gone to dispatch. Rachel hadn't just called her; she'd called 911. The realization shifted everything, made Hall's presence both more explainable and infinitely more dangerous.

"Quite a coincidence," she said, the words bitter as unripe fruit. "Her getting bail again this morning, and now this."

White nodded, watching her face with the focus of a man cataloging tells at a high-stakes table. "I was just as surprised to see you pull up. Following a lead on your witness?"

The lie she'd told at the precinct. He'd remembered despite the pills, despite appearing barely able to focus when she'd left. Hall felt winter spreading beneath her skin even as sweat gathered at her temples.

The bastard had been acting.

"Something like that," she said. "The witness called to cancel, and I was heading back when I heard the call."

White held her gaze for a long moment, then turned toward Room 108. The window had collapsed inward, glass scattered across the threadbare carpet like the aftermath of some violent baptism. Through the jagged opening, Hall could see the motel door standing ajar, framing a slice of darkness from which a man's irritated voice emerged.

"Glass all over the damn place. Jose! Get your ass over here and sweep up this mess!"

White pushed away from the wall with a fluid grace that surprised her—his body remembering what his mind had begun to forget. "Manager's worked up. Says this is bad for business." His mouth twisted around the word. "Like this place had a reputation to protect." He surveyed the parking lot, contempt settling into the lines around his eyes. "Fifteen years ago, this place was nothing but pimps and hookers. Now it's parolees and people hiding from something." He paused, letting the silence expand between them. "Or someone."

The implication hung there, delicate and dangerous as the glass shards catching sunlight. He knew Rachel was hiding from him, and he was letting Hall know he could find her. Faster than she ever could.

Hall turned from White's steady gaze. The motel curved before her—a crescent of identical doors facing the asphalt, each with its window beside it, curtains drawn against a sun that offered no warmth. Three doors stood open along the row, faces hovering in the shadows: a woman whose stained t-shirt strained across her flesh, an old man with skin that had surrendered to gravity years ago, a younger man whose neck bore the rising tide of blue-black ink.

"You think it's random vandalism?" Hall asked, though the words tasted false even as she spoke them. Keep up the façade.

"In this neighborhood?" White's laugh was dry as autumn leaves. "Kids throw rocks through windows here between breakfast and lunch. Or meth heads looking for something worth pawning." He shifted his weight, and in that small adjustment, Hall glimpsed the man she'd left at the precinct—the slight wince as he moved, the careful redistribution to ease pressure on his right hip. "Though the timing is interesting."

Hall didn't ask what he meant. Didn't need to. The timing wasn't just interesting—it was damning. Rachel granted bail, Rachel checking into a motel, a rock shattering her temporary sanctuary. Cause and effect as clean and brutal as winter.

The uniformed officers approached, their shoes crunching on loose gravel. Sweeney and Davis—partners long enough that they moved in unconscious tandem, like planets locked in mutual orbit.

"Detectives," Sweeney nodded to them both. "Homicide?"

White straightened, slipping into authority like an old coat. "Room 108. Rock through the window. Room's registered to Rachel Fenimore. We arrested her last week. Bail."

Sweeney's eyebrows lifted. "On a homicide?"

"Right?" White agreed, his voice flat as the horizon.

Sweeney and Davis exchanged a look that Hall recognized—that wordless communication between people who had worked together long enough to read the silences. She and White had once shared that language too, before the dictionary between them had been rewritten.

"We'll take her statement," Davis said, moving toward the open door. Sweeney followed, one hand resting on his holstered weapon—not from fear but from habit, the way some people touch wood or cross themselves.

"Where is she?" Hall asked as the uniforms disappeared into the room. "Rachel."

"Inside," White said, tilting his head toward the door. "Pale as milk left too long in sunlight. Nervous in a way that makes you wonder what else she's hiding." He ran his hand over his face, erasing something only he could see. "This place was her choice, by the way. After bail, she could have gone anywhere. She picked this shithole in a neighborhood where rocks through windows are as common as cigarette butts."

Hall nodded, saying nothing. The silence between them had once been comfortable; now it stretched taut as a tripwire.

"Right," White said, drawing out the word until it frayed at the edges. "Questioning. Let's see if we can revoke her bail." He gestured toward the open door, where shadows waited. "Shall we? I'm sure Ms. Fenimore will be thrilled to see us both."

The words sank into Hall's stomach like stones dropped in still water. White knew. Knew she was lying. Knew Rachel had called her. How much he'd pieced together remained unclear, but the danger was real, present, standing right beside her in the shimmering heat of the Starlight Motel parking lot, where even the air felt complicit.

"After you," Hall said, the words nearly sticking in her throat.

She lingered at the threshold of Room 108, letting her eyes adjust to the dimness. The space was smaller than she'd imagined, made claustrophobic by the gathering of bodies. A king-sized bed dominated the room, its comforter a faded garden of flowers no one had ever seen in nature, rumpled where Rachel must have been sitting when violence found her again. Glass glittered across the floor, each shard reflecting fractured light from a lamp whose shade listed to one side like a ship taking on water. And there, amid the wreckage of this latest intrusion, sat Rachel Fenimore on a chair that looked salvaged from some other decade, her face bloodless, hands clasped in her lap so tightly that her knuckles pressed against skin like they might break through.

The rock sat on the floor where it had landed—not a small stone but a chunk of concrete the size of a grapefruit, dense with malice and gravity. Heavy enough to kill. Officer Sweeney crouched over it, his department camera clicking in rhythmic counterpoint to the soft scratch of Davis's pen across his notepad. The motel manager hovered near the bathroom door, a short, balding man whose sweat-darkened shirt spoke more of inconvenience than concern, his face arranged in the particular frown of someone whose day had been ruined by other people's drama.

"—tell me again what you were doing when it happened," Davis was saying. His voice carried the particular weariness of a man who had transcribed thousands of human misfortunes into the formal language of incident reports.

Rachel looked up, her gaze finding Hall's with an immediacy that felt like recognition. Something moved across her face—relief perhaps, or a more complicated desperation that made Hall's ribs constrict around her heart. "I was sitting at the table," Rachel said, her voice steadier than the tremor in her hands would suggest. "Watching TV. I'd just checked in about an hour ago. I registered the address."

Davis nodded, his pen never pausing. "And you didn't see anyone outside before the rock came through the window?"

"No." Rachel's gaze dropped momentarily to her hands—pale islands in her lap—then lifted again to find Hall's with an intensity that seemed to compress the stale air between them into something thinner, harder to breathe. "The curtains were closed. I didn't hear anything either, just the sound of glass breaking and then the rock hitting the floor."

Sweeney finished with the rock and moved to the window, capturing the jagged teeth of remaining glass in the frame. Outside, a maintenance man approached with the resigned posture of someone for whom disaster was merely Tuesday. He carried a push broom and dustpan, his stained uniform suggesting he had swept up the aftermath of countless small catastrophes.

"Ms. Fenimore," Davis continued, thumb flicking to a fresh page, "can you think of anyone who might want to harm you or frighten you?"

Rachel never looked away from Hall. "Besides the cops who arrested me for a murder I didn't commit? Or my ex-girlfriend who changed the locks on our apartment and threw my things onto the street?" Bitterness edged her words, but beneath it lay something more vulnerable, like the soft flesh under a crab's shell. "No, I can't think of anyone specific."

Davis glanced at Hall and White, then back at Rachel, his expression carefully neutral.

Hall felt White shift beside her in the doorway, the heat of his shoulder almost but not quite touching hers. Rachel's eyes flickered to him, then back to Hall, something unspoken passing between them. Her gaze dropped meaningfully to the concrete chunk, rose again to Hall, then deliberately slid toward White.

Davis pressed on. "The ex-girlfriend—does she have a history of violence? Any threats, any restraining orders?"

"No," Rachel said, her voice flattening like water freezing. "I. I give up. Okay? I just want to be left alone."

White moved into the room, glass fragments singing beneath his shoes as he passed Hall. He circled with the deliberate grace of a man accustomed to controlling spaces, positioning himself near the broken window where he could observe both Rachel and Hall simultaneously. Hall tracked his movement, noting how he surveyed the scene with the clinical interest of a scientist who had already determined the outcome of his experiment.

"Officer Davis," White said, his interruption so smooth it seemed almost courteous, "when you're done with Ms. Fenimore's statement, I'd like to ask her a few follow-up questions about the Lewis homicide. Now that she's out on bail again, there are some details we should clarify."

Davis nodded, yielding to rank without hesitation. "Almost finished here, sir."

What little color remained in Rachel's face drained away, leaving her skin the pallor of old paper. Her eyes sought Hall's again, a drowning person spotting a distant shore.

Hall moved between them—not dramatically, not in a way that would register as interference, but enough to fracture their sightline. "I think we should let Ms. Fenimore rest after she finishes with Officer Davis," she said, her voice a careful construction of professional detachment. "She's had quite a shock."

White's gaze found hers, cold and measuring. Something moved across his face then—not quite a smile, more a brief rearrangement of features into an expression of satisfaction, like a man who has just confirmed a long-held theory. It vanished so quickly that anyone who didn't know him might have missed it entirely.

That fleeting non-smile confirmed what Hall had feared since she'd first seen the rock. This was White, continuing what he'd begun in that alley where Ira Lewis had died. This was another attempt at the "Mercy" he'd planned for Rachel—a mercy that had nothing to do with compassion and everything to do with silencing.

"Of course," White said, the words slipping like oil on water. "Ms. Fenimore has been through quite enough today. The Lewis case will keep." He turned toward Davis, his authority unquestioned. "Have someone sweep the perimeter when you're finished. Our rock-thrower might have left us something more than just the obvious."

White moved toward the door, passing close enough that Hall caught the scent of his aftershave—that same brand he'd worn for years, a scent that carried memories she preferred not to revisit. At the threshold he paused, his gaze making one final circuit of the room, taking in Rachel, the rock, the constellation of glass shards scattered across the worn carpet.

That smile again. Quick and satisfied, there and gone like heat lightning.

Hall watched through the fractured window as White crossed the parking lot, his footsteps crunching on loose gravel before fading into silence. He slid behind the wheel with the easy confidence of a man who had never doubted his place in the world. The patrol officers followed shortly after, dutiful satellites to his planet, heading out to canvas neighboring rooms. Hall knew they'd find nothing. Places like the Starlight operated on unwritten rules: see nothing, say nothing, survive.

The motel manager cursed again—not with any real feeling, just the perfunctory profanity of a man for whom ugliness had become wallpaper, always present but no longer noticed. "Jose!" he called through the open doorway. "Get your ass in here with that broom!"

Jose appeared, push broom in hand, his face a study in boredom. He was younger than Hall had initially thought—perhaps twenty-five—but with eyes that had aged decades beyond his years, eyes that had witnessed things they could never unknow. He began sweeping glass toward the center of the room, each stroke producing a sound like small, frightened creatures seeking shelter.

Rachel remained motionless in her chair, hands still clasped in her lap. The tremor in them was visible now that White had gone, as though his departure had removed some invisible restraint. She watched Jose's methodical sweeping, her gaze following the glittering path of broken glass, her composure a thin veneer beginning to show hairline fractures.

"You need to take that rock," she said suddenly, looking up at Hall. "For evidence. For proof."

Hall glanced at the chunk of concrete resting on the floor—jagged-edged and substantial, heavy enough to have shattered more than glass had its trajectory been different. "It's not my case," she said, tasting bitterness in the words. "This is just a rock through a window. It goes nowhere."

"And then what?" Rachel's voice cracked, the fear she'd controlled in White's presence now seeping through like groundwater. "No one will connect it to him."

The manager looked up from his examination of the window frame. "Connect it to who? You know who did this?"

"No," Hall said, cutting off Rachel's response before it could form. "She doesn't. And speculation won't help the investigation."

The manager shrugged, his interest evaporating like cheap cologne. "Whatever. I need to call my glass guy." He jerked his thumb toward Jose, who continued his sweeping without acknowledgment. "Three hundred should cover it."

"I don't have that kind of money," Rachel said, her voice small and distant, as though she were speaking from the bottom of a well. "Everything I had went to the bail bondsman."

The manager's words hung in the air like cigarette smoke, acrid and impossible to wave away. "Not my problem," he said, already turning toward the door. "You got until checkout time tomorrow to figure it out, or your stuff goes on the curb." He paused in the doorway. "Jose, make sure you get all that glass. Don't need some lawyer type suing us over cut feet."

Jose nodded without speaking, his broom continuing its steady rhythm across the floor, the sound of glass fragments tinkling against each other like distant wind chimes. The manager left, his footsteps receding down the concrete walkway, fading into the hum of traffic beyond. Jose soon followed, closing the door with a soft click that seemed to seal them inside their predicament.

Hall felt something twist inside her—not pain exactly, nor purely compassion, but a complicated knot that pulled tight beneath her ribs. She studied Rachel's face, the hollows beneath her cheekbones more pronounced now, her eyes ringed with the particular exhaustion that comes from fear sustained too long.

"I can't stay here," Rachel said, her voice barely audible, as if speaking the words might summon the danger itself. "Not when he knows where I am."

Hall crossed to where Rachel sat and lowered herself to one knee, bringing their faces level. The cheap carpet pressed against her skin through her slacks. She could smell Rachel's fear—like copper and salt.

"Rachel," Hall said, her voice low, intimate. "I need you to listen carefully."

Rachel's eyes fixed on Hall's face with terrible intensity, her gaze both present and somewhere else entirely, like someone watching the horizon for an approaching storm.

Hall reached into her pocket and withdrew her wallet. "You have to stay here. Just not this room. I'll pay for the window. You get a room higher up, on the inside."

"No. I'm not stay—"

"You can't leave. Condition of bail. I'll arrest you."

"I'll be safer in jail."

Hall sighed, a sound that contained all her professional certainties collapsing. "You said yourself the jail is full. They won't keep you. You're low risk."

"Carolyn, I can't." Tears began to fall, cutting clean tracks through the day's grime on Rachel's cheeks.

Hall looked around the room—at the broken window, the glass still scattered in the corners Jose had missed, the thin walls that had never protected anyone. She leaned closer, close enough that she could feel Rachel's breath on her face. "I'll come back. Protect you. Okay?" She held Rachel's gaze, searching for something to anchor them both. "Please. Get a safer room. Order food from the Starlight café, have them leave it at the door. It will be okay. I promise."

Rachel drew a ragged breath and nodded, a movement so slight it might have been mistaken for a tremor.

Hall had never imagined crossing this line—this invisible boundary between duty and something else, something without a name. Using her personal money, keeping secrets from her partner, from Internal Affairs, from everyone. The rules had always seemed so clear before, like lines on a map. Now they blurred and shifted.

Rachel's hand moved to Hall's, cool and dry against her skin. "Thank you," she whispered, the words heavy with meanings neither of them could afford to acknowledge.

Hall nodded once, then turned toward the door. She needed to leave now, before the weight of what she was doing settled fully upon her, before whatever was growing between them took clearer shape.

Outside, the heat pressed down like a judgment, the smell of hot asphalt rising in waves that distorted the air. Hall walked to the office, each step deliberate, as if testing ice that might not hold. She paid for the window, for another room. She requested receipts, knowing that White would find a way to use this against her, that every action left a trail. She had to be as above board as she dared while breaking every rule that mattered.

In her car, Hall sat with her hands on the steering wheel, not yet turning the key. The vinyl seat burned through her clothes. She started the engine, and the air conditioning pushed hot air through the vents before it began to cool, like the last gasp of something dying. As she pulled out of the Starlight Motel parking lot, Hall caught a glimpse of Rachel walking toward the lobby, shoulders hunched against invisible blows.

At least she was still alive. For now.

Chapter 19

The weight of betrayal settled over Hall like a second skin as she stood outside Room 512, her shadow stretching long beneath the sickly fluorescent hallway light. This was wrong—crossing a line that couldn't be uncrossed. Yet somewhere between duty and instinct, she'd made her choice. Her witness needed protection, and the list of people she could trust had dwindled to a dangerous few.

Her fingertips hovered near the door, not quite touching. White might be a killer. Barnes and Rocha had leaked the investigation within hours, then strapped a wire to her chest and called it protection—as if a recording device could stop a bullet. The division had already marked her: Matthews's grip on White's shoulder had been a message written in pressure and silence. And Rachel? A murder suspect who kept surviving attempts on her life, who had called Hall directly, who had somehow known Hall would help. The thought nagged at her like a splinter beneath skin.

The hallway light buzzed overhead, an electric insect trapped in glass. Hall watched her shadow shift against the threadbare carpet, stretched and distorted like the truth she was pursuing. Trust was a luxury she'd pawned somewhere between the first body and the fourth. She raised her hand and knocked, three short raps that felt like confessions whispered in a darkened room.

Footsteps approached from the other side, hesitant as a heartbeat. A pause, then the metallic whisper of the security chain sliding free. The door opened, and Rachel stood there, framed in the doorway, her face pale as old paper in the half-light.

"Thank you," Rachel said, stepping back to let Hall enter. "I thought—" She didn't finish the sentence. She didn't have to.

Hall stepped inside, closing the door behind her. The lock engaged with a click that sounded like finality. She surveyed the room: a bed too wide for one person yet too narrow for comfort, two chairs arranged for utility rather than conversation, a television reflecting nothing, a coffee maker with its red light burning like a distant warning. Everything temporary, nothing meant to be remembered.

"Did you eat?" Hall asked, the question floating between them like smoke.

"I'm fine," Rachel said. She hugged herself, arms wrapped tight across her chest, fingers digging into her own flesh as though holding something inside that might escape if she relaxed her grip.

Hall moved past her to the coffeemaker, not acknowledging the gratitude. She wasn't sure she deserved it. Wasn't sure she believed Rachel, not completely. But she believed enough to stand here now, in this room that smelled of industrial cleaner and other people's sleep.

"Are you hungry?" Hall asked, pulling open the refrigerator door. Cold emptiness breathed against her face. "I can order something."

"I don't want anyone to know I'm here," Rachel said, her voice catching on the edges of words.

Hall tilted her head, considering. "I'll pick up something from the café downstairs. Pay cash." She paused, studying the shadows beneath Rachel's eyes. "What do you want?"

Rachel nodded, drifting to stand at the kitchen counter that separated the small cooking space from the living area, her fingers tracing invisible patterns on the laminate surface. "Wine sounds good. Food too, if it's not—" She stopped herself. "A burger?"

"You got it," Hall said, moving toward the door. "I'll be back in a few minutes."

In the elevator, Hall watched herself fragment in the mirrored walls, a woman divided into panels and seams. This wasn't about helping Rachel, she told herself as the floors ticked downward. It was about keeping her alive until Hall could prove who really killed Ira Lewis. The lie tasted metallic, necessary.

The hotel café yielded two burgers wrapped in foil, fries going limp in their paper container, and a bottle of wine that cost more than it was worth. Hall returned to the room, the bag warm against her side, the wine bottle cool against her palm—opposing sensations that matched her divided loyalties.

Rachel's face softened when Hall entered, relief washing over her features like water. "God, that smells good," she said, hunger making her voice deeper. "I'm starving." Hall extracted the wine bottle from the bag and held it up, the dark glass catching what little light the room offered.

"I can't tell you how much I need a drink," Rachel said, watching the bottle as though it contained something more valuable than fermented grapes.

The cork surrendered with a soft pop that seemed to expand in the quiet room, intimate as a whispered secret. Hall reached for cupboards, finding only empty space behind the doors.

"Straight from the bottle it is," she said, setting it down on the small table in front of Rachel. "Hope you don't mind." The smell of grease and salt mingled with the mustier scents of the room, creating something almost like comfort. "After today, I think it's the only way to drink."

Hall settled into a chair and unwrapped her burger. Rachel had already spread her meal before her, half the fries scattered across the foil like abandoned plans. Hall leaned back, her body gradually yielding to the chair even as her eyes remained vigilant—moving from door to windows to Rachel's face and away again, mapping escape routes and entry points.

"You're safe here," Hall said, though the words tasted hollow. Nowhere was truly safe, not if White had decided Rachel needed to die. Not if he'd already orchestrated four deaths disguised as accidents, suicides, robberies gone wrong—deaths that looked natural until you stood far enough away to see the pattern.

Rachel's fingers tightened around the wine bottle, knuckles paling. "Am I? He found me at the motel." Her eyes lifted to meet Hall's, dark with a knowledge that went beyond fear. "How long before he figures out I'm still here?" She tipped the bottle to her lips and drank slowly, as though measuring out time in careful sips.

"He knows you're here. He'd arrest you for breaching bail conditions if you left," Hall said, the words hollow against the weight of what remained unsaid. "That's why I'm here."

Rachel set down her burger after a single bite. "Is anyone doing anything about him? He tried to kill me today. That rock—" Her voice caught, a small fracture in her composure. "If I'd been sitting closer to the window, it would have hit me in the head."

Hall watched color rise in Rachel's cheeks, a flush that spoke of fear transmuted to anger. "There are things happening. I can't tell you too much, but things are happening."

"I don't understand," Rachel said. "I was nothing but kind to him. After his surgery, I sat with him when the pain was bad. I held his hand. I talked to him for hours because I knew how lonely it could be, stuck in a hospital bed with nothing but your own thoughts." The careful control she'd maintained at the motel began to unravel, her voice rising with each remembered kindness. "And now he wants me dead because someone else's surgery didn't fix him."

Hall studied her burger as though the answers might be layered between lettuce and meat. She took a bite, the soft surrender of wilted greens filling the silence between them.

"It struck me as odd," Hall finally said, "that he was there so quickly. At the pawnshop, here at the motel. There before physics allows."

"Because he was already in the area. Each time. His car in the parking lot." Hope flickered in Rachel's eyes—not hope for safety, but the more essential hope of being believed. "He threw that rock, I'm sure of it. He wanted to scare me, to let me know he could find me anywhere."

Hall chewed slowly, buying time. The meat was stringy between her teeth, the bun crumbling like dust against her tongue. She barely tasted it. Instead, she tasted doubt—about the Internal Affairs meeting that morning, about the wire she'd worn and then removed, about Barnes and Rocha dismissing her concerns while insinuating inappropriate relationships.

Some secrets weren't hers to share. Not the report she'd filed with Internal Affairs. Not the journal from White's apartment with its four drawings marked "Mercy," each date matching a death. Not yet. Not until she could see where this winding path led.

"Eat," Hall said instead, gesturing toward Rachel's abandoned dinner. "You'll need your strength."

Rachel picked up her burger again. Her hands no longer trembled. "For what?"

Hall looked toward the apartment door—solid but penetrable, locked but vulnerable. Not truly secure against someone like White, who knew how to slip past barriers, how to find those who wished to disappear.

"For whatever comes our way," Hall said. She sipped her wine, but it did nothing to wash away the strange taste of the word 'our' that had settled at the back of her throat like an unexpected intimacy.

Rachel ate a fry and reached for the wine bottle. It was half empty now, easier to lift, easier to pour a more generous measure. The kitchen clock read 7:15 P.M. Outside the windows, New Hanan settled into evening, streetlights flickering on one by one like uncertain stars.

Hall watched as Rachel drank, her movements steadier now with food in her stomach and walls between her and the darkening world.

"You want to know why he hates me so much?" Rachel asked, her voice softer than before, pitched for just the two of them though no one else existed in their temporary sanctuary. "Why I'm on his list?"

Hall nodded, gathering their wrappers and dropping them in the trash. "I wish he'd talked. Just talked about how he was feeling, what was happening."

"I was there for his worst moments," Rachel said, staring at the bottle as if reading a forgotten history in its dark glass. "After the surgery, when the anesthesia wore off and the pain hit him. I was the one on shift. I was the one who held his hand."

Hall settled back onto her chair, close enough to hear the soft catch in Rachel's breath, the slight tremor that had returned to her voice despite the wine's false courage.

"The first night was bad," Rachel continued. "He woke up disoriented, trying to get out of bed. I had to talk him down, remind him where he was, why he was there." She took another sip of wine, the glass lingering against her lower lip. "He cried. Did you know that? Your partner, this big tough detective who took a bullet and lived to tell about it. He cried like a child that night, clutching my hand so hard I had bruises the next day."

Hall tried to imagine it—White stripped bare by pain, clutching a stranger's hand like a drowning man might grasp driftwood. The image refused to settle against what she knew of him: the man who sealed himself in compartments, who wore his stoicism like armor, who had returned to his desk while surgical staples still pulled at his flesh because absence felt more like failure than presence ever could.

"I warned him," Rachel said, her gaze rising to meet Hall's across the table's small geography. "I think that's what he couldn't forgive. I told him the post-operative instructions weren't suggestions. That forcing recovery would break what had been mended. That pain would become his constant companion." A sigh escaped her, soft as confession. "He wouldn't listen. They never do—those who've built identities on being unbreakable. They mistake mortality for weakness."

Hall recalled White at his desk, fingers curled around orange plastic, the careful redistribution of weight when he shifted in his chair. "And this became your fault? When the pain persisted?"

"I became the messenger who lived while the message proved true," Rachel said. "The surgical team made the first cut, but I spoke the prophecy." She lifted her wine, a gesture that seemed both toast and surrender. "All I did was tell him how bodies heal. How they break when denied proper mending. Then I watched it unfold exactly as medicine promised it would."

A siren wailed somewhere beyond the windows, its urgency rising then falling as it traced the city's arterial streets. Hall reached for the bottle. This Rachel Fenimore—the one who spoke with quiet resignation of a man's broken body and fractured pride—seemed impossibly distant from any woman who would plunge a blade into a stranger's flesh. Here instead sat someone caught in the undertow of a drowning man's desperate thrashing.

"Tell me about Dr. Strickland," Hall said. "Her suicide—you mentioned disbelief." It remained for Hall an absence with shape, a darkness that needed illumination.

Rachel's face transformed, softened by memory in a way Hall hadn't witnessed before. "Victoria possessed that rare brilliance that doesn't burn those nearby. A surgeon's precision with a poet's heart. She took time with patients, ensured they understood what was happening within their own bodies." The momentary warmth ebbed. "And she embraced life—her husband, children, work—with a hunger that left no room for despair."

Hall drank, the wine nearly gone. Night had claimed the city outside, turning the windows into dark mirrors that reflected two women leaning toward one another, faces suspended in the pendant light's harsh island of illumination.

"The week before she died, Victoria invited me to her daughter's birthday celebration. Six years old. She'd commissioned a unicorn cake with rainbow layers inside, hired a magician who specialized in children's wonder." Rachel's voice caught on something sharp and hidden. "That isn't the choreography of surrender. Those aren't the actions of someone preparing to exit."

"The medical examiner ruled it suicide," Hall said. "Was there a note?"

Rachel's eyes flashed, sudden as heat lightning. "A typed note. Victoria wrote everything by hand—birthday wishes, thank-you cards, even patient notations when protocols permitted. She wouldn't have typed her final words." She leaned forward, wine forgotten. "And she would never—not in any version of this world—have abandoned her children."

Hall thought of the journal, of White's meticulous script. Another thing he shared with Strickland, perhaps.

She remembered his reaction to the bail notification that morning: rage briefly uncaged before being forced back behind bars, the pill bottle clutched like something that might be weapon or salvation. She recalled the rock that had shattered glass at the motel, White materializing at the scene with suspicious promptness, the satisfaction that had briefly claimed his features when he believed himself unobserved.

Between them now stood the empty bottle, hollowed of purpose like the evening had emptied Rachel of her careful defenses. Exhaustion had reclaimed her, the brief respite of food and wine fading to reveal a woman who had been running through darkness with no promise of dawn.

Hall studied Rachel's face beneath the pendant's unforgiving light—the violet shadows beneath her eyes, the tension that had colonized her jaw, the way her attention still darted toward the door as though expecting it to fracture inward at any moment. And Hall saw something else: a truth that aligned the scattered pieces of this puzzle into a pattern more coherent than any she had yet discerned.

"We should get some rest," Hall said, though she knew sleep would be a stranger tonight, a visitor who might knock but never enter. "Tomorrow we figure out what to do."

Rachel nodded, her gaze lifting to meet Hall's. Something passed between them—fragile, wordless. Two women connected by the thin thread of circumstance, by fear that hummed beneath their skin like electricity. Two women joined by a man who had walked the space between them, scattering death like seeds. Now they had only each other in a world where trust had become as brittle as the glass that separated them from the night.

They moved to the bed—the room offered nothing else. Hall lay on top of the covers while Rachel curled against the headboard, pulling the blanket across her legs, creating a soft barrier between herself and everything else.

The wine had loosened something in Rachel. Stories of the hospital spilled from her now—patients who slipped away beneath her hands and those who didn't, twelve-hour shifts that bled into eighteen when bodies were scarce but need was not, the surgical team that had become family until death claimed them one by one, a slow and methodical harvesting.

Hall offered her own stories in return—the hollow victories and defeats that punctuated office life, the peculiar solitude that existed even in rooms full of people who knew your name but not your dreams.

The phone's ring sliced through the quiet apartment. Hall glanced at the screen and felt something cold slide down her spine: WHITE. For a moment, she considered the silence of letting it pass unanswered, but that silence would speak too loudly. White knew her habits, knew she always answered, especially for him. Especially before.

Rachel's face changed, the half-formed smile vanishing like breath on cold glass. "Is that—?"

Hall pressed a finger to her lips, nodding once. She rose and drifted toward the table, each step widening the space between them, creating a pocket of false privacy for whatever was coming.

"White," she answered, her voice a mask she'd worn a thousand times before.

"Hall." His voice came through with a clarity that felt like an accusation. Almost friendly. Almost. But beneath the familiar cadence ran something new, something that made the fine hairs on her arms rise. "Hope I'm not interrupting anything important."

She turned away from Rachel, facing the kitchen window where city lights smeared against the darkness, constellations formed by human hands. "Just finishing dinner. What's up?"

"Thought I'd check in. See if you'd heard anything more about our Internal Affairs friends and their little inquiry." The casual words carried an edge that hadn't been there before, like finding a blade hidden in a familiar drawer.

Hall's fingers tightened around the phone. Behind her, Rachel's presence filled the room like smoke—silent, watching, waiting. Every word between them now was a stone dropped into still water, ripples expanding outward.

"What the hell would I know about that?" The words came sharper than she'd intended. "If you hadn't told me about it, I wouldn't even know it was happening."

A pause stretched between them, filled with the soft static of distance and years.

"That right?" White asked finally. His voice had changed again, cooling by degrees. "Because I heard an interesting rumor today. When I got back to the office, after that little incident at the Starlight." He let the words hang, a hook baited with memory. "Seems someone from Homicide has been talking to Barnes and Rocha. Frequent visits to the eighth floor. Very cozy."

Sweat gathered at the base of Hall's spine, a cold line tracing her vertebrae despite the warmth that filled the apartment like stale breath. "The eighth floor gets all kinds of traffic, White. Everyone has to report to IA sometimes."

"Not everyone," White said, his voice dropping to a murmur, intimate as a secret shared across a pillow rather than miles of city darkness. "Just the ones with something to report."

Hall drifted to the bathroom, turned on the faucet. Water rushed over her free hand—the shock of cold against her skin cleared away the wine's lingering fog, leaving her thoughts sharp-edged and dangerous.

"Are you sure they're actually after you?" she asked. "Maybe it's routine, something about an old case."

White laughed, a sound she'd heard countless times across desks and crime scenes and late-night drinks. Never like this—brittle as ice over deep water, cold and without depth.

"I'm a damned good detective, Hall. You think I can't tell when I'm being watched? When reports are being pulled, when witnesses are being re-interviewed?" His voice hardened into something she barely recognized. "I will find out who did this. Who went to Barnes and Rocha behind my back. And when I do—"

The sentence remained unfinished, but its shadow stretched between them, long and dark as evening.

"White—" Hall began, the single word holding everything she couldn't say, everything she didn't know how to begin.

"Don't," White said, cutting her off. The words fell soft now, almost tender, which made them somehow worse than shouting. "Seven years. Partners. Family." He paused, each word settling like dust. "And someone's trying to take it all away, trying to paint me as some kind of monster." A breath escaped him, not quite a sigh. "They'll be sorry. When it's over, they'll wish they'd never heard my name."

The water continued to run over Hall's hand. She watched it, feeling the cold creep up her fingers, then her wrist, a numbness that seemed to mirror something spreading inside her chest. A heaviness, like swallowing river stones.

"No one's trying to take anything from you," she said. The lie tasted metallic, like pressing her tongue against a filling.

"We'll see." White's voice had returned to something closer to normal, the menace receding like a tide that would inevitably return. "Good night, Hall. Sleep well. We'll talk more tomorrow."

The call ended without ceremony. Hall set the phone on the counter and turned off the faucet. She dried her hand on a towel lumped on the counter, her movements precise, deliberate, disconnected from the thoughts circling her mind like birds above a field.

He had threatened her. He had threatened Barnes and Rocha, hadn't he? Or had he merely promised consequences? The line between the two blurred in her memory.

Rachel stood in the narrow space between living area and bathroom, blanket abandoned, her face drained of color in the half-light. "What did he say?"

Hall moved past her to the living room, lifted the wine bottle they'd left on the coffee table. The familiar weight of it steadied her, gave purpose to hands that wanted to tremble. "He knows someone's been talking to Internal Affairs. He doesn't know it's me, not for certain, but he suspects."

"He threatened you." Not a question.

Rachel followed her to the sink, watching as Hall rinsed the bottle, placed it in the garbage. The simple ritual of disposal, as if clearing evidence.

"He said he'd find out who reported him." Hall turned, leaning back against the counter. "And they'd be sorry."

Rachel wrapped her arms around herself—a gesture Hall had seen before, a holding-together when everything threatened to come apart. "He'll kill you," she said. "Just like the others. Just like he tried to kill me."

"Maybe."

Hall moved past her, back to the living room where case files lay scattered across the coffee table. Files she should have been reviewing instead of sharing wine with a murder suspect in her apartment. Files that seemed insubstantial now, paper ghosts against White's quiet promise.

"Or maybe he's just angry. Lashing out because he feels trapped."

"You don't believe that." Rachel's voice hardened, frustration cutting through fear. "Not after everything I've told you. Not after what you've seen yourself."

Hall straightened, arms crossing her chest. Armor. "What I believe doesn't matter. What matters is what I can prove." She brushed past Rachel and picked up the TV remote. Sound filled the space between them. "He's smart, Rachel. He knows he's being investigated. He knows who's involved, and he knows there isn't enough to arrest him." She paused. "IA probably hasn't even suspended him yet."

"So we just wait?" Rachel's voice rose. "Wait for him to kill us both?"

Hall met her eyes across the room. The distance between them seemed vast suddenly, unbridgeable. "No. We don't wait." She checked her watch—9:06 P.M. "But we have to be careful. White isn't some common criminal who makes stupid mistakes. He's a cop. A good one. He knows how to cover his tracks, how to make murders look like accidents or suicides. Robberies gone wrong."

Rachel sank onto the bed. The brief flare of anger drained from her, leaving behind a woman who had been running on fear for days. "He's a monster," she whispered. "He won't stop now."

Hall moved to the window. Outside in the courtyard, the glow of a cigarette rose and fell in the dark—someone standing alone, smoking, unaware of the fear filling this motel room like invisible smoke. She remembered other nights at other windows, watching other lives continue while hers seemed suspended.

"No," she agreed, her breath clouding the glass. "He won't stop. Which means we're running out of time."

She turned back. Rachel sat small and vulnerable on the bed, a target White had missed repeatedly. A cat with a mouse. And Hall knew with terrible clarity that she was a target now too—that her questions, her suspicions, her visits to the eighth floor had placed her in White's sights as surely as Rachel's connection to his surgery had placed her in his.

"We need to get ahead of him," Hall said, decision crystallizing as she spoke. "Find proof that will stick. Evidence that Barnes and Rocha can use." She didn't finish the thought: before White tries again.

Rachel looked up, her eyes meeting Hall's across the room. Something passed between them—an understanding, unspoken but binding. They were tethered now by White's rage, by the deaths trailing behind him like shadows, by the knowledge that they might be next.

"Tomorrow," Hall said, the word hanging between promise and prayer. "We start tomorrow."

Chapter 20

The bedroom lay in darkness save for the knife-edge of yellow streetlight slicing through the curtains' gap. Hall sat with her back against the headboard, sheets pooled at her waist, Rachel's body a warm weight against her side. Rachel's head nestled in the hollow of Hall's shoulder, dark hair spilling across Hall's skin like ink on parchment—something both startlingly new and achingly familiar. The digital clock on the nightstand pulsed 11:04 P.M., red numbers measuring time in a world suddenly compressed to this room, this bed, this borrowed sanctuary carved from danger.

Hall combed slow circles through Rachel's hair, each strand sliding between her fingers like water remembering its flow. The press of Rachel against her felt right in ways Hall hadn't anticipated, hadn't permitted herself to imagine. Three years without touch—maybe four. The endless shifts, the black moods, the silences that stretched until they became a language of their own. The weight of other people's tragedies carried home night after night. Everyone eventually retreated from it.

"Not you," Hall whispered into the darkness.

Rachel tilted her face upward, features half-illuminated by the angled light. "Not me what?"

"You understand a cop's life." The word hung there, unadorned.

Rachel shifted, creating a small pocket of coolness between their bodies. "More than you realize. Cops and nurses—we're both witnesses to strangers on their worst days. Then we move to the next, and the next." She settled back against Hall. "We're both caretakers."

Heat rose to Hall's face, the darkness a merciful veil.

"I..." She paused, searching for words that wouldn't collapse under their own weight. "I wish we'd met differently. Not hiding in this motel from my partner who might be—"

"A serial killer," Rachel finished, her voice steady as a surgeon's hand.

"Yes." A single syllable, inadequate against the horror they'd uncovered.

Rachel melted back against Hall's shoulder, her breath warm against skin gone cool. "I wish that too."

Silence stretched between them, comfortable despite everything. Outside, a car horn sounded, then faded down the street. The city continued its nocturnal rhythm, oblivious to their small island of quiet.

"Do you ever get lonely?" Rachel asked, fingers tracing invisible constellations across Hall's stomach. "Being a homicide detective?"

Hall considered the question, weighed the easy deflection against the truth that would expose too much. Rachel's touch decided for her—patient, expectant, deserving of honesty.

"Yes." The word fell like a stone into still water. "All the time. The job walls you off, even surrounded by other cops. You can't speak about the cases, not really. Not the details that follow you home at night—a victim's face, a family collapsing, the smell of death that clings to your clothes no matter how many times you wash them." She felt Rachel's hand grow still against her skin. "You learn to bury it all inside where it feeds on itself, growing teeth."

"Nurses understand that," Rachel said softly. "We witness terrible things—children broken beyond repair, elderly patients abandoned by those who should love them. But we can't speak of it, not to friends outside the hospital, not to family who'd only hear horror stories." She eliminated the small space between them, her body seeking Hall's warmth. "HIPAA protects the patients, but who protects us from carrying all those stories alone?"

Hall nodded, her chin brushing against Rachel's hair. In all her years wearing a badge, no one had articulated so precisely the particular burden she carried. Not department therapists, not other officers, not civilians with their morbid fascination about crime scenes. The isolation of bearing witness was a specific kind of loneliness, one Rachel understood without explanation.

"Some nights," Hall said, words rising unbidden, "I dream of them. Not just the victims, but those left behind. Their faces in that first moment of knowing someone they love isn't coming home." She swallowed against the tightness in her throat. "Those haunt me more than the bodies do."

Rachel's arm tightened around Hall's waist, anchoring her against memory's undertow. "I dream of the ones we lose. The flatline that won't reverse no matter what we do. That moment when medicine becomes mourning." Her voice caught. "And the ones we save but send back to situations that will destroy them anyway."

Like White.

Hall pressed her lips to the top of Rachel's head, a benediction of sorts. The shared understanding between them felt like the first clean breath after years of shallow ones, of parceling out pieces of herself with careful calculation. Even with White, her partner, the man she'd trusted with her life, she had maintained a certain opacity, kept rooms within herself locked. Now, those barriers seemed like premonitions rather than protection.

Rachel's breathing had deepened into the slow rhythm of near-sleep, her body growing heavier against Hall's side. The clock's red digits read 11:21 P.M. Ten hours until morning, until whatever waited beyond this room would demand their attention. Ten hours of borrowed safety, if White hadn't already set his machinery in motion.

Hall closed her eyes, surrendering to the warmth of Rachel's skin against hers, the cadence of her breathing, the nocturnal pulse of the city beyond her window—a world continuing its indifferent rotation despite the danger that had entered her particular corner of it. For tonight, in these stolen hours, they existed in suspension. Tomorrow would arrive with its own terrors. But here, in the darkness, Hall allowed herself to feel something beyond fear, beyond duty, beyond the four deaths and the shadow of more to come.

The silence in her head wasn't deafening anymore. That was the thing she couldn't quite reconcile—how quickly solitude could become memory rather than condition.

Rachel shifted beside her, unaware of the realization forming in Hall's mind. "What are you thinking about? You went quiet."

Hall turned toward her, pushing the half-formed strategy back into the shadows where it belonged. "Just processing everything," she said. The half-truth lay between them like a small, necessary betrayal. She couldn't name this new feeling, couldn't add its weight to what Rachel already carried. "We'll figure it out. Tomorrow."

Rachel studied her face for a long moment, reading the spaces between words. Then she nodded, accepting the boundary without pressing against it. "Tomorrow," she agreed.

She moved closer, her hand rising to cup Hall's face, fingers light against her skin. The touch asked a question that required no voice. Hall answered by leaning forward until their lips met.

This kiss held something different from those they'd shared earlier—less desperate, less tethered to fear. This was something else entirely, a promise neither could articulate nor guarantee in the world that waited beyond morning.

When they separated, Rachel reached for the lamp, her hand finding the switch in the darkness. The room fell into deeper shadow, the streetlight outside now the only illumination breaking the night.

"Sleep," Rachel whispered, settling back against the pillow, drawing Hall down beside her.

Hall let herself be guided, turning onto her side so that Rachel could curve against her back, arm draped over her waist, breath warming the nape of her neck. Outside, the city continued its nighttime conversation—distant sirens, the occasional car washing past beneath her window, the mechanical hum of air conditioners pushing back against summer's lingering heat.

Somewhere in that darkness, White was waiting. Planning. Perhaps even now arranging pieces on a board she couldn't yet see. But for tonight, in these hours before dawn, Hall allowed herself the small mercy of Rachel's presence, of sleep that might come if she could quiet her mind enough to permit it.

Chapter 21

The dashboard read 9:32 A.M. when Hall pulled into the visitor space outside White's building. For a moment she remained motionless, her fingers pressed against the steering wheel's worn leather, feeling the subtle indentations her hands had made over countless drives. The morning light caught dust motes floating in the car's interior, making them seem suspended in time, like her decision to come here. White would still be home.

She sat listening to the engine tick as it cooled, a sound that had accompanied so many stakeouts and quiet confessions between partners. The holster at her hip felt suddenly conspicuous, its weight an accusation. She couldn't walk into his apartment armed—couldn't let him see the gun and understand she'd anticipated violence from a man who had once covered her back without question. She removed it, the familiar heft in her palm a reminder of everything that had changed, and locked it in the glove compartment. The latch clicked with a finality that made her pause. This was a conversation, she told herself. Not an arrest. She needed to believe that, even as certainty dissolved around her.

The lobby smelled of furniture polish and recycled air. Hall used her key without announcing herself—no point in calling first. White would either flee or craft his defenses. Better to arrive unannounced, to witness the first unguarded reaction when she mentioned the journal, the four names, Rachel. Seven years of partnership had earned her that much truth, even if it shattered everything they'd built.

The elevator ascended with a smoothness that belied her internal turbulence. Her heart quickened against her will. She focused instead on Rachel waiting at the Starlight Motel, trusting Hall to find something that would save them both. The thought anchored her as the elevator chimed at the fifth floor.

White's door was exactly as she remembered—solid oak with brass numbers that caught the hallway light, the small scratch near the peephole from the afternoon he'd attempted to change the lock himself, cursing softly as the screwdriver slipped in his usually steady hands. She had laughed then. She knocked now.

"I hardly expected to see you at my door."

White's voice stilled something in her, a momentary paralysis that she disguised with a slow smile, her breathing controlled through discipline.

He filled the doorway completely, his broad frame leaving no space unclaimed. His expression held a detached curiosity, as though she were a puzzle he hadn't expected to encounter this morning.

"Robert, we need to talk."

"No, we don't."

Hall drew a breath that tasted of his aftershave and the coffee he'd clearly been drinking. "I need to hear it from you." Her voice emerged steadier than she felt, betraying nothing of the cold certainty settling in her bones.

White tilted his head, regarding her with eyes that revealed nothing while seeing everything. "Come in." He stepped aside, the door held open like an invitation she couldn't refuse.

She swallowed and crossed the threshold.

"I know it all." The words fell between them, heavy with implication. Hall recognized the moment with sudden clarity—she had stood in rooms like this before, across from suspects who believed themselves beyond reach. Talking with a suspect was just that, regardless of how clever he believed himself to be. Regardless of who he was.

Except he locked the door behind her. She was in his territory now.

"You know." White's tone remained conversational, but something shifted in his gaze—a coldness creeping inward from the edges, like frost forming on a window pane. "And what exactly is it that you know?"

The oldest deflection in the world. Get the cop to reveal her hand, then dance around the evidence.

White's fingers drifted to his hip, a gesture she'd witnessed countless times over their partnership—reaching for the spot where an old injury sometimes flared. Now she wondered if he sought reassurance of his weapon instead, if their history would end with her blood on his walls.

"Why are you here, Hall?" White asked, his voice hardening like cement setting. "What do you think you know?"

The silence between them hummed with potential energy. Hall chose her path, stepping into a current that would carry her beyond any possibility of return.

"I went to Internal Affairs." Each syllable felt like a small betrayal, impossible to reclaim once spoken. "After I found your journal. After I connected you to the deaths of Dr. Fowler, Dr. Strickland, Sandra Kim, and Jennifer Moss."

White's expression remained unchanged, but his breathing quickened slightly—a tell she might have missed had she not spent years reading his body language across interview tables and crime scenes.

"I found the entries where you tracked them. The dates marked 'mercy' that matched when each of them died. The surveillance notes, the planning." Her voice strengthened as certainty replaced fear. "I took photos of everything. IA has them now. They're investigating you."

A sound whispered through the apartment—perhaps the refrigerator cycling off, or the building settling into itself beneath the weight of midday heat. White remained motionless, his gaze fixed on her with that particular stillness he had once employed during interrogations, a stillness that had made reluctant witnesses speak into the silence he created. Now it made him something else entirely.

"You've been busy." His voice came soft, almost tender, at odds with the weight of what hung between them. He shifted, leaning against the door in a posture that might have appeared casual in another context, in another life. "You broke in?"

"Used the keys. Including the key to your filing cabinet."

White's eyes rolled upward, a brief surrender to irony. "The ones I gave you. Damn. Still, illegal. Breaking into my home. Going through my private papers. Running to Barnes and Rocha with tales of conspiracy and murder."

"Not tales." Hall held his gaze, refusing to look away though something cold and primitive gathered at the base of her spine. "Evidence. Facts. Four dead people who all worked on your surgery. Rachel Fenimore targeted next. The murder of Ira Lewis. The car. The rock." She paused, the air between them thinning. "You're torturing her, aren't you?"

"Am I?" White's mouth curved into a shape that resembled a smile the way taxidermy resembles life. "And tell me, partner, what did Barnes and Rocha say when you showed them this 'evidence' you illegally obtained? Did they thank you for breaking the law, for violating my privacy, for betraying seven years of partnership based on suspicion and conjecture?"

The question found its mark with surgical precision. Hall remembered Barnes's face when she'd removed the wire—the subtle withdrawal, the professional distance reasserting itself. Rocha's careful warning about lawful evidence acquisition. Their promise to investigate properly, a promise that had yielded nothing but silence in the days since, like a stone dropped into still water with no ripple returning.

"They're investigating," she said, the words hollow as bird bones.

White laughed, a sound devoid of mirth, dry as autumn leaves. "Investigating. Of course they are." He straightened, a flicker of pain crossing his features as weight settled onto his bad leg. "And now you're here, looking for what? More evidence to illegally collect? More private information to take to men who see us all as potential criminals?"

"I need you to tell me why you're doing this. This isn't you, Robert," Hall said, refusing to be drawn into his narrative where she became the betrayer, the villain of their shared story.

"First names are for friends, Hall."

White pushed away from the door and moved into the living room. His gait was uneven but purposeful, each step claiming territory, marking boundaries of a space he controlled absolutely. Hall shifted position, maintaining distance, her mind mapping exits, cataloging potential weapons, calculating relative speed. The living room seemed to contract around them, the walls drawing closer, the air growing dense with unspoken things. White lowered himself into his armchair, leather creaking beneath him like a confession. He gestured toward the couch across from him. When she remained standing, something altered in his expression—pride displacing caution, as though some internal scale had finally tipped.

"You know," he said, his tone conversational, intimate, "I've always wondered what it would be like to tell someone. To really explain the art of it all." He settled back, hands resting on the chair arms, a monarch regarding a subject. "Seven years as partners, and you never really saw me. Not until Rachel Fenimore opened her mouth."

Hall's throat constricted. "You're admitting it?"

"You wearing a wire?"

She exhaled, a sound caught between derision and disbelief. "No, White." She emphasized his surname, a small reclamation of distance. "Not wearing a wire. I'm not investigating you. IA is. I just want to understand why you would sink so low."

"Low?" White's laughter rose genuine this time, rich with authentic pleasure. "I'm proud of it. Four perfect executions. Four deserving targets removed from this world." His fingers tapped against the leather, a patient rhythm, like rain on a windowpane. "Sandra Kim was first. The easiest. The smallest."

White's gaze hardened. "Don't look at me like that. You think it was easy for me? To just...switch?" He snapped his fingers, the sound sharp as a bone breaking. "I needed an easy one first. An easy win."

Hall remained still, watching White lick his lips. The mask of the partner she'd known for seven years was slipping away, revealing something underneath she had never seen before—or perhaps had never allowed herself to see, like a shadow glimpsed from the corner of one's eye that vanishes when confronted directly.

"I watched her for weeks. Learned her routine, where she parked every day, where the cameras were positioned." White's voice took on a storyteller's cadence, a man sharing a cherished memory. "I waited for the perfect night. No one around. Kim was half-asleep after a long shift. Twelve hours, I think. She didn't hear me, didn't even turn around."

Hall's stomach contracted as White described it, his tone casual as if recounting a mundane errand rather than murder.

"I used a baseball bat I bought with cash at a hardware store forty miles away. Made it look like a robbery." White's mouth curved slightly, as if savoring a private amusement. "The parking garage was nearly empty. No witnesses. I wore a ski mask, gloves, clothes I'd never wear normally. Took her purse, phone, watch. Made it twenty feet before I vomited."

"Evidence," Hall said, the word barely audible.

White shifted, the vinyl chair creaking beneath him. "No murder is perfect. But Carpenter and Robbins are idiots. I chose Mercy's parking lot specifically because it was their jurisdiction. I knew they'd get the case. Robbins practically genuflects when I walk into a room, so when I offered assistance, he jumped at it."

"You undermined their work from inside."

"Robbins actually bagged the vomit as evidence." White's voice lilted with amusement. "I told him, 'It's a hospital, people get sick all the time.' He bought it completely. Tossed it himself."

Hall looked up, her gaze catching on White's satisfied expression. "Review of recovered items," she murmured. "Jesus, White."

Something flickered in his eyes—recognition of her praise, perhaps. She wondered if he could see her methodology, the careful construction of rapport.

"Then Fowler?" she prompted.

"Then Fowler. The surgeon who promised to fix me. Who said I'd be normal again in six months. Who lied."

"You watched him too?"

"Three weeks. Learned his routine, his alarm code. It's remarkable what a good zoom lens captures these days." White leaned forward, his voice dropping. "His wife had book club every Thursday with other doctors' wives. I waited until he was half-asleep in front of the television. The back door was unlocked—imagine that. A man of his wealth, his importance, and he relied solely on his security system."

"How could you be certain?"

"I wasn't. I checked three separate nights. The third time, he made his mistake."

Hall settled into the chair opposite him, the metal cold through her slacks. She should have worn a wire. Should have activated the recording app on her phone. Should have been prepared for this confession that now unspooled between them like a toxic thread.

"With Kim's case still open, there was always the risk of reexamination. So with Fowler, I needed resolution. I used a crowbar on the back door frame. Created the appearance of forced entry." White's expression softened into something like nostalgia. "Then I ensured Pryor took the blame. Small-time burglar who'd hit three houses nearby that month. Arrested each time, bailed each time. Planting evidence from Fowler's house in his apartment was almost disappointingly simple."

"Why choose him?"

"Why not?"

The question hung in the stale air. Hall thought of Pryor—a young man serving life for a crime he hadn't committed. A man whose conviction she had helped secure. The knowledge crystallized inside her, sharp-edged and immovable.

"Jennifer Moss," she said, her voice steadier than the tremor in her fingertips.

"Ah, Jenny." White straightened, animated now. "Perhaps my finest work." He leaned closer, as if sharing a confidence. "Moss lived outside our precinct, and I wanted to keep you away from it. I cared about that, Hall. About protecting you. But once I started, I..."

He paused, his gaze distant for a moment before his features rearranged into a smile.

"I was meticulous. Waited until your vacation. She had that boyfriend—Parrish. Kevin Parrish. Volatile, jealous, history of bar fights. It was perfect casting." White's smile deepened, genuine in its terrible sincerity. "I observed them arguing at a restaurant. Followed her home. Timed it so the neighbors would hear through those paper-thin walls. Mimicked his voice, shouted the same accusations from dinner. Then I strangled her wearing the gloves from Kim's murder. Velázquez nearly spotted the fibers. Sharp detective. I sent him for something trivial, cleaned her neck. Evidence gone."

White stretched, arching his back against the chair. He settled himself with the unhurried movements of someone entirely at ease. Hall remained motionless, her body a collection of rigid angles.

"Strickland required more finesse," White continued, warming to his narrative. "She was vigilant. Perceptive. Always scanning her environment." His voice softened to something like reverence. "Did you know she had children? Two little girls she adored above everything. That's why suicide made such perfect cover. No one wants to believe a mother would take herself from her children. But when confronted with the evidence—the pills, the alcohol, the note—what choice do they have but to accept it?"

"Two girls," Hall said, remembering Rachel's words like a distant echo. "She would never have killed herself."

White shrugged, the gesture almost elegant in its dismissiveness. "It was a small detail. No one else questioned it."

"You are really okay with this?" The question hung between them, fragile as spun glass.

White stared for a moment, something ancient and terrible moving behind his eyes. "More than okay."

Hall's hand drifted toward her weapon—a movement so slight it might have been mistaken for a breath—but White noticed. His eyes tracked the motion with predatory precision, belying his relaxed posture.

"Not yet," he said softly. "I'm not finished with my story."

"And Rachel?" Hall asked, though the answer already lived in her throat like a stone. "Why wait so long for her?"

White's face transformed, hardness giving way to something that might have been tenderness in another life. "Rachel was special. The kind one. The one who held my hand when the pain was unbearable, who sat with me for hours just talking." The momentary softness calcified. "The one who warned me to take it easy, to follow the recovery plan, to not push myself too hard too fast. Advice I ignored, to my eternal regret."

His fingers found his hip, pressing against the epicenter of his suffering as if to confirm its constancy. "I wanted to kill her in the alley, but Lewis..."

"He saw," Hall said, the two words carrying the weight of everything that followed.

"It should have been perfect. I knew about her sleepwalking, knew she sometimes ended up outside her apartment building. All I had to do was wait." Shadows gathered in the hollows of White's face. "But that damned Ira Lewis came out of nowhere. Started yelling, tried to kick me. Hit my damaged leg." His fingers whitened against the chair arm. "I had to improvise. Let her take the fall like Pryor and Parrish. Stab him instead. Flee."

He extended his leg with a grimace that became a weak laugh. "Flee as best I could, anyway."

"It was a game with her," Hall said, recognizing the pattern now, seeing how the pieces had always fit together.

"I tried to run her down with my car a few days later," White continued, his voice as casual as if discussing the weather. "Missed by inches. The rock through the window at that disgusting motel was just to remind her I could find her anywhere." His smile bloomed slowly, reaching his eyes with an intimacy that chilled her. "The fear in her face when she saw me there—it was beautiful."

Hall felt something fundamental fracture inside her—not merely trust or friendship, but a more essential faith: the belief that one human being could ever truly know another.

"You're insane," she whispered, the words barely disturbing the air between them.

White's smile deepened. "No, Hall. I'm just in pain. And I decided those responsible should feel it too."

Chapter 22

White rose from his chair, his body betraying him with each increment of movement. He crossed to the kitchen counter that separated the living room from the cooking space, placing his palms flat on the surface, leaning forward like a professor about to deliver his most important lecture. Morning light filtered through the blinds, striping his face in alternating bands of illumination and shadow as he shifted his weight. Hall stood, her legs remembering their purpose before her mind commanded them.

"So, what do you think, Hall?" White asked. "I always thought it was bullshit when we tell suspects that if they confess, they will feel better." His fingers drummed against the counter, each tap like a tiny gunshot in the apartment's stillness. "But it's true. I feel better."

"The notes of your journal—" she began, clinging to evidence, to procedure, to anything solid in a world suddenly liquid with betrayal.

He smiled, genuine amusement warming his features. "I've already disposed of the journal. Barnes and Rocha can dismantle my apartment with a proper warrant and they'll find nothing."

White laughed, the sound bouncing off the kitchen cabinets and returning to her altered, wrong. "How was your sleepover?"

Heat rushed to Hall's face—not embarrassment but the sudden, visceral understanding of exposure. How did he know? Had he been... Of course he had.

"Oh yes," White said, reading her like a book he'd written himself. "Did you think I wouldn't watch the motel? Not your room, of course, I'm not a pervert." His smile widened, revealing teeth that seemed too sharp in the striped light. "Detective Hall sleeping with a murder suspect, breaking into her partner's home, reviewing files she had no right to review. It doesn't look good for you."

"Wh—" The syllable died in her throat.

"Did you like the knife plant?" he asked, cutting off her protest. "I carried that damned thing around the whole time, waiting for... something. Anything. And there it was. You and your girlfriend away from the car. Unlocked door." He savored the memory visibly. "You bought it. Even a half-assed defense attorney wouldn't, but you did."

"I knew it was you." The words tasted like ash.

"Bullshit," White said, the single word like a slap. "You arrested her. Not me. You. I couldn't have asked for better."

"You won't get away with this," Hall said, hearing the hollow ring of cliché even as the words left her mouth.

"I already have." White pushed away from the counter, each step toward her in the living room deliberate, a predator's approach disguised as a man's walk.

He stepped closer, and Hall felt her body tighten against the instinct to retreat. To show weakness now would be fatal. The man before her was no longer her partner—the transformation had happened so gradually she'd missed it entirely, like a photograph developing in reverse, revealing not what was created but what had always been there.

White's bulk eclipsed the door. The distance between them had collapsed to nothing, his presence a weight against her skin. His arrogance made him careless. While he savored his own cleverness, his own narrative of triumph, Hall's fingers began their slow pilgrimage toward her weapon.

Then memory intruded with brutal clarity. Her gun. The car. The careless decision that would cost everything.

"You're going to leave here," White said, his voice falling to the register reserved for confessionals and deathbeds. "You'll tell Barnes and Rocha everything I've said. They'll believe you. Rachel will corroborate." He regarded her with the weary pity reserved for lost causes. "But that's not how this ends, Hall."

His hand drifted to his hip, not seeking the familiar territory of old pain, but something more immediate, more final.

"Your end is here. Now." White drew his service weapon with the fluid economy that comes from ten thousand repetitions, muscle memory perfected in empty ranges and sleepless nights. "This ends with a story—my partner became unstable, dangerous. I had no choice." His words fell between them like stones. "This ends with me alive and you a footnote in tomorrow's report."

The barrel rose toward her heart, unwavering as a judge's gaze.

She moved before thought crystallized—pure animal reflex propelling her forward even as White's weapon tracked her movement. The collision was intimate, her shoulder finding the soft hollow beneath his ribs, driving breath from his body in a harsh exhalation. The gun discharged, a thunderclap in the confined space. Plaster rained down like confetti, marking the moment.

Metal skittered across hardwood. Disarmed.

But then his arms enfolded her, massive and inevitable, his weight bearing her down as gravity reclaimed them both.

Pain blossomed where her shoulder met the floor, White's body pressing the air from her lungs in increments. His face hovered inches from hers, features she had memorized over countless stakeouts and shared meals now contorted into something she had never truly seen before—the mask finally slipping to reveal what had always waited beneath.

"You stupid bitch," he whispered, the words warm against her skin. "This is how it ends."

Hall's knee sought his groin but found his thigh instead, connecting with the old injury he'd nursed for months. White's face transformed, pain stripping away the last veneer of humanity. His hands found her throat with the precision of someone who had studied anatomy, who understood exactly how fragile the human body truly was.

Darkness gathered at the edges of her vision, a curtain drawing closed on the final act. Her fingers scrabbled against his, seeking purchase against the inevitable. How strange that it should end here, in this apartment where she had once accepted coffee, shared jokes, felt safe in the presence of his family photographs and worn furniture.

With the last reserves of oxygen-starved strength, Hall twisted beneath him. Her hips bucked upward, legs searching for leverage against the treacherous smoothness of the floor. The unexpected movement loosened his grip for half a heartbeat—enough. The heel of her hand connected with the bridge of his nose, cartilage yielding with a sound like wet kindling breaking.

Blood erupted between them, warm and copper-bright, baptizing them both in the sacrament of violence. White reeled backward, hands flying to his face, a sound escaping him that belonged to no language Hall had ever heard.

She rolled away, drawing air through a throat that felt scorched and narrowed. Each breath was rebirth, painful and precious. The coffee table separated them now—a border neither substantial nor reassuring. White rose to his knees, blood threading between his fingers, staining the shirt she had complimented just last week. His gun lay somewhere beyond reach, lost in the geography of their struggle.

"You're dead," he said, the words thick and distorted, blood painting his teeth in the half-light. "You're fucking dead."

He lunged across the coffee table, sending it skating away, a constellation of magazines and coasters scattering in its wake. Hall's back found the entertainment center, the solid edge of oak pressing against her spine like an accusation. His fist connected with her jaw, snapping her head sideways. Blood filled her mouth where teeth had pierced flesh, the taste of pennies and childhood falls.

Pain bloomed through her skull, but instinct commandeered what conscious thought could not. She tucked her chin, protecting her throat as White swung again, his fist glancing off her shoulder instead of finding her face. His weight trapped her against the entertainment center, shelves digging into her spine, a picture frame toppling to shatter beside them—one more broken thing in a room suddenly full of them.

White's breathing came in wet, ragged gasps, each exhale misting blood across Hall's skin. His eyes had gone wild, pupils blown wide, a man transformed by some terrible alchemy of rage and pain into something barely recognizable as the detective she'd known. He reached again for her throat, fingers seeking the tender places already darkening on her skin.

Knuckle to the Adam's apple.

White gagged.

Hall pushed against his chest with everything she had, creating just enough space to bring her knee up between them, driving it into the soft vulnerability of his stomach. He doubled over, and she shoved him sideways, sending him crashing into the coffee table that had already capsized in their struggle.

She lurched away, tasting copper, feeling the throb of what would become something more lasting than memory across her ribs. White lay amid the wreckage of his coffee table—a tableau of violence rendered in mahogany and flesh—blood from his nose pooling on the hardwood floor beneath him. He pushed himself up on one elbow, eyes finding hers, a smile spreading across his ruined face.

His hand moved toward something beneath the shattered remnants of the table—his gun, Hall realized with a clarity that seemed almost separate from her pain, hidden by the debris of what they had become to each other.

Hall stumbled toward the door, her free hand fumbling behind her for the doorknob, fingers slipping on the metal, slick with sweat or blood—distinctions that seemed suddenly academic.

The door yielded at her touch, the hallway beyond empty, silent, offering a reprieve if she could just reach it without turning her back on the man whose transformation she had witnessed like some terrible privilege.

"This isn't over," White called after her as she backed into the hallway. "It's just beginning."

Hall fled, hands searching for her phone. Her footsteps echoed off the walls like distant gunshots, the space between them and whatever White might become growing with each stride. The stairwell door loomed ahead—she couldn't risk the elevator, couldn't bear being sealed in a metal box if White decided to follow through on his promise.

She took the stairs three at a time, each landing sending shocks through her bruised ribs, each breath a negotiation. Five flights down, air coming in painful gasps, the taste of blood still coating her tongue like a memory she couldn't spit out. The lobby stretched before her, her car and what passed for safety just beyond.

Emergency call. 911. Tap.

She pushed through the lobby doors into midday sun, obscenely bright against the darkness of what had happened in White's apartment. Her car waited where she'd left it, keys still in her pocket, somehow intact through the struggle, as if some things could remain unchanged while others fractured beyond repair.

Hall slid behind the wheel, locking the doors, fingers clumsy with her phone.

"911, what's your emergency?"

"Detective Carolyn Hall."

She leaned across the seat.

"Badge number 4-7-2-9."

She unlocked her glove compartment. Retrieved her gun.

"Officer needs assistance." Her voice emerged thick, words catching on split lips. "Suspect is armed and dangerous. Robert White, detective, New Hanan PD. He has his service weapon."

"Ma'am, what's your location?"

"17 Waller Street apartments, parking lot. I'm in my car—" She glanced at the building's entrance, expecting White to materialize at any moment, a nightmare stepping into daylight. "I can't—"

"That's okay, ma'am. Are you injured?"

"Yes. Assault. I need—" Hall's breath hitched. "Send units. He's in apartment 5F. Robert White. He's armed. Do not approach alone. He's—" She stopped, the truth of what White was—what he had always been beneath the surface—catching in her throat like something swallowed wrong.

"Units are en route, Detective Hall. Stay on the line with me. Are you safe where you are?"

Hall stared at the building's glass doors, at the elevator visible through them, a frame within a frame, waiting to deliver something she wasn't prepared to face. "I don't know."

White didn't emerge. No figure came limping through those doors, no pursuit materialized. The seconds stretched, each one carrying away a small measure of the adrenaline that had sustained her, leaving pain and confusion in its wake.

Why wasn't he coming after her? He'd said she wouldn't leave the apartment alive, had confessed to four murders, had tried to kill her with his bare hands. Yet here she sat, watching an empty doorway, waiting for an attack that didn't come, as if violence, once unleashed, should follow its own inexorable logic to the end.

Sirens wailed in the distance, growing louder as backup approached. Hall touched her split lip, wincing at the sting, the reality of what had happened beginning to settle into her bones. Her partner had tried to kill her. Had confessed to four murders. Had almost succeeded in making her the fifth.

Chapter 23

Hall's fingers trembled as she dialed Rachel's number, the phone slipping in her blood-slick grip like a bar of soap in wet hands. Each breath sent pain radiating through her ribs—delicate fractures of trust made physical—while copper lingered on her tongue, a penny-bright reminder of mortality. The sirens crescendoed now, yet her gaze remained fixed on the lobby doors of White's building, waiting for the man who had been her partner, her friend, to emerge with murder in his eyes. How strange that she could still recognize those eyes after discovering she had never truly known them at all.

The call went straight to voicemail. Rachel's phone was off—or worse, White had somehow reached her first, impossible as that seemed within the collapsing timeline of betrayal. "Rachel, call 911. Get police officers near you. White is on a rampage." Her voice sounded foreign to her own ears, as if belonging to someone she had once been.

A flicker of movement drew her attention to the side exit, where White's massive frame appeared, limping but purposeful, moving toward a dark sedan with the determined grace of a wounded predator.

"No, no, no," Hall whispered, the words a prayer without faith as she fumbled with her keys. White climbed into his car, and she watched with a curious detachment that sometimes accompanies moments of pure terror. She started her engine just as White's sedan roared to life, tires releasing a high, animal scream against asphalt.

White's car shot past her, missing her front bumper by inches—close enough that she felt rather than saw the displacement of air. He accelerated hard, blowing through the lot's exit and onto the street without hesitation, as if the rules that governed ordinary lives had ceased to apply to him. Perhaps they had. Hall slammed her car into drive and followed, phone pressed to her ear as dispatch answered again.

"Suspect is mobile," she reported, voice raw from White's assault, from the memory of his hands at her throat. "Black sedan heading east on Waller Street from suspect's residence. I am in pursuit." The operator acknowledged, asking if Hall needed medical attention. The question seemed absurd, disconnected from the urgency of the moment. Hall ignored it, her focus narrowing to the back of White's car as it weaved through traffic ahead of her—a dark ship on a receding tide.

"Detective Hall?" the dispatcher pressed, voice tinny and distant.

"Send units to Star—" Hall yanked the wheel left to avoid another car, her phone tumbling to the floor like a discarded thought. "Starlight! Starlight!" She shouted, hoping the operator could hear.

Faster.

The car surged forward as she pressed the gas pedal to the floor, her body cataloging every bump and turn with sharp reminders of the fight she'd just survived. Pain blossomed between her ribs, bright as neon, then faded to a dull throb that matched the pulse in her temples.

White took a hard left onto Parkhill Avenue, cutting across two lanes and forcing a delivery truck to brake suddenly. Hall followed, her tires releasing a plaintive wail as she navigated through the gap White had created before it closed, like threading a needle with trembling hands.

"Come on, move!" she shouted at an SUV hesitating before her. The family inside—a mother, father, two children in the back—stared with wide eyes as she swerved around them, their faces a tableau of ordinary life suddenly interrupted by violence. How many such moments had she witnessed from the other side, she wondered, before becoming the interruption herself?

The chase led them away from New Hanan's commercial district, past storefronts that had once seemed familiar but now blurred into unfamiliar shapes.

Faster.

She was gaining on him, the distance between them contracting like a wound healing in reverse.

White blew through a red light, narrowly missing a crossing courier on a bicycle who wobbled but maintained balance. Hall followed, wincing as horns blared and brakes screeched around her—a discordant symphony of near-misses. Her pulse pounded in her ears, drowning out the voice of reason that told her to back off, to let other units pick up the pursuit. That voice sounded suspiciously like White's from earlier days, when he had still been the senior partner she trusted.

They tore down Alameda Boulevard, past restaurants where outdoor diners froze mid-bite, forks suspended between plate and mouth, past pedestrians who became momentary witnesses to a chase they would later describe with increasing embellishment.

White's brake lights suddenly flared red—bright as fresh blood—his car skidding as he came to an abrupt stop in the middle of the street. Hall had only seconds to react, yanking her wheel hard left. The g-force slammed her injured body against the door, a fresh wave of pain washing over her as her car swerved to avoid collision. She overcorrected, clipping a parked car before wrestling control back from momentum and panic.

By the time she'd steadied her vehicle, White was already accelerating again, making a sharp right onto Hemsfield Lane, a narrow, one-way residential street lined with trees that had witnessed a hundred years of the city's secrets. Hall cursed, fighting her car back into the proper lane, precious seconds lost in the maneuver, seconds in which White might disappear like a memory one tries desperately to hold upon waking.

"Officer in pursuit of suspect on Hemsfield, heading north," she called out to her phone, not knowing if the line remained open, not caring. Her words dissolved into a gasp as pain lanced through her ribs, the adrenaline no longer sufficient to mask her injuries or the deeper wound of betrayal that had preceded them.

She reached the turn White had taken, only to find her path barricaded by pedestrians crossing the street—a cluster of teenagers drifting through the intersection with that peculiar teenage languor, as if time belonged exclusively to them. They moved in their own bubble of laughter and slouched shoulders, utterly disconnected from the desperation pulsing through her veins. Hall's palm struck the horn, sharp as panic. The sound scattered them like startled birds, but not swiftly enough. Through the gap in their ranks, she watched White's car shrink into the distance, swallowed by another turn at the far end of the block.

"Move!" The word tore from her throat. "Police!"

The last of them cleared her path with reluctant, backward glances. Hall pressed the accelerator, feeling the car lurch forward as the tires caught and slipped on the trolley tracks embedded in the old cobblestones. Their metal edges gleamed dully in the afternoon light, wet from an earlier rain. By the time she reached the intersection where White had vanished, the street offered nothing but strangers' cars crawling through the arteries of downtown—brake lights blinking like red warnings, none of them his.

Hall wrenched the wheel, cutting across traffic toward the expressway entrance. Her eyes dropped briefly to the floorboard, searching for her phone. The empty space where it should have been made her stomach tighten. "Starlight Motel!" she shouted into the void, hoping the open line to dispatch hadn't disconnected in the chaos.

The car surged onto the expressway ramp, suspension groaning as it tilted upward. For one weightless moment, Hall felt herself lifting slightly from the seat. Then gravity reclaimed her as the midday sun caught her windshield, transforming it into a blinding sheet of white light. She squinted, one hand raised against the glare as she merged into traffic.

Three exits to go. She slipped into the left lane where cars moved faster, then to the center to pass a slow-moving truck, then back left again. Weaving through the current of vehicles like a needle through fabric. Horns protested her passage. Brake lights flared around her like sudden wounds.

Two exits remaining. The silence from dispatch pressed against her ears. Another quick glance at the floor—still nothing. Hall couldn't spare the mental space to worry about it. Her focus narrowed to the road, to the distance remaining, to the knowledge that with each second, White drew closer to Rachel.

Next exit. Just two blocks beyond the highway. Almost there.

Hall eased off the accelerator as she approached the motel, her eyes scanning the vehicles lining the curb. Dread pooled cold and heavy in her stomach. There—wedged between a fire hydrant and a pickup truck, its front wheels mounted on the sidewalk at a hasty angle—sat White's black sedan. A smear of blood marked the driver's window, dark and damning. Confirmation that her former partner had indeed come for Rachel.

She pulled in behind White's car and killed her engine. Her hand found her phone on the floor where it had fallen during the chase. It rang immediately. Dispatch, their voice taut with concern. "White's vehicle is at the Starlight Motel," she said before they could speak. "He's inside. I'm going in."

"Detective Hall, wait for—"

She ended the call. The words died against her thumb. She had no patience for caution, for protocol, for anything that would place more time between Rachel and safety. White was in that building. Rachel was in that building. And between them stood Hall, the only person who understood the full architecture of White's crimes, the only one who could prevent him from completing his grotesque mission.

Hall drew her weapon as she approached the entrance, its weight familiar against her palm. Her badge waited in her other hand, cold metal warmed by her grip. The office manager looked up as she entered, his eyes fixing immediately on the gun, widening with alarm.

"What the hell—"

Hall closed the distance to the desk in three quick strides, badge raised like a shield.

"New Hanan Police Department. Did a man come through here? Big guy, bloody nose, limping?"

"Five minutes ago." The manager's voice thinned with nervousness. "Cop too."

Hall turned toward the elevators, her body already in motion. The hallway stretched before her, cluttered with the debris of hotel life—luggage abandoned against walls, room service trays waiting for collection. Each obstacle forced her to twist, to sidestep, sending fresh waves of pain radiating from where White's hands had marked her. She jabbed the elevator call button once, then again, as if repetition might summon it faster, might compress the seconds ticking away above her.

Chapter 24

Not fast enough.

The stairwell door opened onto a different world—colder, harder, honest in its utilitarian purpose. Concrete and steel held no pretense of comfort, no warmth. The air smelled of dust and disuse. Hall took the first flight two steps at a time, her left hand sliding along the metal railing, its chill seeping into her skin. Her right hand gripped her weapon, the textured handle pressing reassurance into her palm.

By the second flight, each footfall sent a jolt through her injured body. White's rage had left its signature across her ribs, her back, her shoulders—bruises blooming beneath her clothing like a map of his betrayal. Cuts from earlier stung with the salt of dried sweat. The metallic taste of blood lingered at the corner of her mouth where her lip had split against her teeth.

Her phone vibrated against her hip. Dispatch again, no doubt, calling with instructions to wait for backup, to follow procedure, to remember her training. Hall let it ring. Time was a luxury Rachel didn't have, a currency Hall couldn't spend on caution.

Third floor. Hall's breathing came in controlled bursts now, measured against the pain. The academy had taught her this—how to push through physical discomfort, how to maintain focus when the body pleaded for rest. Fourth floor. No training had prepared her for this particular betrayal, for the knowledge that the man she'd trusted with her life for years had been hiding a monster beneath his badge.

As she neared the fifth-floor landing, voices filtered through the stairwell's concrete acoustics. A man's voice, deep and insistent, followed by the higher pitch of a woman's response. White and Rachel. Hall slowed her ascent, each step now deliberate, silent. She eased the stairwell door open just enough to slip through, wincing at the slight creak of the hinges that seemed to echo in the corridor like an announcement of her arrival.

The hallway stretched before her, an endless corridor of identical doors that seemed to recede into infinity, with 512 waiting at the vanishing point. Hall ran. Pain bloomed across her ribs, but her body relegated it to background sensation—the way it always did when survival became the only calculation that mattered. Her mind sharpened, edges of perception crystallizing with the peculiar clarity that arrived only in moments when death felt close enough to touch.

The door handle to 512 turned with excruciating slowness.

A sliver of light appeared as the door eased open, revealing fragments of the room beyond—the edge of a laminate table, the rumpled corner of a bed. Nothing in this partial geometry revealed where White and Rachel waited within. Hall slipped through the narrow opening, weapon raised before her like a divining rod.

Rachel stood flattened against the far wall, her body tensed beneath the oversized T-shirt Hall had brought her days earlier. Her hands hovered uselessly before her chest, neither surrender nor defense. Her face had gone the color of old paper, eyes dilated with terror. White stood between them, his back to Hall, shoulders bunched beneath fabric gone stiff with dried blood. His service weapon extended toward Rachel with the terrible steadiness of absolute conviction.

"Drop the gun, White." Hall's voice cut through the room's stale air, each syllable precise as a scalpel. "It's over."

White's body registered her presence—a nearly imperceptible tightening across his shoulders, a fractional shift in his stance—but his arm remained extended, the weapon unwavering. For one terrible heartbeat, Hall saw the future collapse into a single possibility: White's finger tightening on the trigger in one final act of spite, a last rebellion against whatever remained of order in his world.

"I was wondering when you'd show up," he said, voice eerily calm, as though they were meeting for coffee rather than this final reckoning. "Figured you'd come for her. Always had a savior complex, Hall." He turned then, a deliberate pivot that kept his weapon trained on Rachel even as his face came into view. "All these years, and I still can't predict everything you'll do." The words emerged as a rasp, dragged across vocal cords gone raw.

The sight of him struck Hall with physical force. Blood had dried in dark rivulets from his nostrils, painting his mouth and chin a grotesque mask. His shirt—once white, now rust-brown and black in places—crackled slightly when he moved. He favored his right leg, his bad hip clearly punishing him for their earlier struggle.

Hall advanced, letting the door whisper shut behind her.

It was his eyes that froze the breath in her lungs. She recognized that gaze—had seen it in men who'd crossed invisible lines and knew there was no crossing back. The hollow stare of someone who had abandoned tomorrow and existed only in the desperate now, a man already haunting himself.

"Put the gun down," Hall repeated, edging deeper into the room. The familiar space had transformed into alien territory. The table was no longer furniture but obstacle, the bed no longer for rest but a River Styx between them. White's presence had transmuted the ordinary into a killing ground. "This doesn't have to end with more blood."

White's laugh held no humor, just a hollow acknowledgment of some private joke. "That's where you're wrong, Hall. That's exactly how it ends."

Behind him, Rachel had gone preternaturally still, as if motion itself might trigger catastrophe. Her eyes found Hall's for the briefest moment, a wordless plea passing between them. She was searching for direction, for some signal. Hall kept her face deliberately blank, unwilling to telegraph intent across a room where White could intercept every glance.

"You're surrounded," Hall said, measuring another step forward, closing the distance between them by careful increments. "Units on the way. There's no path out of this building that doesn't lead to a cell."

White gestured with his weapon, a small movement that made Rachel flinch as if he'd struck her. "You think I care about jail? You think that matters to me now?" His voice rose, cracking with an emotion that seemed to surprise even him. He swallowed, steadied himself. "There's nothing they can do to me that's worse than what I live with every day. Nothing."

Hall calculated distances with the cold precision of someone whose life depended on geometry. Fifteen feet of hardwood separated her from White, another fifteen beyond him to Rachel. No clear approach that wouldn't place Rachel in a crossfire. She had a clean shot at White, but his weapon remained trained on Rachel. A perfect stalemate with no elegant solution.

"Partner."

The word hung between them, freighted with history. White's attention shifted fractionally toward Hall, the barrel of his gun drifting almost imperceptibly away from Rachel. Hall tracked the movement, waiting for an opening that might never come.

"They're coming."

Sirens wailed in the distance, growing louder with each second. Promised salvation, moments away. White heard them too; his head tilted slightly, tracking the sound, measuring his remaining time just as she was.

"You can still walk out of here," Hall said, offering a lie they both recognized in its shape and weight. "Put the gun down, White. Let Rachel go, and we'll get you help. Real help this time, not just pills and promises."

White's laugh contained a genuine warmth that disoriented her, like finding a flower blooming in winter frost. "Help? From who? The same medical system that hollowed me out?" He shook his head, his features tightening as the movement pulled at his wounds. "No, Hall. We've crossed that threshold now."

He shifted toward Rachel, who pressed herself harder against the wall. The salmon-framed print beside her surrendered to gravity, tumbling with a crack that scattered silence like birds from a wire. Hall and White flinched in unison—a moment of shared humanity that vanished before she could grasp its significance.

For half a heartbeat, White's attention drifted to the fallen artwork.

Hall felt her muscles coil, her body preparing without conscious command. The space between decision and action narrowed to nothing.

But White recovered with the instinct of someone accustomed to pain's interruptions. His weapon steadied on Rachel once more, his gaze finding Hall with a lucidity that acknowledged her calculations. The feverish light in his eyes had crystallized into something Hall recognized from a hundred interrogation rooms—the peculiar serenity that comes when someone finally surrenders to their darkest impulse.

"It ends today," White said, his voice carrying the flat certainty of a man reading his own obituary.

He adjusted his stance, a grimace flickering across his face as his damaged leg protested. The gun remained level, an extension of his will rather than his flesh. Hall could see the layers of him peeling away—the professional mask, the patient mask, the reasonable man mask—revealing the architecture of obsession beneath. She had witnessed this unveiling before, this moment when suspects finally allowed themselves to speak the unspeakable, to articulate the logic that had seemed so sound in the echo chamber of their minds.

Hall kept her weapon aligned with White's sternum, her finger resting alongside the trigger guard. She said nothing, allowing silence to fill the space between them like rising water. Let him believe the current still flowed his way.

Behind him, Rachel's eyes measured the distance to the bathroom doorway, a prey animal calculating escape routes. Hall gave an almost imperceptible shake of her head. Not yet. The timing wasn't right; the variables weren't aligned.

"We can figure this out, you and I," she said, her voice pitched to suggest intimacy, as if they were the only two people who could possibly understand each other.

A bead of sweat traced the topography of White's face, cutting through dried blood like a river through ancient stone. His breathing had quickened, shallow and uneven. Pain was eroding him from within—not just the familiar demon in his hip, but the fresh injuries from their struggle. Hall could see mortality pressing against him from all sides, time contracting around his body.

Outside, sirens layered over one another, a dissonant chorus drawing nearer. White tilted his head at the sound, listening with the distant curiosity of someone hearing music from another room. "They're coming for me," he said, the words floating detached from emotion, a simple observation of fact.

"Yes," Hall confirmed. "It's over, White."

He shook his head—a small, tight movement, like a man trying not to disturb something broken inside. "Not until it's finished. Not until the circle is closed." His gaze returned to Rachel, the gun an unwavering point of convergence.

The sirens reached their crescendo before cutting to silence—tactical teams positioning themselves around the building. Hall could feel the operation unfolding beneath them: the perimeter establishing itself, SWAT units preparing entry points, the command center assembling its nervous system. Soon the hallway would fill with men and women trained to end situations like this, one way or another.

"It's over, White," Hall said again, her voice gentling, the way she might speak to someone standing too close to an edge. "They're here now. There's no path out of this building. No way to complete what you started."

"I could complete it right now," White said, the gun shifting almost imperceptibly, finding the center of Rachel's chest with terrible precision. "One more shot. The last one."

"And then what?" Hall asked. The question hung between them, heavier than the gun. "The pain will still be there. Killing Rachel won't alter that equation."

Something shifted in White's expression—perhaps exhaustion finally claiming territory, or recognition seeping through the cracks of his resolve. The hand holding the gun trembled, a hairline fracture in the foundation of his control.

"It has to stop," he said, and Hall couldn't tell if he meant the pain or the killing or his own existence. "It has to end somehow."

"This is how it ends," Hall said, maintaining her aim, her voice steady. "Not with another death. Not with more blood. It ends with you putting down the gun and walking out of here alive."

She'd rehearsed these words in her mind a dozen times since they'd tracked White to this apartment, but speaking them aloud felt different—like offering a prayer she didn't quite believe in.

Hall watched White's shoulders bend, aging him before her eyes. The man who had once filled doorways with his presence now seemed to collapse inward, as if some internal architecture had finally given way. She heard movement in the hallway outside—the soft tread of tactical boots, the whisper of body armor, the nearly silent communications of a SWAT team preparing to breach. Each sound distinct yet part of a familiar choreography she had witnessed too many times.

White heard it too. His head tilted toward the door, eyes closing briefly as he processed the reality of his situation. When they opened again, something had changed—the wild desperation replaced by a quiet resignation that unsettled her more than his rage ever had.

"It's really over, isn't it?" he asked, not looking at Hall now but at some middle distance, some future suddenly rendered in perfect clarity.

"Yes," Hall said. "It's over."

White nodded once, a short, sharp movement like the period at the end of a sentence. The gun in his hand lowered, not dropping completely but no longer aimed at Rachel. His body seemed to settle into itself, like sediment after a storm.

"Okay," he said, the word barely audible over the approaching footsteps. "Okay."

Chapter 25

"O kay."

The word hung between them like frost on a window—delicate, temporary, obscuring what lay beyond. Hall maintained her aim, searching White's face for deception. Experience had taught her that surrender came in stages—acceptance, then bargaining, then sometimes a final, desperate act. The gun in White's hand had lowered, but not enough. Not yet. Behind him, Rachel remained still, her breathing shallow and quick, her gaze fixed on the weapon that moments before had been her executioner.

Something crumbled in White's expression—the last wall of justification, of righteous anger that had fueled him through these terrible days. He looked down at the gun as though it were an artifact from another life, something excavated rather than chosen.

"I'm so tired," he whispered. "I'm just so goddamn tired, Hall."

The door shuddered. "Police! Open up!"

"One!"

White's massive frame seemed to diminish, shoulders curving inward like a man suddenly aware of his own mortality.

"Two!"

"I'm sorry," he mouthed, the words without sound, meant for her alone. In that moment, Hall saw a flash of the partner she had known—the man who had once pulled her from a burning car, who had stood beside her at her father's funeral.

"Three!"

White's arm snapped up with terrible purpose, the gun arcing toward Rachel with the inevitability of a pendulum completing its swing.

"No!" The shout tore from Hall's throat as she recalibrated her aim. But White was faster, years of muscle memory and desperation driving him forward when everything else in him had surrendered.

He twisted, pivoting on his good leg, and fired a single shot. The sound fractured the air, echoing off walls thick with old fear. Behind him, Rachel's head snapped backward. Bone and drywall; a white bloom across wallpaper. Her body remained upright for a heartbeat before sliding downward along the wall, a marionette with severed strings.

White barked out a laugh, the sound primal and broken, as if something ancient had escaped from deep within him. His eyes met Hall's across the room, and she saw nothing of her partner there—only a terrible completion, the look of a man who had finally scratched an itch that had been just beyond reach for years.

Hall pulled the trigger.

The first shot punched White under the collarbone. Fabric parted, skin ruptured, bone yielded. He staggered back half a step, surprise washing over his face like cold water. Hall fired again, the second round hitting three inches lower, center mass, the impact folding him at the waist. The third shot followed without thought, her finger moving on instinct born of countless hours on the range. This bullet caught White at the sternum, and something essential gave way inside him.

His gun clattered to the floor. White looked down at the three spreading circles of red on his shirt with mild bewilderment, as if confronted with a puzzle he couldn't quite solve. He opened his mouth to speak, but found no words. Instead, he sank to his knees, then toppled sideways onto the hardwood. The sound of his body hitting the floor was dull and final—a book closing on the last page.

"Officer down!" Hall shouted, the words seeming to come from someone else.

The door burst inward, splintering at the frame. Black-clad figures swarmed into the room, weapons raised, voices calling commands that blurred into white noise. The world had narrowed to two fixed points—White on the floor, blood pooling beneath him like spilled wine, and Rachel crumpled against the wall, unmoving.

"Officer down! Officer down!" someone was shouting, the words reaching Hall as if through water. "We need medical in here now!"

Hall moved without conscious thought, her body on autopilot while her mind remained trapped in the moment before—the instant when White's finger had tightened on the trigger. She stepped over his hulking form, her foot mechanically nudging his weapon farther away, a gesture of procedure embedded so deeply it survived even this. Three long strides carried her to Rachel, each footfall echoing strangely in her ears as though coming from somewhere else, someone else.

Her gun slipped from nerveless fingers, forgotten before it clattered to the floor. She knelt beside Rachel's still form, her knees settling in warmth she refused to acknowledge.

"I need assistance!" The words tore from her throat, unfamiliar and raw. "Officer down and civilian hit! Medical, now!"

Someone spoke beside her, syllables washing over her like water, meaning nothing.

Her hands hovered above Rachel, training battling the terrible knowledge that spread through her body like cold poison. The wound left no room for hope—a neat, almost delicate entry at the temple had become catastrophe on exit, taking with it fragments of bone and matter that now decorated the spines of Hall's books like macabre confetti. Rachel's eyes remained open, fixed on some distant point Hall couldn't see, the first cloudy veil of death already drawing across them.

Hall reached toward Rachel's throat, two fingers extended in a gesture of procedure rather than possibility. A hand caught hers before she could complete the motion.

"Hall." A voice cut through the cottony silence in her head. Fingers gripped her shoulder, trying to pull her away. "Detective Hall, we need to clear the scene."

She shrugged off the touch, remaining beside Rachel, unable to process the finality of what lay before her. Seven years of partnership had culminated in this tableau of blood—a woman dead because Hall hadn't moved quickly enough, hadn't recognized the depth of White's obsession, hadn't seen the monster growing beneath his skin.

Someone spoke into a radio nearby, the words "coroner" and "multiple casualties" floating disconnected through the air. Another voice methodically checked for signs of life. The phrase "no pulse" drifted across the room, confirming what the stillness had already told her.

"Detective." The hand returned to her shoulder, more insistent now. "We need to clear the scene for medical. Come with me."

Hall looked up to find a uniformed officer she didn't recognize, his face young beneath his tactical helmet. His eyes held the wary compassion of someone approaching an animal that might either collapse or attack. She allowed him to help her stand, her body rising with the wooden compliance of shock.

The officer guided her toward the door, one hand firm on her elbow. "Where—where is my gun?" she asked, raising her empty hands before her eyes as if seeing them for the first time.

As they stepped into the hallway, the reality of what had happened crashed over Hall like a physical wave. The corridor tilted beneath her feet, the walls seeming to breathe in and out with unnatural rhythm. Her stomach heaved, and she doubled over, vomit splattering the tile between her feet.

She sank to her knees, dimly aware of the officer calling for assistance. The taste of bile mixed with the copper tang of blood where her split lip had reopened. Hall pressed her forehead against the wall, its coolness momentarily anchoring her as the world continued its sickening spin.

"Easy," someone said, a woman's voice. Cool hands pressed against her back. "Take a breath. Keep breathing. That's it."

Hall obeyed without thought. In. Out. The mechanical action of drawing air provided momentary structure in a world suddenly without foundation. Down the hallway, the elevator dinged, and a new wave of personnel spilled out—paramedics with equipment, more officers, someone from the medical examiner's office carrying a case that seemed too small for its purpose.

The hallway had filled with neighbors, their faces a blur of curiosity and horror. A woman in a bathrobe pressed fingers to her mouth, eyes wide. An elderly man with a newspaper tucked under his arm shook his head slowly, muttering something about the neighborhood going to hell. Back inside folks, it's all under control.

Hall closed her eyes, shutting them out. Behind her closed lids, she saw Rachel's face in the instant before White fired—the dawning realization, the beginning of fear cut short by the bullet. She saw White's laugh, the satisfaction in his eyes as he completed his mission. She saw the end of everything in blood on the motel room floor.

Someone draped a foil blanket over Hall's shoulders, the material crinkling with each shallow breath. Gentle hands guided her toward the elevator. Outside, the cold air struck her face like a rebuke. She hadn't realized she was shaking until the chill settled around her like a second skin. Voices continued to wash over her, questions she couldn't process, instructions she couldn't follow.

"I need to get her to the ambulance," someone was saying. "She's in shock."

Hall wanted to protest that she was fine, that she needed to stay, to explain, to understand—but when she opened her mouth, no words came. Only a sound that might have been a laugh or a sob escaped, a noise she didn't recognize as her own. The world contracted to a pinpoint of light, then expanded into darkness.

Epilogue

Rain drummed against the window of Benny's Coffee, a steady patter that kept time with Hall's thoughts. She curled her fingers around a cup gone cold twenty minutes ago and watched a moving truck pull away from her old apartment building across the street. The world had folded itself around her absence, creased and smoothed where she once had been. New tenants in her old place. Green shoots rising through cemetery soil. Only Hall remained caught in that fraction of a second when White completed his design, when Rachel's blood transformed the wall into something terrible and beautiful.

The couple who'd taken her apartment seemed kind enough—young professionals with easy smiles. The woman had laughed earlier that morning as they carried a potted fern up the front steps, the sound traveling to Hall through layers of rain and traffic noise. It struck her as right that someone could laugh in those rooms again.

Her reflection ghosted in the window glass, and Hall looked away. The face there belonged to no one she recognized—cheeks hollowed like river valleys after drought, shadowed half-moons beneath her eyes, hair hanging limp as forgotten laundry. Her polo shirt draped across shoulders that had carried more flesh three months ago. The department psychiatrist had a clinical term for the vanishing of twenty pounds. Hall understood it differently, as penance.

A waitress approached, coffeepot tilted in offering. "Refill?"

Hall shook her head. When she lifted her hand, it trembled—a slight vibration, like a tuning fork struck too softly for anyone else to notice, but she had learned its warning.

"Actually," she said, her voice rusty hinges rarely opened, "just the check."

The moving truck disappeared around a corner. Her apartment existed now only in memory, furniture either sold or abandoned when they posted the papers on her door. Her car had vanished from its accustomed space after the second payment failed to materialize. The police department had a phrase for what they'd done to her—"disability leave"—and Captain Washington had said, "until you're ready to come back," but they both recognized the lie beneath the words. She had become a ghost in her own life.

The review board had cleared her. No criminal charges. White had killed Rachel Fenimore and then shifted his weapon toward Hall. Any officer would have responded the same way. Barnes had said so. The board had concluded it. Her own memory confirmed it.

But memory was water, taking the shape of whatever vessel held it. In dreams, time stretched like taffy. In dreams, she felt her finger against the trigger, the pressure building as White's arm began to move toward Rachel. Always, she woke at the same moment—when she understood there had been nothing to be done.

The coffee shop hummed around her. A woman at the next table laughed into her phone, the sound like metal against glass. Two men debated numbers by the counter, their voices rising and falling in waves that broke against Hall's consciousness. A child dropped something metal—a spoon perhaps—and the clatter traveled through Hall's body like an electrical current. The world had become too sharp, too present, too insistent.

Her hand shook harder now. Time for the pills. The bottle nestled in her pocket, always within reach. The psychiatrist had written the prescriptions with a flourish—this one for the constant dread, that one for when the panic rose like floodwater. They were meant to soften the world's edges, but they did nothing for the dreams.

The waitress returned with her check, eyes narrowing. "You okay? Something about you seems—"

"Fine," Hall said, fishing in her wallet for what remained of last week's cash. "Just tired."

The word had become a talisman after three months. Fine was the answer when your partner revealed himself as something monstrous. Fine was what you said when you watched possibility bleed out across linoleum. Fine was the shield you raised when the department therapist asked about night terrors. Fine was the distance you placed between yourself and anyone who might glimpse the empty rooms where you once lived.

She left a tip that wouldn't be enough—her savings slipping away like sand—and stood, pulling her jacket around her. The pill bottle rattled, a tiny percussion instrument keeping rhythm with the rain. She twisted the cap and swallowed one with the dregs of coffee, bitterness lingering on her tongue as she stepped through the door into the waiting storm.

The cold struck her like a physical memory. November in New Hanan carried a pointed chill—the kind that settled beneath skin, that whispered promises of the longer dark to come. Sleet mixed with rain now, tiny pellets that stung Hall's face as she walked without destination or purpose.

The city had altered in three months, or perhaps it was only Hall who saw it differently. The glass towers downtown no longer impressed—just empty reflections, mirrors returning nothing. The park where she once ran lay sodden, grass matted with old rain, trees stripped to bone. Even the people had changed, hurrying with downcast eyes, faces pinched against the weather, gazes sliding away from contact.

Or perhaps the change was in her, in the eyes that could no longer find beauty where it had once seemed abundant. The world shifted its angles when viewed through certain memories. Colors dulled and sounds warped when sleep came broken by reaching hands, by the phantom weight of metal, by the futile attempt to rewrite what had already been inscribed in someone else's blood.

Hall walked, letting cold numb her cheeks, letting rain seep through the inadequate shell of her jacket. Each step carried her from what had been—the apartment, the certainty, the woman who had believed in order and reason and the fundamental benevolence of things.

That woman had vanished somewhere between a trigger pull and the wet sound that followed. In her place moved this hollow-eyed stranger whose hands trembled when the medication wore thin, who startled at car doors slamming, who existed in a city turning steadily toward winter.

The Coste Motel crouched at the edge of Highway 16, its vacancy sign flickering like a faltering pulse. Hall climbed the exterior concrete stairs to the third floor, rain dripping from her hair, each step releasing a small squelch from her shoes. Three months ago, she would have seen this place rife with evidence to be collected. Now it was home. Room 312. The key scratched by so many careless hands that its number had nearly vanished. The air inside held industrial cleaner layered over decades of cigarettes and perfume and waiting. The rent came due weekly, and no one asked questions as long as she paid.

The lock resisted, as always. Hall worked the key, shoulder pressed against peeling paint, until the mechanism surrendered with a reluctant click. Inside waited the familiar smell—mildew from the bathroom, the chemical ghost of bug spray, and something older, something that lived in the walls themselves. She dropped the key onto the particle-board dresser where it slid across water rings left by strangers.

The room remained as she'd abandoned it that morning—sheets twisted from restless sleep, a plate with toast crumbs on the nightstand, blinds drawn against November's thin light. A cheap print hung crooked, mountains faded to suggestions of themselves. The carpet wore its stains like a history she avoided reading. Ninety square feet of anonymity, her life distilled.

Hall sank into the chair by the window without reaching for the light switch. Darkness had become familiar, almost companionable in the weeks since she'd arrived. She pulled the cord that controlled the drapes, shutting out even the meager glow of approaching evening. In darkness, she could pretend herself elsewhere. Anywhere.

But shadows harbored their own dangers. In the absence of light, memories circled—Rachel's head snapping backward, the slow-motion spray that followed, the impossible sound. White's face as understanding arrived a moment after Hall's bullets. The wet pull of his final breath. The copper smell that had soaked into floorboards and lingered sometimes at the back of her throat, waiting to be tasted again.

Rachel slid down the motel wall, leaving a crimson smear across the stems of wallpaper floers. White collapsed with the finality of an old oak, his bulk sending tremors through the thin carpet when he struck the floor. And there stood Hall between them, gun still raised, tendrils of smoke curling from the barrel, the shots that had dissolved their partnership still echoing in her bones long after the air had gone quiet.

Hall jerked her head sideways, not to dislodge the memory but to acknowledge its persistence. Her fingers trembled against the cool glass of her phone screen, its harsh light catching the fine lines around her eyes, transforming familiar features into a topography of exhaustion. Forty-two, and the face reflected back seemed borrowed from someone decades older.

She tapped the search she'd been refining for days: "affordable apartments midwest queer friendly." The screen populated with possibilities—Chicago's brick-lined streets, Minneapolis's river paths, Madison's university corridors, Columbus's renovated warehouses. Places where her name would be just syllables, where her history could dissolve like sugar in rain.

The listings blurred as she scrolled. After the creditors had taken their due, her savings had dwindled to a sum that felt both substantial and insufficient—enough for a security deposit and first month's rent, perhaps a secondhand sedan with high mileage, enough to craft the skeleton of another life. Not enough to buy forgiveness.

A listing caught in her vision—one bedroom above a vintage clothing shop in Chicago's Lakeview. The photos revealed hardwood that had absorbed decades of footfalls, east-facing windows that would fill with morning, walls whose emptiness seemed less like absence than possibility. The rent stretched her budget thin, but her disability checks would cover it if she learned to live small.

Her thumb hovered over the contact number. Chicago. Years ago, she'd spent three days there for a conference, remembered only in fragments: wind that found every gap in her jacket, buildings that seemed to grow from the water's edge, streets that felt both anonymous and inevitable in a way New Hanan never had.

Far enough, perhaps. A state line between her and the ghosts of White and Rachel.

Thunder cracked the sky open, closer now than before. Rain lashed the window, driven sideways by wind that probed the motel's aging joints and seams. The building seemed to inhale around her, timber and plaster settling into the rhythm of the storm.

Chicago would have its own storms, she thought. Winter would push across the lake, burying unfamiliar streets in drifts that would make her scars contract—the visible ones mapping her shoulder and hip, and those other wounds no one could catalog. The cold seemed fitting somehow. Not as punishment, but as counterpoint, a physical echo of what lived inside her.

Her thumb pressed the call button.

The storm intensified outside, rain striking the glass like hurried whispers. Thunder rolled across the low clouds, and for a moment, the neon vacancy sign of the Coste Motel flickered out. In that brief darkness, Hall could see nothing but afterimages—the phone's glow, the rain-streaked window, her own reflection suspended between what had been and what might yet be.